THE NEW DESTROYER:
CHOKE HOLD

BY WARREN MURPHY AND JAMES MULLANEY

The New Destroyer: Guardian Angel
The New Destroyer: Choke Hold
*The New Destroyer: Dead Reckoning**

*Forthcoming

THE NEW DESTROYER:
CHOKE HOLD

Warren Murphy and James Mullaney

TOR®

A TOM DOHERTY ASSOCIATES BOOK
NEW YORK

This is a work of fiction. All of the characters, organizations, and events portrayed in this novel are either products of the authors' imagination or are used fictitiously.

THE NEW DESTROYER: CHOKE HOLD

Copyright © 2007 by Warren Murphy

All rights reserved, including the right to reproduce this book, or portions thereof, in any form.

A Tor Book
Published by Tom Doherty Associates, LLC
175 Fifth Avenue
New York, NY 10010

www.tor.com

Tor® is a registered trademark of Tom Doherty Associates, LLC.

ISBN-13: 978-0-7653-5760-1
ISBN-10: 0-7653-5760-7

First Edition: November 2007

Printed in the United States of America

0 9 8 7 6 5 4 3 2 1

For Adam Koffman and Morgan Abbotts;
for Samantha and Adelaide Coles,
for Thomas and Tyler Hering...each one a joy.

For Bob Salvatore, with thanks.

For www.warrenmurphy.com,
where one of us can be reached;
for www.jamesmullaney.com, where the other one can.

And for the Glorious House of Sinanju, e-mail:
housinan@aol.com.

For some reason that morning, on the day he would die for unleashing an unimaginable plague on an unsuspecting world, Dr. John Feathers remembered the screaming girl.

He did not even know her name. He had met her three years before on a commuter train to New York. The girl must have been a college student somewhere because she carried a textbook before her like a shield, and with jutted chin seemed to dare the seated passengers she passed to comment on the title. All the other seats were full, and so she and her fat book had wound up next to John Feathers.

She attempted to appear casual as she angled the book so that John could read the title. The book was called *Modern Feminists from Abzug to Zeigert* by Nora Personning. John would have preferred to ignore it and the girl, but every time the train jostled, her book hand managed to bump against him and it was either allow her to bruise his ribs all the way to Grand Central Station or ask her what she obviously wanted him to ask.

"Good book?" John queried politely.

The girl who had been trying to get his attention for five minutes turned to him as if his question were as welcome as a dead horse in the Russian Tea Room.

"It's brilliant," she accused.

She was pretty, but exposure to academic life was clearly putting her through a metamorphosis to perpetual anger. She wore no makeup and her hair was cut too short. Her clothes were lumpy and formless, yet here and there when she moved was fleeting evidence of bumps and curves that suggested a good figure, one that might even emerge like a moth from a chrysalis when her twenty-something flirtation with militancy ended and her real life began. She had the very ordinary college-age bearing of someone with an infinite number of opinions but not one single thought of her own.

"Dr. Personning is a genius," the young woman said. "She's opened my eyes to the reality of this bourgeois patriarchal society."

John didn't think anyone still said "bourgeois" these days, and under normal circumstances he might have mentioned this. But this girl did not seem likely to respond well to criticism, so all he said was, "Hmm."

"Abzug was a pioneer, of course," the girl said, whacking the book cover with the back of her hand, "but Zeigert is a fascinating figure. A proto-feminist from the early twentieth century, but she couldn't stand the slowness of societal change, so she just dropped out. Disappeared in the 1940s."

"Sort of like Greta Garbo," John suggested mildly.

The girl's eyes narrowed. "Who?"

"She was a famous actress who dropped out of the limelight, I guess at the height of her celebrity or something. They chased her around for years after, trying to snap pictures of her, but she just wanted to be left alone."

The girl looked for something in his words to snarl at, but finding nothing she hummed a little noncommittal hum and sank into her seat. They rode in silence for a few long, awkward minutes until some vestigial polite impulse that Dr. Nora Personning and her fellow professors had not been able to eradicate completely surfaced in the girl and she asked what John Feathers did for a living.

"I'm a research scientist for Cheyenne Tobacco," he replied with a friendly smile.

The next thing he knew, the girl was on her feet screaming bloody blue murder. At first he thought she must be accusing him of improperly touching her or something, but through the bugging eyes, frothy spittle and her finger pointing straight at his nose, he picked up a few words.

". . . mass murderer . . . innocents . . . baby killer . . . dying in the streets . . . worse than heroin . . ."

She accused him of being a bigger murderer than Hitler and George W. Bush combined.

"Please. Sit down," John Feathers begged.

But the girl would not stop. She just stood in the aisle, screaming and spitting and pointing, until John was forced to get off at the next stop and catch a later train.

That was three years ago, and it had been the last time he ever admitted to a stranger what he did for a living.

But on this morning, the last of his life, John Feathers felt even greater shame than he had that day on the train. On that day, he had walked a gauntlet of embarrassment past his fellow passengers, melting inwardly as he passed each set of accusing eyes. But this morning, he walked amidst peers who scarcely noticed him, so busy were they cheering one another and popping champagne corks. A white-coated scientist spied John skulking by and grabbed him in a bear hug.

"This is the guy," said the man, whose name tag read "Neil Speckman." "This guy is responsible for the addition on my house that the old ball-and-chain has been nagging me for, and the brand-new, heated inground pool I'll be building to get away from her. Ain't it the truth, Tonto?"

John hunched uncomfortably among the group of scientists. Although Neil Speckman was smiling, the rest sneered silent resentment at John as they scratched their arms and faces.

That outbreak of skin-itching at the Cheyenne Tobacco

labs had started a few months before and had been growing steadily. The little red bumps were worse around the mouths and right hands of most of the men and women.

"Tonto here is going to make us all rich," Speckman roared, gesturing with a Styrofoam cup of champagne. Sparkling wine sloshed over the rim.

"Knock off the Tonto stuff, Neil," someone nearby suggested.

"Johnny doesn't mind, do you, John?" Speckman asked. "I mean, look at him. He looks about as Injun as I do. Hey, is that really true what they say, John? You really Indian?"

John nodded. "Excuse me," he said, and extricated himself from the man's bear hug.

"No way. Can't be Indian," Neil Speckman whispered boozily as John headed for the exit. "Guy's whiter than my lab coat."

One woman was still trying to hush the man silent as John Feathers stole out of the lab and into the hallway.

There was a portrait on the wall outside the lab. A man with stony visage, steely gaze, and robust bearing stared unflinchingly at passersby. A tiny plaque at the base of the picture read, "Edgar Rawly, CEO Cheyenne Tobacco."

The caption was unnecessary. There was no one at the Cheyenne Tobacco complex who did not know their company's founder and chief executive officer. Rawly was the picture of health, with an athletic red glow to his chiselled cheekbones and a hint of a smile on his full, manly lips. On his knee rested one hand, and between his fingers was a cigarette. The cigarette was painted so brilliantly white it should have had a halo.

In portrait form, Edgar Rawly was living proof of the health-giving qualities of all tobacco products.

The picture nearly made John Feathers retch. Panting, he raced down the hallway, away from the portrait, away from the labs. In the stairwell, John leaned against the wall. And then it came back to him. . . .

. . . *mass murderer . . . baby killer . . . worse than heroin.* . . .

That incident had been three years ago and now, still, the shrill, accusing words of that young college student on a Manhattan-bound commuter train echoed in John's head as if she were shouting them up from the depths of the stairwell. He wanted to cover his ears, to run screaming from the building.

From upstairs, he could still hear the happy buzz of his fellow workers. There were big bonuses all around, thanks to him. Most of the workers were stockholders as well, and their stock in Cheyenne was about to go through the roof. There were sales projections from marketing that had the guys from corporate doing cartwheels down the hallway. In three years, maybe less, Cheyenne would corner the world tobacco market. It was simple, it was neat, and the only things John had traded away in the deal were his soul, his people and the world.

And for what?

The Cheyenne Smooths.

The first great tobacco product in a century. A gold mine of curling smoke that would make them all rich beyond their wildest dreams. And they could not have done it without Dr. John Feathers.

For John Feathers, knowing what he had done—what he was about to do—it was all he could do to keep his breakfast from launching up out of his churning stomach.

He took the back stairs down to the parking lot. Two men and a woman were smoking near a trash bin.

"I wish I'd never tried these things," one of the men commented, hacking a viscous glob of mucus onto the pavement.

"It's cheaper now anyway," the woman said. She was puffing away as if possessed, launching plumes of curling white smoke at the eight-story glass and steel building across the parking lot. The Cheyenne Tobacco world headquarters reflected the yellow sunlight and brilliant blue of the West Virginia sky. "I figured it out. Back when we started, when the stuff was so hard to come by, it used to cost Cheyenne five thousand dollars a puff."

The second man was suddenly racked by a coughing

spasm. Doubled over, he held his cigarette far away from his face as he fought to catch his breath. The woman, careful to keep puffing, patted him on the back.

"You okay, Stan?" she asked once the spasm subsided.

Stan sniffled, cleared his throat and stuffed his cigarette right back between his lips. "I hate this," he said, his voice hoarse. He was nearly in tears. "It was never this bad with my old brand. I get up in the middle of the night to smoke now. I even dream about these damn things. If it wasn't for that son of a bitch John Feathers, I wouldn't have that spot on my lungs, I know that for damn sure. Someone should shoot that scumbag."

The woman noticed John walking by and nudged her companion in the arm. Stan glanced at John, scowled and turned away. But he and the others never stopped puffing.

John noted that each had a rash around their mouths. The rashes were older now, and the early-stage cherry redness was now a lunar surface of tough, jaundiced boils. Although the morning was humid, each wore rubber gloves on their right hands, filched from the Cheyenne labs. Still, the rash was faintly visible on their forearms.

John did not blame them for giving him the cold shoulder. He deserved whatever anyone gave him and much more. Like a zombie, he walked to his car. From his coat pocket, he removed a book of official Cheyenne Tobacco matches and slipped them in his trousers. After, he took off his lab coat with its ID tag and dropped it to the pavement. He would not be needing the tag any longer. He was never coming back to this place of death.

John drove to the airport, bought a ticket to Montana, and flew back to the land of his people, to his home, back to the place where he was known as Johnny Crow Feathers of the Chowok Tribe. It was the father of Johnny Crow Feathers who picked up his troubled son at the airport.

His father was waiting in the parking lot, perched on the hood of his old Dodge. He had not gone inside the terminal to wait for his son. William Eagle Feathers had told his son when he called from the plane that the health fascists did not allow smoking inside the terminal building.

It broke Johnny's heart to see the red rash on his elderly father's face and hands. Like Johnny, William Eagle Feathers was light-skinned, with only a broadness to the nose that might have indicated Indian blood.

His father tried to hug him, but Johnny leaned away.

"I warned you about those things, Dad. Can you please not smoke?"

It took all of the old man's willpower, but he stubbed out the cigarette on the bumper of his car. Johnny noted with great guilt that his father did not toss away the half used cigarette, but slipped it into his pocket.

Johnny shook his father's hand, his left hand, where the rash was fainter. At the touch of his father's weathered fingers, the floodgates burst. All the guilt he was feeling for what he had done poured out and he began weeping.

"This is all my fault, Dad."

"No, Johnny," his father insisted. "A man makes his own decisions. They might be stupid, but they're his to make and no one else's."

Johnny didn't argue although he knew that was a load of crap. He had the test marketing data to prove it. Free will might open the door a crack, but Johnny's work would make sure that door was kicked down and a loaded gun was held to the homeowner's head.

Without exchanging another word, they rode to the Chowok reservation.

The Chowok were a puzzlement to researchers, and had been featured in many articles and documentaries through the years. DNA testing had proved that they were related to other North American Indians, yet there had been great influence from European immigrants. On his people's land, John saw white-skinned and fair-haired men and women smoking. Worse, and to his eternal shame, many of the pink-skinned children he passed were puffing as well. And not just stupid teenagers, but kids as young as nine or ten.

There were signs in front of every package store and the little main market: CHEYENNE SMOOTHS, A WHOLE NEW TASTE IN FLAVOR! Hand-painted signs made by the store owners read, "Smooths Available" and "Smooths Inside!"

Johnny had heard the cigarettes were already being sold on certain reservations. The government had not yet gotten wind of that.

When Johnny was a boy, the main village abutted pristine wilderness. Now he and his father drove past cultivated fields of gently waving leaves. The four-foot tall plants had already been pruned to direct nourishment to a few leaves. Although only recently transplanted, the plants had been manipulated for rapid growth and were racing toward maturity and would be ready for harvest in a few short weeks. In the distance were the greenhouses where the next crop of seedlings was being tended and big barns for drying the tobacco leaves. Other buildings would eventually be constructed for blending, shredding and packaging. Right now, all that work was taking place off the reservation.

"I've unleashed a great evil on the world," Johnny said as he watched the results of his handiwork speed past.

"Now you stop saying that," his father replied. The old man was gripping the steering wheel too tightly. More than once his blistered hand strayed out of habit to his pocket and his pack of Cheyenne Smooths. But then he remembered his son in the passenger seat and his shaking hand would retreat to the steering wheel.

"It's true, Dad. I should never have told them about it. I never should have come back here for it. It was dead, and I brought it back to life."

"It's history and history makes its own decisions. That plant was important to your ancestors," William Eagle Feathers insisted. "We only have to learn how to use it wisely, as they did."

"There's no evidence they used it wisely at all, Dad. Have you seen PBS? Every documentary says something nearly wiped out the Chowok. Only we know the truth. We survived because of the 'yellow fire' that burned the old crops. From the oral histories, it sounds like that was a lightning-sparked fire, so you must have some god or other to thank for that. Maybe he was trying to help our people out, Dad."

His father shook his head firmly. "It was not spirit aid, but wrath that destroyed the sacred crops, Johnny. Our people were able to smuggle out only a few dried leaves, but they were dead and could not be planted again. We kept them as sacred objects for hundreds of years. Then you came along with your science and genetics and you brought it back to life. You've restored our history. You're the savior of the Chowok, Johnny, the savior, and don't you ever forget it."

The savior of the Chowok felt sick to his stomach. He slouched down in his seat and closed his eyes on the freshly planted fields and new buildings.

The legend of the sacred plant was one of the most mysterious of the Chowok past. The great migration from the east had come long before the forced resettlement of other North American tribes—before, in fact, there was a United States. Even without their sacred plant the Chowok were a mysterious people. So many of the tribe possessed white features that there was doubt until genetic testing came along that the Chowok were even true Indians.

They were a strange people. And thanks to Johnny Feathers and a few dried leaves that he had brought back to life, illness and death would ensure that they—and many others around the world—would soon vanish into the mists of history.

Fields led to a few scattered houses. William Feathers stopped in front of a modest ranch and the two men went inside.

His father had turned his son's childhood bedroom into a small study. John Feathers tossed and turned on the couch until eleven o'clock before he kicked off the old afghan his late mother had knitted and climbed to his feet.

He carried his shoes in his hand. The floor still creaked in all the old spots, but Johnny knew just where to step to get out to the porch in silence.

Outside, he went to his father's toolshed. There was no

lock, just a piece of twisted wire looped through the holes where a padlock would go. Inside the shed, he found what he was looking for in the same place it had always been. Johnny picked up the heavy can of gas his father kept filled at all times and carried it to the trunk of his father's Dodge. The reservation was deep in slumber as he drove out to the big tobacco fields.

There were no lights in the new buildings. This was all costing Cheyenne a pretty penny, but the Chowok reservation was a forgotten backwater. Cheyenne relied on security cameras rather than actual guards. There were none nearby that Johnny could see, but even if they spotted him he no longer cared. He was going to do what was right.

Rain had been scarce in Montana during the past two weeks. The night was warm and the soil dry. The automated sprinklers would not kick on until early the next morning.

Johnny lifted a bare arm to the breeze and felt the short hairs blow. The wind was to his back and away from the settlements. The conditions were ideal.

Unscrewing the cap on the gas can, Johnny sloshed gasoline along the eastern edge of the field. He worked as quickly as he could, careful to soak the plants nearest the road. When they caught, the adjacent rows would go up as well, until the whole field was ablaze. He would go get more gas for the field on the other side of the road, as well as the greenhouses. He would steal a tanker truck if he had to. Johnny could not let the evil he had helped revive be unleashed on the world. He would wash the shame from his soul with a cleansing fire, just like the fire that had saved the Chowok before the great migration hundreds of years ago.

The world would know. The fire would attract the media. Washington would be alerted. Cheyenne would be stopped.

He reached in his pocket for the matches he had brought with him from the Cheyenne Tobacco office complex in West Virginia.

Johnny was surprised at his own calm. His hands were rock steady as he tore a single match from the book.

As long as the wind did not shift, he would be fine. If not, so much smoke from the genetically altered tobacco leaves might be deadly. There was no way of knowing what such a high dose could do to a human.

Johnny brought the match to the book.

"Dr. John Feathers."

The cold voice behind him made him jump, and he fumbled the matchbook out of his hand. Instinctively, he tried grabbing for it as it fell, but wound up swatting it away. He heard the matchbook rattle a big tobacco leaf a few feet away on its way to the ground.

Johnny turned. A dark figure stood behind him.

"What? I—I . . ." he stammered. "It's okay. I'm from Cheyenne Tobacco, from West Virginia. Corporate HQ."

It was a stupid thing to say, he knew. The person had known his name. They knew who he was. Maybe they had followed him from West Virginia, knowing that he was about to snap. But how could they? Even Johnny hadn't known what he was going to do until he got here. But now that he was here, standing next to the field with a useless match still in hand, they would know. Certainly they could smell the gasoline he had dumped all over their expensive crop.

"Look," Johnny said. "You're just a night watchman or something? Well you don't know what this stuff is." He waved a hand at the field. "This is not ordinary tobacco. This is genetically altered plant life. We brought back a form of tobacco that has been extinct for hundreds of years."

"And you're proud of that, aren't you?" the cold voice demanded.

Johnny saw something rise up in shadowed hands. A weapon. He quickly raised his own hands in surrender.

"Whoa," he said. "Hold on. No. No, I'm not."

"Dr. John Feathers, you have been judged in absentia for crimes against humanity," the voice intoned.

"What?" John said, confusion darkening his brow. "Listen, there's no problem here. I'm not fighting, okay? I'm going to lower my hands. Let's just go sit down and—"

A loud pop, as crisp and clear as the bright stars in the moonless Montana sky.

Johnny felt a sharp pain in his chest, to the right of his sternum. Shot. He'd been shot. Gasping disbelief, he grabbed at the bullet hole he knew must be there.

But there was no bullet wound. His searching fingers found something flat, rounded. Hard like metal.

Another shot. The impact trailed the pop, and he realized now this was much slower than a normal gun. More pain. The last pain. Straight into the heart.

Johnny fell to his knees.

The shadow moved and he felt something press against his chest. Feebly, he tried to brush it away.

"You have been found guilty," his executioner said.

And before the final pop, an image sprang unbeckoned to the mind of Johnny Feathers. It was of the young college girl, textbook in hand, screaming on that long ago train.

Murderer!

He saw the faces of the men and women who had watched him slink guiltily down the aisle. Saw through the window the look of smug satisfaction on the anonymous girl's face as he stood on the platform and watched the train pull out of the station.

And then he heard a voice, but it was not the voice of his killer, or of the girl on the train, or of his father, or of any of the great spirits that the Chowok prayed to. It was a voice from inside his head, but which seemed to roll to him in warming waves from the very center of the universe. And the voice assured John Feathers that his murder would be avenged, and that his people had been mistaken these hundreds of years, and what had been thought a scourge would return once more with purifying vengeance.

Johnny wanted to ask this voice of the heavens what it meant, but before he could there was another loud pop that seemed to come from inside his head, which was followed by another sharp pain to his chest. But this pain was less than the last, because he was already dying, and then he was on his back on the ground in a puddle of gasoline, and his killer was backing away and Johnny no longer cared.

And as he watched the stars above him wink out one by one, Johnny was content to know that all would be made right. And then the black shroud of eternal night drew over and, as would be the same one day for all men, the shadow claimed Johnny Crow Feathers as its own.

2

His name was Remo and he hoped this day would not end with another dead body.

It was an odd wish coming from Remo Williams who could not count the number of living, breathing humans who had surrendered to death at his hands. Years before, he had attempted to add them all up but very soon in the count he had felt ill and not very long after he had given up. There were some things one did not dwell on, especially when professional assassination was one's bread and butter.

It was not that Remo could not count them all; it was that, once faced with the cruel reality of his life, he had no desire to tally up the dead.

But this day was different. This day would not end in death, as had so many of Remo's days, but in life. It was a notion that sparked a tiny glimmer of hope in his breast, and he smiled at the thought.

"Why you smiling?"

Remo was jolted from his reverie. He turned to find a pair of suspicious eyes staring at him. The eyes and their owner were an arm's length away. The sounds of many sets of lungs breathing heavily and of tired feet trampling brittle grass came to Remo's ears from all around.

"Just thinking."

"Ain't nothing funny out here. Ain't nothing anybody should be smiling at, that's for damn sure."

"You're right." The smile fled Remo's face, replaced with a look of grim seriousness.

The woman next to him studied this new visage and seemed to accept it, but only reluctantly. She turned her attention from Remo. "Why you here anyway, mister?" she asked. "Fella like you don't look like he likes crowds too much."

She was right. Remo mostly worked alone or with only one other individual. He glanced to his right. A line of men and women stretched across the wide field. To his left, a dozen more. They walked slowly across the field, using sticks to push aside tall grass as they went.

"I was watching the news—" Remo replied.

The woman nodded and quickly cut him off. "I seen it on the news, too," she said. She was black, late middle-aged and had a kind face. She was the sort of woman who laughed easily, sang hymns while doing housework, baked cookies for her grandkids and swatted their knuckles with a wooden spoon if they tried to filch more than one before dinner. "I just had to come out here," she said as she pushed aside a tall clump of weeds with a five-foot-long pole each searcher had been issued. "Poor little girl, getting taken like that. Shouldn't happen in this country, no, sir. I got four of my own, and five grandchildren. Can't think what I'd do if one of them was to be taken like this. Terrible thing. Just terrible what people can do. You from around here, mister?"

"No," Remo said.

"Didn't think so. I know everybody in town an' everybody, they know me. Lot of faces I see today ain't from around here. I 'spect they're all just like you. Just want to help. You lucky you got in. Police got so many volunteers wanting to help they turning folks away." A big hand swatted a fly on her neck. "Dang skeeters gonna eat us all alive out here," she griped.

She wore a tiny backpack that she'd filched from one of her grandchildren. She fished inside and pulled out the can of Away! bug spray they had each been issued. Closing her eyes, she squirted a cloud into the air and walked through it. The insect repellent mingled with the sweat that glistened on her dark skin. She applied some to her arms. When she was done, she offered the can to Remo.

"No thanks."

"Don't be like that," she said. "Them bugs'll eat your skinny behind for supper."

"Really," Remo said. "I'm good."

Her eyes narrowed and for the first time she noticed that there were no mosquitoes buzzing around Remo. The insects were making a veritable feast of the other searchers, swarming around as if the men and women were a moving buffet. Everyone else was slapping bare skin.

Remo wore a black T-shirt and charcoal gray chinos. Not a single fly landed on his bare arms. In fact, now that she noticed, despite the stifling Virginia humidity this thin young man was the only person present not perspiring.

"You a robot or something?" she asked as they walked.

"No. And shouldn't you be watching the ground like everybody else?"

"I ain't missing nothing, honey. You got no flies on you? Well there's no flies on Sadie neither." Sadie swatted a fat mosquito that was at that moment sucking greedily from her neck. "Just my no-flies ain't the literal kind like yours," she said, wiping the squashed fly onto the front of her jeans. "Care to share your secret?"

"You wouldn't like it."

"Try me."

"I've only eaten rice, fish and fresh fruits and vegetables for the past thirty years."

The woman turned instantly away. "Pass."

"Sometimes I have duck," Remo offered.

"Pass," Sadie repeated. "I'd rather get eaten by mosquitoes

than give up living. Whatever cult they got you in, son, get yourself out and have some nice juicy pork barbecue."

The woman returned to beating the underbrush.

For some reason, her comments stung worse than if a mosquito had bitten him.

Remo rarely got the chance to socialize, but this Sadie seemed like a nice woman. She was volunteering her time for a worthy cause and he wouldn't have minded making friends with her, but even in a group of strangers like this one he was always the outsider.

Beside him, the woman whacked aside some grass, then all at once, let out a little gasp. Something round had been hiding in a little gully underneath the clump. At her cry, the nearest searchers glanced over expectantly.

The woman's face fell and she shook her head sadly. "Just a rock," she called. She poked at the big black rock with her stick. "Yep, just a rock. Nothing here but rocks. Lord, I hope we find something soon."

She shook her head and muttered a soft prayer to herself as she moved away.

Remo could have told her that there had been no body in the grass. Bodies gave off certain smells, even ones recently dead. It was not a body and it was certainly not anything living, which is what all the searchers hoped to find. Remo trudged along, hearing the individual heartbeats of every hunter along the line, and of the animals that scurried away from them into the tall grass. He could feel every footstep, both two- and four-footed. Despite the clomping and the crackling grass, if he strained he could have heard the blood coursing through arteries of the most distant member of their search party. There was no human in this field, living or dead, other than the men and women who had assembled with Remo on the road two miles behind.

Yet Remo forged on. It was hope that kept him going, the same hope that sustained the other searchers. Yes, Remo could sense further than the rest, but even Remo's senses had their limits. And every step brought him another pace closer to the shared hope of a happy ending.

It was a strange feeling, to be part of a group effort. Not only was Remo used to working alone, he had come out in broad daylight, a great departure since much of Remo's life seemed to be spent lurking in shadow.

Although his own feelings should have been irrelevant, Remo could not help but feel connected to the strangers around him, a part of something noble, something good.

But, Remo knew, not everyone shared his sentiments. He had found that out earlier in the day when he called his employer to tell him he was going to be out of town for a while.

"For how long?" the tart voice of Dr. Harold W. Smith had asked over the phone. Smith's voice could curdle cream at twenty paces. On the telephone he could make a crystal clear fiberoptic line sound like corroding copper.

"For however long it takes," Remo had replied.

"Remo, this is not a part-time job, you know. If you are abandoning your responsibilities to go wandering around Africa for weeks again, I am going to insist that Master Chiun reduce what we pay for your services."

"You ever try getting a refund out of a Master of Sinanju, Smitty? Ptolemy V was the last employer who tried and they're still finding parts of him floating down the Nile. Since then our number one rule has been etched in stone: 'No refunds.' You want to know our second rule?"

"Not really."

" 'I'll tell you anyway. Rule One is 'No refunds.' Rule Two is 'Never forget Rule One.' And anyway, I'm not going to Africa for a while. This is someplace even hotter."

He told Smith the story he had seen on the news that morning. A little eight-year-old girl from northern Virginia had been abducted on her way to the local community pool.

"The Traci Rydel case," Smith had said.

"You know about it?" Remo asked, surprised. Smith was normally concerned about larger matters—terrorism and wars and threats to America at home and abroad. Human interest stories were lost on the cold, emotionless director of CURE, America's most secret espionage agency, and Remo wondered idly if Smith was developing something like a human soul in his old age.

That brief hope was quickly shattered.

"The story is impossible to ignore," Smith replied. "The networks are covering it as if it were a presidential funeral. I had to instruct the CURE mainframe computers to delete updates on the case from the hourly news digests they send me."

"You're all heart, Smitty."

"Heart doesn't enter into it. The girl will either be found or she will not. It is an unfortunate case, but there are many such cases every day across the nation. We are not here for such small matters."

"See, that's where we disagree," Remo said.

There had been a pause on the line. "Remo, involving yourself in a common child abduction is out of the question."

"You must be asking a different question than me, Smitty, because I say it is. Isn't this what we're in business for? Saving Americans? Well there's an American in trouble in Virginia and she needs our help."

"You can't go."

"That's going to be tough, since I'm already here."

From the sidewalk pay phone, Remo had looked around the supermarket parking lot where the volunteers were assembling. Police were dividing men and women into groups.

He saw faces of every color, which made his heart warm. Climbing onto the bus that would take them to their search destination was a jowly black woman who wore an expression of fierce determination. Others in Remo's group were falling in behind her. One man with greasy blond hair and torn jeans hung back, bouncing from foot to foot. When the final call for Remo's preassigned group was shouted out, he waved a finger "one moment" at a uniformed police officer.

"Gotta go, Smitty. My group is about to pull out."

Smith fumed silently. "If you are looking for my blessing, you do not have it."

"Don't want it, don't need it, don't care," Remo said, and hung up the phone.

That had been hours ago, when the sun was rising higher in the sky and a hum of optimistic chatter filled the air. The late afternoon shadows were growing longer now and there was little talking among the volunteers.

"The sun is going down," Sadie, the woman next to Remo, observed. There was soft worry in her voice.

Sadie had reason to be concerned. The little girl had been missing for more than two days and hope that she would be found alive dwindled with each passing hour.

Remo's group marched on through woods, field and woods again. They combed every square inch they passed, following instructions of specially trained state police officers who walked the line with them. When they reached another road, they set up a new line overlapping the first, and trekked back in the direction from which they had come.

It was dark when they emerged from the woods beside their idling bus. Exhaust fumes hung heavy in the humid air. Some men wanted to go back out, but the state police and sheriff's deputies told them no.

"Relief search groups have already been deployed," a state police officer with a sweat-slick face and a neck as wide around as his skull called out.

The atmosphere on the ride back to town was funereal.

Remo wanted to feel like part of something, and he was. He was part of a failed effort. There was a palpable sense of defeat on the bus ride back to the supermarket parking lot where the authorities had set up base camp.

There were new faces ready to offer relief to those arriving back in the parking lot. The search for Traci Rydel would continue into the night and straight through until dawn when the next set of volunteers would be recruited. Remo was ready to mix in with the new crowd, to glide to the front and ensure that he was picked for the night shift, just as he had done that morning, when someone caught his eye.

A man of about thirty-five stood at the edge of the crowd. His blond hair hung in greasy strands. The hair was dirty as a fashion statement, and he periodically jerked his neck to flick away the bangs that fell over his eyes. He wore an un-tucked white dress shirt and torn jeans, and bounced from one foot to the other as he watched the men and women climb down from the bus. It was the same man Remo had seen standing in the parking lot that morning.

A few searchers offered glum good-byes to one another before climbing into their cars. A kindly hand touched Remo's forearm. "Maybe we'll have better luck tomorrow."

Remo glanced down into his new friend's face and shook his head. "I don't think I'll be back tomorrow."

"Too bad," Sadie said. "Terrible thing." Shaking her head sadly, she offered a wave to a pretty young girl of about twenty who was standing by a nearby car. "My youngest. Now keep your googly eyes in your head, she's too young for you. You take care of yourself, skinny. Try to eat something other than fish. Too much iodine. That stuff'll kill you."

Remo watched her get into the car with her daughter, and smiled sadly at thoughts of the normal family he would never have before turning back to business.

The twitchy blond-haired man watched the bus leave the parking lot. Many reporters remained, as well as local and state officials and groups of private citizens who had come out to gawk at the circus. Remo noted that the young man stayed at the edge of the crowd. Flipping hair from his eyes, he glanced around at the various faces without seeming to look for anyone in particular. At one point he nearly made eye contact with Remo, but Remo was suddenly very inter-ested in a tattered green flier taped to a streetlight that prom-ised to speed up one's "metabali$m" in two short weeks.

The young man turned and skulked off into the shadows.

Remo trailed after him. The bright yellow lights and ex-citement of the parking lot became quiet tree-lined streets. Insects fluttered around dull streetlamps.

Remo did not know what it was that made him trail the young man. Years of training had developed instincts that Remo himself could often not explain. But guilty men car-ried themselves differently, just as did men with guns or

knives. This young man had no apparent reason for being interested in the search for Traci Rydel, yet he had been at the
scene of the rescue effort at least twice. And he had walked,
not driven. It could be that he had no car, but it could also be
that he wanted no one to see his vehicle. His nervous man-
nerisms led Remo to believe that the second possibility was
the right one.

The young man stuck to the shadows between the street-
lights, casting furtive glances over his shoulder as he walked.
His eyes never seemed to find Remo, who remained ten yards
behind but always managed to be in darkness when the man
turned to look in his direction. He steered a steady path in the
man's wake.

A mile and a half away, the young man turned down a
dead end street and walked up a poorly maintained flagstone
front walk to a rotting front porch. He was putting key to
lock when the door suddenly burst open.

"Finally!" a woman's voice whispered hoarsely.

Remo's eyes narrowed when he recognized the woman's
face. He had seen the suddenly famous woman's picture on
TV that morning. She had appeared in a vacation photograph of father, mother and daughter, taken in happier days
on a trip to Disneyland.

Ever since her daughter's abduction, Mrs. Connie Rydel
had refused to appear live on camera. The family said she
was too grief-stricken to answer questions.

Mrs. Rydel did not appear stricken by grief over her missing daughter as she wrapped her arms around the neck of the
greasy-haired young man. "Brad, I was so worried about
you."

Brad was startled by the ferocity of Mrs. Rydel's embrace.
He tried to pull away, but was first forced to peel her arms
from around him.

"Get inside, stupid bitch," he said, glancing nervously out
at the street.

Shoving her even as she tried to wrap her arms around
him again, Brad slammed the door. Remo saw fingers pull at
a curtain and a pair of eyes peer out at the street.

Remo was not worried about being seen. From the shadowed night he watched Brad's shifty eyes disappear and the curtain fall back in place.

The driveway was two strips of cracked, oil-stained cement that led to a detached two-stall garage. The warped doors had been in desperate need of paint thirty years ago. A small corner of the roof had fallen in and one side window was boarded up. Remo went to the other side.

Through the grimy pane, he saw a faded blue panel truck. The vehicle fit the description of the van that had snatched Traci Rydel from the roadside.

Something stirred, white hot, in the coldest depths of Remo Williams's soul.

There was movement in a room off the side porch that ran parallel to the driveway. Remo mounted the stairs silently. Connie Rydel and the man Remo had followed from the parking lot were in the kitchen. Through the window, Remo saw that Brad had backed Mrs. Rydel into the refrigerator.

If Mrs. Rydel had decided to join in the search for her missing daughter, she apparently thought sticking her tongue down a lowlife hairball's throat would recover young Traci. Brad was pitching in, but mistakenly seemed to think Traci Rydel was hidden up under her mother's blouse.

"I can't wait for this to be over," Mrs. Rydel gasped when she came up for air.

"It'll be done soon enough, baby," Brad said. "Soon as I can figure out what to do with my van. Course, if your head wasn't up your ass that wouldn't be a problem for ol' Brad now, would it?" With a flash of anger, he pushed her aside and rummaged in the fridge for a beer.

"I just wanted us to be happy, Brad," Connie said. "It was just taking so long. I'm sorry I used your van. It's all I could think of. I couldn't use George's car."

"Whatever." Brad dropped angrily into a kitchen chair.

Connie came up behind him. Leaning her chin on one of his shoulders, she massaged his back. He grunted irritation, but did not push her away.

"Did you . . . do it yet?" she purred.

"Back off," Brad said. He took a deep pull on his beer. "She's all taken care of."

"Where did you leave her?" Connie Rydel asked.

"She's taken care of," Brad snapped. "Jesus, I told you to back off."

"I only thought—" She stopped, sniffling. "You don't know how hard this is. My sister had to sneak me out of my own house in her car. They're watching me twenty-four hours a day. And George? He's crying like a woman over this. He's not a real man. Not like you. And don't forget. You're the one who said you didn't want any kids. I only wanted to give us both a fresh start."

She had hoped for a sympathetic response from her lover, but the male voice that responded did not belong to Brad.

"This isn't the start of anything for you, June Cleaver—"

Brad and Connie glanced up from the table. A stranger stood before them. The kitchen door was closed at his back.

"—it's the end," finished Remo.

For someone who appeared as if he had spent the past thirty years wasted, Brad's reaction was surprisingly quick. The young man flung his beer bottle at Remo's head while simultaneously diving for a drawer near the stove. His hand wrapped around the barrel of a loaded revolver.

Brad realized on an instinctive level that something was wrong even as he grabbed for the gun. Things were moving so quickly his brain did not have time to sort out that the stranger should have yelped when struck by the beer bottle or, if he had ducked out of the way, the bottle should have smashed against the tile over the sink. Neither happened.

Then Brad saw a very near shadow and glimpsed a flash of movement. He did not see the hand that swatted the drawer shut, only felt the result.

Bones in Brad's wrist shattered and the gun tumbled from useless fingers to the rear of the drawer.

The breath left his lungs. Unable to shout, he squealed in pain. He scratched at the drawer with his good hand, but it would not open. It was as if the drawer had fused with his arm. He wheeled, gasping in pain.

A pair of deepset, dark eyes bored accusing holes through to his black soul.

"Don't go anywhere," Remo warned.

Connie Rydel stood near the door to the hallway, frozen in place with shock and fear. When Remo turned to the woman, Mrs. Rydel gasped and backed into the door frame.

Remo walked slowly toward her. "You kidnapped your own daughter," he said.

She looked to Brad, forearm flattened spatula thin, attached as firmly to the apron drawer as if he were screwed in place, on his knees now and whimpering. Blood from the compound fracture dribbled down the cabinets.

"I wanted to build a new life," Connie explained, voice trembling. "What else could I do?"

Remo kept walking. "You could have tried leaving her with her father for starters."

"I didn't want a long fight in court," Connie Rydel insisted, as if kidnapping and murder were the only logical alternatives to complicated divorce proceedings.

Remo had been trained away from anger. Anger was destructive. It took control of the rational mind and put the body at risk. In his business, that was the difference between life and sudden, violent death.

"I was an orphan," Remo said. "I never knew my mother. But I'm willing to bet that if she lived, she never would have drowned me in the sink or drove me into a lake and claimed it was because she'd run out of Pamprin."

"I don't—" Connie began, but stopped, her eyes growing wild. An idea came to her and she stabbed a shaking finger toward Brad. "It was all his idea."

On the floor, unable to extricate himself from the drawer, Brad snarled, "You lying slut!"

Remo continued as if neither of them had spoken. He stood before Connie Rydel, and she seemed to wither into herself, growing visibly smaller at his unforgiving glare.

"And I know my mom never would have taken up with some bath-deprived loser she met at the local filling station," Remo said. He snapped his fingers. "Hey, you know what? Why don't you ask her?"

"But didn't you say she was—" Connie began.

She could not finish what she had intended to say because a hand had enveloped her face.

Remo held her one-handed, as if holding a basketball, palm covering her mouth, middle finger between her eyes, thumb and other fingers spread out to cheekbones and jaw.

He squeezed.

Her eyes bulged. She tried to scream, but Remo's hand blocked the sound. Her scream was a silent scream, a scream in the vacuum of space.

The last thing the woman who had wanted to murder her own child saw in this life was the vengeful face of an orphan who had at one time wanted nothing more than to feel the loving embrace of a mother he would never know.

Then there came a loud crack of bone. The bulging eyes crossed and the body went limp in Remo's hand.

"Although you're probably not going to the same place as my mother," Remo said. He dropped Connie Rydel to the floor and turned to her boyfriend.

Animals caught in a hunter's trap had been known to gnaw off their own limbs in order to escape. At that moment, if Brad could have reached the knife drawer he would gladly have sawed his own arm off in order to escape the wrath of the dead-eyed killer who was strolling slowly toward him.

Remo reached down and picked the cowering man up by his shirt front with as much effort as if he were plucking a spring dandelion. He brought the kidnapper to eye level. The skin of his flattened arm stretched like Silly Putty.

"Where is she?" Remo said, in a voice so cold it seemed to freeze the humidity from the sweltering Virginia air.

Brad was too frightened to find his voice. He pointed a shaking finger toward the backyard. Remo glanced out the kitchen window and spied a small structure in the back of the yard, overgrown with weeds.

"Is she alive?" Remo asked,

"Yes. Yes."

"You're not."

Remo tossed the man over his shoulder. To an observer it would have looked like a casual throw, but that same observer would know that one does not toss a hundred-and-seventy-pound adult male as if he were an empty beer can.

The arm stretched and detached, the drawer went with him, spilling contents on the floor, and Brad rocketed back across the room. When he struck the wall with bone-crushing force, sending up a cloud of plaster and knocking pictures from walls in the next room, Remo was already outside.

An old tin toolshed rusted in the corner of the fenced-in backyard. The doors slid open in either direction, squealing on a bent and rusted track. In the corner was an ancient wheelbarrow, rusted through in spots and missing its wheel. Remo found Traci Rydel tucked in behind it.

The girl wore white shorts and an oversized red tank top over her swimsuit. There was a sneaker on only one foot. The other was bare. The news had said that a shoe had been found at the scene of the abduction. Her mother had thrown it to the roadside to support the lie.

The girl was gagged and blindfolded, with hands and feet lashed together with clothesline rope. She was shivering in fear and her skin was white and covered in sweat. The young girl was in shock. She shrank from the opening doors.

"Don't worry," Remo whispered gently. "You're safe now."

He manipulated a cluster of nerves at the side of her neck and the girl's head lolled. The shaking stopped.

Remo snapped her bonds and lifted her lightly from the dirty floor of the shed.

There were news vans parked in front of the Rydel house. A hundred cameras flooded light into the front yard of the big colonial. In the wash of brilliant light, as bright as the noon-day sun, no one saw the dark figure that approached the house from the rear.

Remo scaled the garden fence and climbed the back wall

of the house one-handed. On the second floor, he popped a latch on a bedroom window and lifted the unconscious girl inside. It was Traci's bedroom. Remo removed the dirty old stuffed animals from the bed and gently placed the girl on the covers.

Voices filtered up from downstairs. Family and friends who had come to comfort the parents. Remo heard someone wonder aloud where Connie was. He heard Traci's father say that she had taken a sleeping pill and gone to bed early.

The anger he had felt earlier was gone, burned off like morning mist. His eyes, described as cold by so many, many of them targets he had been sent after in his endless battle against the forces that would harm America, were warm now as he brushed a loose strand of hair from the young girl's face.

"It'll be hard," Remo whispered. The girl stirred at his words, but remained asleep.

Remo heard footsteps on the stairs. Quickly, he leaned in close to Traci's ear. "But don't worry, kid. It will get better," Remo vowed. "I promise."

Then he was gone. Out the window and down the wall. The shadow that fled over the rear garden fence a moment later was unnoticed amidst the cries of shock and joy that sounded from Traci Rydel's upstairs bedroom window.

3

Wendy Burdette checked her watch as she hustled along West Forty-third Street in Midtown Manhattan.

"Damn, damn and double damn," she mumbled from one corner of her mouth. In the other corner was a cigarette which she puffed as she ran, sending up plumes of smoke like a locomotive with a bad attitude.

She was late. Parking had been miserable that morning, more so than usual, and the underground garage she ordinarily used on the days she didn't take the train had been full. Traffic was more snarled than usual, too, so much so that she'd nearly had to park in Harlem. She was winded from her twenty-block hike all the way to the bland sandstone tower that housed the Broadcast Corporation of North America.

Wendy was a segment producer for the BCN Evening News, a position she had held for the past seven years. The work had never been particularly fun but it had always been interesting. Most of her time at BCN she had worked under the network's crusty news anchor, a flightly old-timer with a penchant for bizarre, folksy aphorisms. Sometimes, he wore sweaters. The anchor had sat in the center chair for nearly twenty-five years and was as political in his job as any Washington spinmeister. He was finally forced to retire when he attempted to prove that the president of the United States had dodged the Vietnam draft with a phony deferment. His proof positive was a letter, allegedly written in the president's own hand and dated 1969. When the anchor touched the thirty-five-year-old letter on live TV, the ink smeared. His career was over before the fresh ink dried.

After the men in white coats had carted the old anchorman away, BCN announced his replacement. The new anchor would be a former female cohost of a highly-rated morning show on a competing network.

When the news broke, Wendy Burdette had been delighted. The old anchor had not been so difficult to work for as his detractors liked to imagine, but he was still a man, as well as a throwback to the dinosaur age of television journalism. Wendy was looking forward to working for a female anchor, a gender equal who would appreciate what it was like to be a career woman in a world dominated by men.

Wendy's excitement had lasted until nine o'clock on the new anchor's first day at work.

The new female anchor had marched in spitting orders and venom. Her perky smile, cute in her thirties, had at fifty become a snarl of gums and porcelain caps. Botox injections kept the wrinkles from her forehead, but it also froze her expression, preventing anyone from knowing precisely when she was enraged. The staff quickly decided that, immobilized forehead or not, their new boss was angry most of the time.

Work became a nightmare. It had only gotten worse when, by the end of her first week on the job, the new anchor's ratings sank into the basement and stayed there. Now when they heard the sound of the anchorwoman's stiletto heels clacking closer, grown men and women dived into offices and hid under desks.

Wendy had quit smoking five years before, but thanks to her new boss the habit was back with a vengeance.

There had been some calm during the Traci Rydel story. Wall-to-wall coverage of a single story meant that much of the staff could take a breather. And the she-devil anchorwoman was spending so much time on the air, she could not screech at the staff off-air. But the Virginia kidnapping story had ended with a bizarre twist, which meant there would now be more stories exploiting the new angle, as well as an eventual return to more normal news coverage. This, in Wendy Burdette's life, ultimately translated to more time for the new BCN anchor to abuse her staff.

Half the newsroom now had resumes out around town, Wendy included. And at this moment, thanks to a missed train and no place to park her car, Wendy was running up Forty-third, sending clouds of cigarette smoke in her wake and fearing the wrath of the news bitch boss from hell.

Foot traffic was heavy as always in Manhattan, and Wendy darted around slow-moving pedestrians. As she ran around a corner, she tripped and fell over a black body bag that had been dumped across the sidewalk.

Wendy did not even have time to curse, so shocked was she to find herself sprawled on the ground. Something had cushioned her fall. She realized with a frightened start that she had landed atop a second body bag.

Hands grabbed her by the arms. A man and woman helped Wendy to her feet.

"Are you all right, miss?" the woman asked.

"Fine," Wendy said. She had just noticed there was another body bag beyond the second, and dozens more beyond that. Many more had been dumped into the street.

No wonder traffic had been so bad. Judging from the two hundred body bags, there had apparently been a mass murder in Midtown at nine o'clock on a weekday morning.

Wendy's first thoughts were not sympathy for the dead but fear of what the new female anchor would do to her for not being at her desk on time on the day of the most explosive news story to hit New York in over five years.

But if Wendy was going to be eviscerated with a stiletto heel over this, she would not be alone. She noted only a couple of cameras on the scene, none of them network. Maybe Wendy could get the scoop after all.

"What's going on?" she demanded of the couple who had helped her to her feet. Cigarette between her fingers, she pulled out her cell phone and pressed the speed dial.

"I think they're filming a commercial," the helpful woman suggested. She was elderly, broad-faced and had a Midwest accent so thick you could spread it on an English muffin. "We've been watching them set up for the last twenty minutes, haven't we, Mitch?"

"BCN News, how may I direct your call?"

Wendy ignored the operator and hung up her phone.

The elderly tourist was right. Several college-age boys and girls hustled around amid the body bags. Horns honked and drivers cursed as the young people went about their business, uncaring of the madness they were causing. If anything, the college students seemed to puff up with each curse, as if a cabdriver's jeers was helium to their inflating egos. The cameras on the scene were not news cameras but belonged to the young people. They played to the cameras, were given instructions about where to stand and to keep their voices loud. When one of the young men took out a bullhorn and began yelling at the buildings, it finally hit Wendy.

"Oh, God," she hissed.

She quickly pulled her cigarette from between her lips and crushed it under the toe of her comfortable sneaker.

She had not been fast enough. A young woman with a bullhorn hustled over to her.

"Smoking-related deaths account for two million deaths per year in this country!" the girl screamed.

"I've got to get to work," Wendy grunted.

The young girl dogged her down the sidewalk. They both had to step over body bags which, Wendy now knew, were fake.

This was a stunt by the Campaign for a Smoke-Free World. She had seen their ads on television a thousand times. Young people staged hit-and-run videotaped attacks on major urban centers to promote their cause. The privileged kids in the ads were stylish in their clothing, piercings, tattoos and facial hair. The girl chasing Wendy was wearing boots, studded jeans and a too-tight CSFW T-shirt.

"I said two million! That is the same number as Hitler murdered in all of the Second World War!" the girl screamed through her bullhorn. Wendy had to plug a finger in one ear to keep from going deaf.

"Actually, no, it isn't," Wendy said through gritted teeth. "Not including battlefield deaths, Hitler killed more like eleven to thirteen million."

The girl hesitated. "That's what I meant," she bellowed through her bullhorn. "Smoking kills thirteen million people in the United States in a single year."

"Idiot," Wendy said.

"You're with them!" the girl bellowed through her bullhorn. Turning wildly on the nearest pedestrians, she aimed a j'accuse finger at Wendy. "I saw her smoking a cancer stick back there. She's in the pocket of Big Tobacco!"

With that, the girl with the bullhorn spun away victorious. In another moment, she was screaming at a middle-aged stockbroker who had made the mistake of walking out of a building with a pack of Marlboros in his hand.

"Morons," Wendy muttered. She tapped a cigarette from the pack she'd slipped from her purse, lit it defiantly, and marched off to work.

The Campaign for a Smoke-Free World videotaped its latest hit-and-run commercial for ten more minutes. When the police arrived in force to drive them off, the young people gathered up their cameras and body bags, which were stuffed with old clothing and shredded newspapers, and obediently abandoned the scene.

In their haste to clear out, several of the more than two hundred body bags were left behind, including the one Wendy Burdette had tripped over.

Since this was New York City, the black bags were ignored for two days until the smell became so great that someone finally called the authorities. When the police returned and unzipped the bag that had tripped Wendy Burdette, they found a decomposing body.

The man was white, in his forties. The driver's license in his wallet identified him as John C. Feathers.

"Got any idea the cause of death?" the medical examiner asked when he arrived on the scene.

"Someone nailed the poor guy right in the heart," one of the police detectives said. The comment brought chuckles from nearby members of the NYPD.

The medical examiner found that the detective's words were literally true.

Three thin, flat-topped metal objects were embedded in the chest of Mr. Feathers, two directly through the heart. Carpentry nails.

The other body bags were opened, more bodies discovered. Sixteen in all. Unlike the late Mr. Feathers, who it was discovered worked for Cheyenne Tobacco, Inc., the other victims had not died from nail injuries but from many other different, baffling wounds.

When word of the mass murder reached the press, the Campaign for a Smoke-Free World immediately issued a statement blaming Big Tobacco for attempting to discredit their group. It read in part, "They cannot debate us with fact, so in order to intimidate us they have resorted to what they do best. Murder." Representatives of most of the major tobacco companies responded to the accusation with bland press releases assuring that they would, of course, cooperate fully with authorities.

Headlines around the nation screamed that there was a serial killer on the loose who was dumping bodies in Manhattan in broad daylight.

And at BCN, the new female anchorperson clicked into the morning meeting on three-inch spikes screaming bloody murder at her staff and demanding to know why no one had thought to cover the CSFW commercial shoot that had tangled up traffic out front two days before. She neglected to mention that her limo had wended its way through the snarl that morning and she had done nothing because she had been too busy berating her driver for not getting her to her Pilates class in time.

"Sorry," segment producer Wendy Burdette said. "Didn't see a thing."

4

Remo's mood was lighter by the time he returned
home to his Connecticut condominium. He was whistling
the theme from *The Flintstones* when he stepped through the
front door.

"Lucy, I'm home," he called.

A bellowing television was his reply.

Remo shared the condo with Chiun, the Master of Sinanju,
who was Remo's teacher in the discipline of Sinanju, the Sun
Source of all the lesser martial arts. Although his ears were
as sharp as they had ever been, it was not unusual for aged
Chiun to watch the TV at full volume, as any of a dozen
neighbors who had attempted to occupy the other side of the
duplex could attest. When the condo association had complained that they were finding it impossible to sell the unit
next door, Remo finally bit the bullet and bought it himself.
Next door was now nothing but a storage area for his and
Chiun's belongings.

Not that Remo needed the extra storage. When he packed
a lot, he brought a toothbrush and a change of underwear.

Most times he brought nothing, which worked out nicely because he owned very little. Other than a little carved stone figure that he kept on the dresser in his bedroom, he could not think of anything he would worry too much about if the duplex burned to the ground.

Chiun, on the other hand, had a great many belongings. Most of what the Korean master assassin owned was back in his home village of Sinanju, in Communist North Korea. What remained had mostly been squirreled away in fourteen lacquered steamer trucks which Remo had been forced to lug from hotel to hotel for much of their association.

But now they had a home of sorts and a place to put all of Chiun's gewgaws. So the Master of Sinanju's belongings had a home in the empty house next door, which was only empty because Chiun refused to turn down the TV volume no matter how long desperate neighbors pounded on the walls demanding silence.

The big screen television was on now, and loud, and Chiun was nowhere to be found. The TV was tuned to a cable news program.

This was unusual. Remo was used to the TV blaring Mexican or Australian soap operas. Rarely these days, but every now and again, some grainy old tapes of American soaps from the 1970s would get hauled out of one of Chiun's steamer trunks. The picture quality on the thirty-year-old tapes had degraded to smears of moving beige, gray and white, but the stories were still some of Chiun's favorites and would never be parted with. Sometimes the old Korean would watch primetime entertainment shows and offer commentary on the appalling state of American culture. For a time years before he watched the news only to catch a glimpse of a particular anchorwoman for whom he carried a torch. But Cheeta Ching had disappeared from the TV radar a long time ago. These days almost never did the Master of Sinanju watch the news.

And yet the news was on when Remo strolled into the empty living room of the condominium. An anchorman with a salon tan and rings of white around his eyes that made him look like a raccoon in reverse read the news.

". . . are calling a miracle, little Traci Rydel, missing since yesterday morning, was discovered by her father near ten o'clock last night asleep in her own bed. A blue van discovered on the next street led authorities to the home of Brad Swinder, an out-of-work bakery truck driver. The shocker in this tale is that the girl's mother, Connie Rydel, was apparently having an affair with Swinder, according to evidence discovered at Swinder's home, and may have herself been involved in the kidnapping. Unfortunately, the entire truth may never be known, as Mrs. Rydel and Brad Swinder were dead when authorities broke down the door to Swinder's house, an apparent murder-suicide. . . ."

Remo wondered how that possibility was even being considered. Didn't most murder-suicides involve guns or something? Maybe someone thought her boyfriend had crushed Mrs. Rydel's skull with inhuman strength before hurling himself against the wall with the force of a speeding train.

When the truth finally came out, if it ever did, he doubted the reporter would offer a retraction.

Remo nudged down the volume, clicked off the TV, and went in search of the Master of Sinanju.

His teacher was not in their home. Remo found him next door, in the empty condo Remo had been forced to buy.

"I was watching that," Chiun said by way of greeting.

The elderly Korean was a frail wisp in a powder blue brocade kimono. A thin body that looked as if it had been fashioned from pipe cleaners animated the heavy blue fabric. Chiun had never seen one hundred pounds, was five feet if he stretched and, save for a pair of yellowing-white tufts of hair that danced in the eddies of the empty living room, had been bald since Remo had met him over thirty years ago.

The old Korean's bright face bore in its many wrinkles the wisdom of his own hundred years in addition to the collected wisdom of five thousand years of the House of Sinanju, the greatest assassins ever to touch sandal to soil. His wattled neck craned from the collar of his robes, and he turned his benign visage on Remo Williams, his pupil, the boy who, in his own mind, he had rescued from the muck of

Western civilization, had loved as only a father could love a son, and had raised to the pinnacle of everything any man could ever hope to become.

Thus, with the wisdom of the ages and his own long life, spoke Chiun: "Wipe your big baboon feet."

"Little Father, you know I don't have dirt on my shoes."

Chiun grunted a little grunt that indicated he knew no such thing and returned to what he had been doing before he had been so rudely interrupted.

What the old Master of Sinanju had been doing was sorting through the contents of his steamer trunks.

A local clothing retailer had recently gone out of business and, once the regular inventory had been sold off, Chiun had made Remo purchase the store's old clothing racks. They were arranged now in rows in the living room with lines of wooden hangers from which hung Chiun's many kimonos.

Remo had no idea how so many kimonos had fit in so few trunks. The room looked like Chiun had maxed out his credit card at Macy's Annual Christmas Kimono Blowout. There were kimonos in every shade of orange, red, green, yellow and blue. There were dragons leaping, flying, breathing fire and eating one another. There were magnolias, jonquils, calla lilies, orchids—an entire hothouse of rare and beautiful flowers. The racks were full, and still the old Korean found more kimonos tucked in the recesses of his fourteen trunks.

"This looks like backstage at the midget version of *The Mikado*," Remo commented.

"Now you know why I must turn the television up so loudly," Chiun said as he flounced like a fussing hen amid his open luggage. "To drown out stupid comments. And I said I was watching that."

"Unless you're keeping something from me, watching TV through solid walls is not in a Sinanju Master's repertoire." Remo sank to the floor, scissoring his legs beneath him.

"I took a momentary break from the endless babbling of those pretty men who are in love with their own deep voices. Really, Remo, you must talk to Smith about taking those fools off of the public airwaves. It is not often that you make me proud, yet it is too much even for the Master to endure to get news of your exploits from those makeup-wearing news blubberheads."

Chiun shook out a kimono and draped it on a wooden hanger. Remo blinked and picked his jaw up off the floor.

"You're proud of me?"

"Slightly less ashamed than usual," Chiun said, picking an imaginary scintilla of dust off the shoulder of a yellow morning kimono. He did not turn.

Remo had told his teacher why he was going to Virginia the previous day. The wizened Asian had been rummaging through the fire-engine red trunk with the copper hasps and lapis lazuli insets and had not answered when Remo said he was going to pitch in with the effort to locate Traci Rydel. Remo assumed he was storing up the carping for later.

"Aren't you going to rip me a new one for giving away a freebie like that?"

"You went to clomp through the woods with a herd of wheezing, meat-eating whites. That, of course, was stupid beyond measure. If you had done only that I would draw the shades and hide in the basement until the cloud of shame over the roof dissipated sometime next year. Instead, you did what you were trained to do. They say in the talking moments on television that the harlot and her wicked consort killed one another, which is, of course, utter nonsense. Only a fool would not recognize the unfailing hand of Sinanju. Which, sadly, constitutes everyone in this nation but me."

Remo shook his head. "Doesn't matter, Little Father. I mean, I'm happy to have saved the little girl and all, but there'll just be another one like this in a couple of months. I can accept a guy as a psycho, but women seem to be making a mad dash to catch up lately. This whole place seems to be going to hell in a handbasket these days, and I'm the only one who seems to care enough to try to stop it."

A thin thread of beard adorned Chiun's chin, and he stroked it thoughtfully. "There is a saying in my village. No matter how far the lone fool stretches his arms he cannot hold back the flood."

"Which means?"

"Which means there are things a society can do, even one as backward as the United States, to keep things from falling into anarchy. But your country has abandoned reason in these, its waning days, and so you have a situation, the latest of many, like the one you encountered with the mother of that poor young girl. Even when I came to these shores a few short decades ago such a tale would have been unheard of. Now it is commonplace. And so, my son, as well meaning as you may be, you are still the fool with his arms outstretched attempting to stop the flood that is swamping this nation."

"I'm not alone," Remo said. "That's what CURE was set up to do. Smitty is in this with me."

Chiun knew the story well. How an American president, long dead, had determined that the United States had reached a crossroads. Down one path was anarchy, down the other, a police state. CURE was founded as a last-ditch effort to avoid the two ugliest options; as a barrier to the forces that would destroy a nation that was the last, best hope for mankind. Harold Smith had been recruited to lead the organization, and he had later brought Chiun and Remo aboard. As much as he might fear for the country he loved, and as much as he sometimes didn't like Smith on a personal level, Remo knew that he was not alone in the fight.

Chiun, on the other hand, did not hold their employer in quite as high regard as did his pupil.

"Three cheers and a tiger for you," the Master of Sinanju droned. "Together you and Mad Harold can gather the flood-waters up in your arms. If you are interested, the rest of the saying goes, 'In the dry months the wise man builds his dam in anticipation of the flood. The fool flaps his arms when the rains come and eventually drowns.' Your Smith is the biggest arm flapper of them all."

"Smitty's not so bad. And that story sounds like the Sinanju version of the Grasshopper and the Ant."

"The what and the what?"

"It's a fable. The grasshopper hops around all summer having fun, while the ant spends his time storing away food for winter. When fall comes, the ant has plenty to eat all winter because he was prepared, but the grasshopper dies or something because he wasted his time playing around. Or maybe the ant shares his food with the grasshopper. He'd be a pretty asshole ant to just let the grasshopper die like that, especially since I think they were friends. Or maybe I'm getting that part wrong. It's been a while."

Chiun stared at his pupil, vellum lids hanging low over hazel eyes. "What on earth are you babbling about?"

"You never heard of 'The Grasshopper and the Ant'? It's a famous story."

"Here I am attempting to enlighten you with wisdom of the ages that has bearing on your latest lunatic—yes, Remo, I said lunatic—adventure, and you are chattering on about bugs. Where did that idiot story come from? I demand to know who owes us royalties."

"I think it's an Aesop's fable."

The old Korean's face puckered into a cranky knot of leathery wrinkles. "That thieving Greek slave stole everything from us. Who told you that story?"

"The nuns back at St. Theresa's."

"Oh," Chiun said, as if that explained all the woes of the world. He went back to his wardrobe, angrily shaking out a purple autumn kimono.

Remo watched the old man rearrange kimonos for a few long minutes. At last he sighed and shook his head. "The nuns were okay. They did a hell of a job as far as I'm concerned. You know, Chiun, I sometimes used to feel sorry for myself for being an orphan. But lately I'm thinking that orphans back in my day had it easier than kids with two parents have it these days."

"One-parent households do fine. I managed you, didn't I? The girl will do better with but one parent."

"Little Father, she didn't have two parents when she had two parents."

"Then you have done what's right. A child is a gift to tomorrow. Your actions today have delivered this girl to tomorrow, Remo. But next time, get paid."

"Yeah, yeah." Remo rose to his feet. "I'm taking a nap. Wake me when the world is sane again, will you?" At the sliding glass doors, he paused, glancing around their spare condominium. "You realize, Little Father, that this is the most expensive closet in America?"

"As you saved that young girl, so I once saved you. For all I have done for you, I deserve no less."

With that, Remo could not argue. Sliding the glass patio doors shut, he headed back to their living quarters.

5

In a back office in an ivy-covered brick building on
Long Island Sound, Dr. Harold W. Smith scanned the FBI
files, local police reports, and news updates of Traci Rydel's
miraculous return. Smith heaved a sigh of relief.

All morning he had been scrutinizing every scrap of information out of Virginia, searching for anything that might
connect Remo's actions back to CURE.

Years ago, Smith had written an elaborate computer program that sifted through reams of raw data. It searched
specifically for odd and multiple deaths, strange phenomena
directly tied to individuals fitting either Remo's or Chiun's
descriptions, and instances of people exhibiting anything
that might be seen as extraordinary abilities. The basement
mainframes were more than sufficient for the task and performed their duties flawlessly. Yet at times like these, when
Remo's activities brought him so close to the spotlight,
Smith did not trust anything but his own eyes. And his eyes
were telling him CURE would remain safe.

Smith felt guilty second-guessing the CURE mainframes.

The complex computer system, housed behind a secret wall two stories below Smith's cordovan dress shoes might be a cold, analytical collection of chips, wires, metal and plastic, but as such it was a near, dear, bloodless relative to the emotionless Harold Smith.

Smith could not count how many times he had disappointed his own wife and family. Through his decades at Folcroft Sanitarium, which was secret home to the agency Smith tirelessly managed, he had missed many a holiday, birthday, vacation and special family event, and had done so without feeling as much guilt as he felt on those days when he did not trust the Folcroft Four. Perhaps it was because Smith and his four mainframes were such kindred spirits. Human beings were unpredictable, and were thus difficult to manage neatly. Computers, like Smith himself, did not allow the vicissitudes of human emotion to impact their work, and thus were easier for Smith to relate to on a personal level.

No one who met him would have been surprised that Smith related better to computers than to living creatures since Smith looked to have been constructed in shades of gray by the least imaginative of deities. For decades, his work uniform had consisted of a three-piece gray suit with a white dress shirt buttoned up to his bobbing Adam's apple. His thinning white hair was tinged gray and even his skin tone was an unhealthy gray. His rimless glasses, perched on a patrician nose that might have been carved from the granite of his native New England, were kept spotlessly clean, as if dust, allowed to collect on the lenses, might work its way inside and disrupt the circuitry of Smith's brain.

Smith's personality did nothing to dispel the image projected by his cold, gray exterior. He was unimaginative, distant, and stingy, both with his finances and his emotions.

When Smith was a young boy, his mother had bought him a puppy, hoping to stimulate some kind of human empathy in her son.

"What do you want me to do with it, mother?" young Harold had asked as the little black lab mix mutt yipped happily around its new owner's feet.

His mother had been a loving woman, as kind to her son as his father had been emotionally distant.

"What should a little boy do with a dog, Harold?" his mother had asked.

Smith thought of what he had seen the other children do with their dogs. "Take it for walks, feed it, bathe it and clean up its droppings."

"Love it, Harold," his mother had insisted.

Smith looked at the furry little creature slobbering on his highly shined shoes. Then it started gnawing at the laces.

"If you say so, mother."

Smith had dutifully looked after the dog as just another of his daily chores. When a week had gone by and his mother had commented that Harold had not yet named the animal, her son had suggested "Smith."

"That's our name, Harold. A dog should have a name of its own. Something to do with its personality or how it makes its owner feel. What do you think of when you look at your puppy, Harold?"

Smith thought of what a nuisance it was to pick up the needy little creature's poop. But calling the dog "Nuisance" would have hurt his mother's feelings and so, characteristic of a boy without even a spark of imagination, young Smith had called the little black dog "Blackie."

When another week had gone by and Smith's mother saw that her son had not bonded with the animal, she realized that her experiment had failed. She gave the dog to a family down the street with two children who would love it.

Young Harold Smith was relieved to see it go. The dog had seemed a foolish drain on family resources, especially during the Great Depression.

"If it were a chicken, we would have eggs," he admitted to his mother after the mongrel was gone. "A cow, we would have milk. Even a cat will kill vermin. But a dog that small wasn't even good for discouraging prowlers. I failed to see its purpose, mother."

"That's all right, Harold," his mother had assured him, in that sad tone she seemed to use more and more frequently as she watched her dull little boy grow into the drab man he would remain for the rest of his life.

Smith's blandness had served him well in his work as an OSS spy in World War II, and later at the Cold War CIA. General Eisenhower, Supreme Commander of the Allied Forces in World War II, had once written Smith a letter in which he said that the work done by the bland New Englander might well have been the reason the Allies defeated Hitler. Smith destroyed the letter lest his wife stumble across it and begin to suspect that her husband was more than just another faceless paper-pusher.

He preferred his anonymity and if he made an impression at all on those around him, it was only long enough for him to be dismissed as unimpressive. Harold W. Smith looked for all the world as if he had rolled off a Detroit assembly line for unimaginative bureaucrats.

The only time Smith even approached something resembling human happiness was when he was plugged into his beloved computer network. Remo, seeing Smith interact so blissfully with his computers, once suggested that the CURE director would have married a computer "if that tightass WASP church of yours could have fit an ENIAC between the pews." Of course it was a fanciful notion, but on days like today, when lack of trust in his computer system formed that tiny hollow of guilt in his stomach, Smith tried especially hard to force from his thoughts any of the many disappointments he had inflicted on his flesh and blood family.

The reports from Virginia were a relief. There was nothing to tie the Traci Rydel matter to CURE. The girl unequivocally implicated her mother in the actual kidnapping, and Brad Swinder in the plot to murder her. But she did not remember clearly how she had gotten back home. The story in the media was that Swinder had had second thoughts and returned the girl to her home without the mother's knowledge. When Connie Rydel discovered her lover's betrayal, a fight ensued during which the two killed each other.

The police might eventually have something more to say on the matter, but these initial reports would be what the vast majority of Americans would remember. The Traci Rydel case was over and would soon pass into hazy memory.

Smith heaved a sigh of relief, his second of the morning. The noise that escaped his thin lips sounded like an asthmatic balloon deflating.

Actually—and he would never admit this to Remo—Smith was secretly pleased. For a few years, it seemed that priorities of the secret agency had shifted from what they had always been. An inordinate amount of time had been spent in the clandestine war on terror. During that time, Remo had disappeared for long periods of time on heaven only knew what private business. But Remo was back, Smith was at his desk, God was in his heaven, and things were back to normal for CURE. Even Remo acting out was oddly comforting to Smith. Remo had never fully toed the line, at least not as Smith would have wanted him to. As irritating as that might sometimes be, the fact that Remo was acting his old self reinforced Smith's sense of normalcy.

Smith finished reading the latest news update on the Traci Rydel matter, was satisfied once more that CURE was secure, and back-clicked his way out of the story.

The Web site from which he had followed a link to the Rydel story was a clearinghouse of information. Smith sometimes found displeasing the sensationalistic tone taken by the site owner, but it was far more valuable in content than an entire week's worth of nightly newscasts. When Smith returned to the site, there was a flashing red-and-white police bubble icon at the top of the page that had not been there a few minutes earlier. Underneath, red letters blared the legend: MANHATTAN MURDER MAYHEM!

Smith was certainly no fan of yellow journalism, but he was aware that the siren icon was rarely used on this Web site, so the story must be a big one. Clicking on the link, he was taken to a bare bones Associated Press story.

Sixteen bodies had been discovered in broad daylight in New York City. As he scanned the sparse details, Smith's thin lips pursed.

Smith's monitor was hidden beneath the transparent surface

of his onyx desk, the screen canted so that it was only visible to his eyes. A capacitor keyboard was buried beneath the flat surface of the desk before him. Smith's arthritic fingers sought the keyboard. Typing swiftly, keys lighting amber bursts in the wake of confident finger strokes, Smith used the secret access granted by CURE's all-powerful mainframes to pull the relevant files from the New York Police Department.

Before he was finished, a new window popped open on his screen. In their endless trolling of the Web, CURE's computers had found and flagged a report. Smith saw that it was part of the special program that searched for deaths similar to Remo and Chiun's methods.

For an instant, Smith felt the familiar tingle of worry in his stomach. He assumed he was going to be reading a report out of Virginia. But instead of the Traci Rydel case, Smith was surprised to find that the report was the one out of New York he had been in the process of locating.

Entirely on their own, the mainframes had found something in the New York affair that might interest Smith.

The director of CURE read the police reports with interest. He found that there was not much more than had been in the AP story, save one difference: the condition in which some of the bodies had been found.

Smith arched an eyebrow as he read about the nails in the chest of John Feathers, but his eyes widened when he scanned the details of injuries to the other bodies.

Fingers racing, he quickly tracked back Remo's and Chiun's whereabouts over the past several days. Except for Remo's jaunt to Virginia, credit card, phone and travel records did not indicate that either of them had been away from home long enough to be involved in the other deaths.

Smith felt a knot he had been unaware of loosen behind his breastbone.

The rest of the police report was short and dry. Apparently the bodies had been discovered where a commercial had earlier been filmed. Smith noted that it was for the anti-tobacco group Campaign for a Smoke-Free World.

Leaning back, Smith swiveled in his chair.

A picture window of one-way glass offered a picturesque view of Long Island Sound. Frothy waves broke on the jagged shore where a rotting boat dock extended from rolling green lawns. It was summer and, scattered across the sparkling black water, sails of white sought gusting wind.

CURE had been established to save America from forces that would use her very freedoms against her. Over the years, that mandate had been expanded to include all threats against America, both domestic and foreign.

Since one cloudless September morning five years before, Smith had taken seriously anything that seemed to give off even a faint whiff of terrorism, especially where New York and Washington were concerned. John Feathers had been found with nails in his body, but the others apparently died in ways unfamiliar to the police, a few in a way eerily familiar to Smith.

Remo had been looking for something to keep him occupied. If another matter like the Rydel case turned up, he might be off again.

And as quickly as that, the decision was made.

Spinning from the window, Smith reached for the blue contact phone. He paused as he touched the receiver.

Smith thought once more about CURE's return to the status quo, something that had given him brief satisfaction just a few moments before.

As he brought the receiver to his ear, Smith commented with a bitter sigh, "The world is back to normal in more ways than one."

"Why are we here?" The Master of Sinanju eyed with
distaste the grimy exterior of the New York city morgue.

"Smitty says a bunch of guys got themselves killed," Remo
said.

"People are always getting themselves killed. Fires kill.
Guns kill. Beef kills. If we do not get paid for it, why should
I care?"

"Smitty says we'll care about this."

"An emperor thinks the world has come to an end if his
porridge is too hot or too cold. In fact, Master Kik even
wrote a story about that very thing for Charles V of France.
The story, about three bears and a thieving peasant girl who
eats their porridge, was stolen from us as well."

"The point being?"

"The first point being, if you want to hide something from
the French, wrap it around a bar of soap and sink it in the bottom of a pail of warm water. The second, that Smith's cares are
the cares of the Master of Sinanju only on the day his madman
coffers run low. Otherwise, I remain a disinterested bystander."

As proof of his disinterest, the old Korean tucked his hands inside the voluminous sleeves of his kimono and stared off, bored, as they mounted the stairs.

"Not me," Remo said. "Smitty didn't give me any details, but he sounded worried. And not the usual kind of Smitty worried, but the big kind of worried. But he wouldn't say why, 'cause he said he wanted us to have a fresh perspective just in case his computers are wrong, whatever that means."

Chiun grunted the grunt of a disinterested bystander. Remo noticed some writing above the main entrance. In an attempt to keep the Master of Sinanju from lapsing into silence for days, something he often did to prove a point, Remo nodded to the words.

"I assume that doesn't say 'Welcome Shriners.'"

Chiun cast a bored eye across the words. "It is Latin. It reads, 'Let conversation cease. Let laughter flee. This is the place where death delights to help the living.'"

"Hmm," said Remo. "Sounds like it could be our motto. Although I suppose 'Cash up front' embroiders easier on a pillow."

The shoes of those they passed clicked hard and echoed loud. Remo's loafers and Chiun's sandals made not a sound as they walked side by side along polished floors.

At the main desk, a woman with orange spray-on tan, purple fingernails and saline chest cast a bored eye over Remo's phony FBI identification.

"Where's his ID?" she asked.

"This is what I mean when I tell you this country is backwards, Remo," Chiun said. "The singular visage of the Master of Sinanju is enough to gain entrance to the courts of majesty the world over, yet here I am asked to present a shiny piece of plastic merely to get inside a charnel house."

"Where's the ID Smith gave you?" Remo asked.

"The dog ate it," Chiun sniffed.

"Sorry, can't let you in," the woman said. "Security."

"Security can't be all that great," Remo said. "I saw a movie once where Fonzie and Batman were running an escort service out of here. Diane from *Cheers* played a high-priced hooker. Talk about suspension of disbelief."

Remo could see that the woman planned to be difficult, so without her even realizing it, he took her hand and with his index finger slowly, then more rapidly, tapped the inside of her wrist. The woman's face flushed underneath her orange tan. She was panting and sweating in a moment, and just before her eyes rolled back in her head, she gave Remo and Chiun two guest badges.

"Ten minutes," she said. "Then I come looking for you, brown eyes."

"Tell me, Remo," Chiun said after they had passed the reception desk and were heading down a long corridor. "When was it that you first realized you were an exhibitionist?"

"I thought you were a disinterested bystander."

"Would that I could be. Every time I try to ignore you, like a child acting out, you do something gross to attract my attention."

"I didn't see you stepping up to get us through the front door."

"Perish the thought. And if you are going to engage in such repulsive public displays, the least you could do is get the techniques right."

"Hey, ten thousand satisfied customers can't be wrong," Remo said with a grin.

This brought a string of muttering in Korean that lasted all the way down to the basement to the room where the bodies from the Campaign for a Smoke-Free World commercial shoot had been warehoused.

Dozens of stainless steel doors lined one wall. Remo rolled back the nearest.

The very white body of Johnny Crow Feathers was even paler in death. Remo noted the three puncture wounds in the Indian's chest where the nails had been removed.

"Hey, disinterested bystander, come and take a look at this," Remo called.

The Master of Sinanju padded over and examined the body.

When he saw the wounds in the Indian's chest, the old Korean clucked his tongue in irritation.

"Something was shot into this man," Chiun said. "Metal, judging from the lacerations. There is not the uncertainty of the human hand. Whatever it was was not moving fast. See the punctures in the skin? Tears from a bullet or similar projectile are much sharper."

Remo was glancing at a chart affixed to the slab. "Says here they found three nails in the poor guy. Probably fired at close range from a nail gun."

"There are guns that fire nails?" Chiun asked, eyes narrowing to thin slits of suspicion.

"Sure. They use them for construction all the time. Easier and faster than using a hammer."

"Now I have heard everything. You whites are so lazy you cannot even be bothered to drive in a nail by hand. Not only that, but you take the device you invented out of laziness and use it as a tool of assassination. How soon will it be before you are murdering one another with waffle irons and corn-popping machines?"

Chiun slid the slab back and slammed the door closed with a sound of thunder.

Remo had already slid open the next drawer. When he saw the condition of the corpse, he frowned.

"Here's something you don't see every day."

There was a raised welt dead center in the dead man's forehead. The blow was perfectly placed. More perfect, in fact, than Remo had ever seen delivered by someone trained in the lesser martial arts.

"That is, of course," Remo added, "unless you're us."

Wearing a puzzled expression, Chiun joined his pupil beside the slab. When he noted the fatal injury, the only visible wound on otherwise pale and perfect flesh, the old Korean's eyes squeezed to slits of vellum concern.

"It's pretty good," Remo said. "Sloppier than you'd do it, and you'd kill me if I was that bad, so that rules both of us out. And the last other guy on the planet trained this far in Sinanju was chopped to fish bait and tossed in the sea five years ago. So what's the deal, Little Father? You have any half-cousins or uncles on your mother's side who you've been ashamed to tell me about all these years?"

"This is not Sinanju," Chiun said firmly.

"It looks like a pretty good knockoff to me."

Chiun was not listening. In a swirl of kimono silk, the old Korean twirled to the next door, flinging it wide open. The next corpse had a similar forehead injury. The one beyond had an injury unseen by Remo, but which caused an angry gasp to slip from the Master of Sinanju's thin lips. Hands moved, and something was pulled from the body.

The corpse on the following morgue slab bore mirrored incision marks, one on either side of the neck, from two blades that had crisscrossed and slashed down. A chart identified the man as Charles Merrick. When Chiun saw these wounds, like fish's gills, he stopped opening drawers.

"While I yet take breath," the old Korean said, his voice colder than the chilly morgue air. "The impertinence. That they would climb up from their hole in my lifetime."

"Who?"

Even as he asked the question, Remo heard a sound at his back. Across the room, the rustle of fabric. The air shifted, cooler on his back, lifting the hairs on the back of his neck. The swinging doors had opened smoothly and had closed quickly and quietly.

"You may ask them yourself," the Master of Sinanju said, in a tone of low doom. He was staring past his pupil toward the doors.

When Remo turned he saw four figures standing at quiet readiness just inside the closed morgue doors.

The men were slight; not one weighed over one hundred thirty pounds or stood taller than five-foot-five. They wore loose-fitting black fighting costumes. Black hoods covered heads. Cloth masks ran from side to side over noses and mouths. Catlike eyes peered from between hood and mask.

Remo was impressed by their stealthy silence, and Remo did not impress easily. There were only two sets of human ears on earth that would have heard their soft movements, and the ears of both Masters of Sinanju were trained on the four figures standing across the room.

"Oh, swell," Remo said. "We've got ninjas."

"These are not ninja." In a rustle of silk, the old man held aloft a gleaming silver object.

The object had a round center the size of a fifty-cent piece. Three triangular blades, blunt on one side and curved at the tip were arranged around the central disk. Remo saw several characters etched into the side of the small killing item which Chiun had removed from one of the morgue bodies.

Chiun hissed a few words in a foreign tongue. One of the masked men replied in the same language. Remo did not understand the words, but recognized the language as Chinese.

Remo was surprised. Their costumes were similar to ninja garb, which would have made them Japanese. And yet the dark cloth across their mouths was not black, but the deepest purple. The eyes were Asian. Remo could see that they were clearly Chinese. And then the light dawned.

"Moshuh nanren?" Remo asked.

Remo did not need the Master of Sinanju to reply. Across the room, four sets of eyes shifted to Remo, a flicker of surprise that a white would know that name.

"Hey, cool beans," Remo said. "I thought these jokers went the way of the dodo four hundred years ago."

The hands of the men were hidden in black tunics. From their movements, Remo sensed that unseen hands held weapons. Pommels and grips of swords were visible over shoulders.

"Remain alert," Chiun warned. "These Chinese robbers are not the run-of-the-mill killers you bump into on the streets of America. Americans will at least have the decency to rob you after they kill you. These creatures will have their hand in your wallet during the first thrust of the blade. Guard your gold with your life, my son."

The old man began to glide away from his pupil. Remo moved in the opposite direction.

Across the room, the four moshuh nanren were slowly fanning out, advancing in a semicircle. Remo was surprised yet again at the softness of their footfalls. There was a comfortable glide to their steps that was eerily familiar. It was crude compared to his and Chiun's confident movements, but similar enough to stir a proprietary anger in the soul of the latest Reigning Master of the House of Sinanju.

A dark notch formed between Remo's eyes. "Remember, Chiun, we keep one alive for questioning."

"And why are you telling me?" Chiun sniffed.

"Because it's your turn."

"I took the last turn."

"No, you were supposed to take it, but you didn't, so we were left with a pile of severed limbs and no one to question. It's your turn this turn."

"That is not how I remember it. Yet I will do your work for you yet again, as I have need to question these thieving creatures myself."

If the four men who had been called moshuh nanren were troubled by the nonchalance of the two men they were stalking, their dead eyes did not show it. To the far right, movement. A hand slipped suddenly from a black sleeve. Remo saw a flash of silver and almost simultaneous with its appearance, the silver something was zipping through the air toward Remo's exposed throat.

The killing object came in fast. But most people thought that bullets were fast. Collapsing buildings were fast if they fell on your head. However, an object thrown at a Master of Sinanju at the height of his abilities, be it a spear, a spitball or a spinning silver disk of deadly blades, all had the same chance of striking home. Namely none.

The moshuh nanren weapon flew in at ninety miles per hour, vicious sharp blades glinting in the dull fluorescent morgue light. An inch away from Remo's Adam's apple, he reached up and plucked it between thumb and forefinger.

"I appreciate the gesture," Remo said. One fingernail was slightly longer than the others, and honed to a sharp edge. Remo scored a few quick marks over the Chinese characters, a trapezoid bisected by a single line. "But Christmas is still a few months away."

In a movement that looked relaxed, he let the silver object leave his fingers. A last second snap of the wrist and he returned the gift at supersonic speed. The disk sank an inch deep into the forehead of its owner.

A shocked sigh slipped from unseen lips and the moshuh nanren collapsed to the floor.

The shock of seeing their comrade so easily killed was like a jolt of electricity through the three remaining men. They twirled, they jumped, they crouched. Hands appeared from black tunics, some holding more killing stars, others clutching gleaming knife blades. Twirling, slashing blades before him, one man charged Chiun.

"I see your bandit's toys are useful for attacking air," the wizened Korean intoned. "See you now what it is to have one's weapons always at hand." Chiun turned his palms like delicately opening blossoms, revealing ten razor-sharp fingernails.

A knife slashed at Chiun's throat. Like crossed swords, the old man met the downward blade with the leading edge of his index fingernail. There was a snap of blade and forearm bone. The broken half of the knife skittered across the floor. The arm broken by the immovable object that was the Master of Sinanju's arm failed to pain its owner. To feel pain one had to have a functioning nervous system, and ten sharpened talons slicing through one's spinal column were better than a hundred Advil for putting the whack on impertinent pain impulses.

Chiun removed his fingernails from between the killer's vertebrae, and the dead moshuh nanren slipped with a silent sigh to the floor.

The third killer was on Remo. Blades crisscrossed as he lunged for Remo's throat in the same downward slashing movement that had robbed Charles Merrick of life. The move would have appeared impressive to most anyone, but an eye trained in Sinanju saw a dozen wide-open opportunities. Remo took the most obvious one. As the blades slashed across one another, bearing down on Remo's soft flesh, Remo simply leaned back.

Without a target, the moshuh nanren lost his balance, and

in that split second of uncertainty, Remo reached out and slapped the man's hands. The knives crossed, and the stunned moshuh nanren was left with two bloodied stumps where his hands had been. A stream of panicked Chinese issued from beneath the man's purple mask.

"Steal our moves, lose your hands," Remo said.

From across the room, Chiun snapped, "Remo, stop playing with that one."

The old Korean produced the throwing star he had fished from the corpse and hurled it at the handless man. The killing disk struck throat with a wet thwack. The swirling buzzsaw cut through soft flesh and hard bone, severing the spinal column on its way out the far side. Head wobbling on a neck now as formless as overcooked spaghetti, the third moshuh nanren weaved in place for a moment before toppling over.

"Hey," Remo complained. "That one was mine. Do I do yours? Since when do you do mine?"

"You're welcome," Chiun said. "You may repay the favor by collecting that last specimen that I might question it."

Remo shook his head. "My turn again." He turned to the final moshuh nanren. "Okay, Lone Ranger, hands up."

Seeing the ease with which his companions had been removed, the last moshuh nanren had backed off to a cautious distance. A chattering tear of what sounded like Velcro revealed a belt around the man's midsection from which hung a number of knives and stars as well as a pair of what appeared to be brass knuckles with clawlike appendages. With darting movements, the silent moshuh nanren harvested four stars, hurling them one after another at Remo. Each star struck Remo solidly in the chest. Or, rather, they should have.

There was no way the stars could have missed. Remo was standing halfway across the room, an easy target. But when the stars were thrown, he was suddenly no longer standing in the same spot. He was now standing a foot away from the moshuh nanren, smiling and waving "hello" as the four stars buried themselves harmlessly in a stainless-steel morgue door on the far side of the room.

"Should I be impressed now?" Remo asked.

The moshuh nanren lunged for his belt, but Remo had already snatched the man by the scruff of the neck. Shaking him as if he were a dirty rug, Remo watched items fall from the man's belt like icicles from warm eaves, clanking and scattering across the cold morgue floor.

Remo carted the wriggling man at arm's length over to the Master of Sinanju.

"Why do we even bother taking turns if you're never going to take yours?" Remo asked. The moshuh nanren wiggled. Remo banged his head against the wall. "Quiet, you."

The old Korean extended an imperious finger to the floor. "Put that creature down."

Shrugging, Remo dropped the moshuh nanren in a heap at Chiun's feet. The man was wobbly from the knock Remo had given him. When he tried to crawl away, Chiun dropped a sandalled heel to the man's throat. Reaching down, he tore the black hood and purple mask from the killer's face.

He was in his late twenties, with short-cropped black hair slick with sweat. His smooth skin was flushed and his narrow eyes betrayed panic.

Chiun asked the man something in Chinese. Apparently he did not get the response he desired, for he swatted the moshuh nanren hard across the cheek.

"Can we do this in English?" Remo asked.

Grunting disapproval, the Master of Sinanju asked the cowering man another question. The young man shook his head, fearfully glancing at Remo.

"That is one mark in his favor," Chiun said. "He does not speak English."

"Okay, then ask him why they killed all these people."

"I already did. He does not know. They only returned to retrieve their lost throwing star lest this violence be traced back to them. Such sloppiness is not surprising. There are three levels of moshuh nanren, ending with their master. This group was at the lowest level of training. They know nothing of their mission, and only do as they are told." The old Korean regarded his pupil with hooded eyes. "Perhaps I should count that in their favor as well."

"Har-de-har-har," Remo said. "Find out who trained them or where he trained them. We can track from there."

Another question in Chinese and an answer that obviously did not sit well with the Master of Sinanju.

"They trained in China. He does not know where. They were brought to their training ground in secret. He knows his teacher only as 'master.' Actually, Remo, I think I am beginning to like this cringing Chinese dog."

"No pets," Remo said. "Can't he tell us *anything*?"

Chiun questioned the man again, and this time as he searched for something to offer, his eyes brightened.

"These four were instructed to leave the fifteen bodies of the men they killed after the commercial people were finished. He does not know why."

"He doesn't know a lot," Remo grumbled. "Okay, I guess we're through with him." A thought suddenly occurred to him. "Wait, did you say—"

But Chiun's hand had already moved. The leading edge of his hand struck flesh, then bone. So fast was the move, not a fleck of blood kissed the Master of Sinanju's wrinkled palm. The moshuh nanren's head rolled off his shoulders, thudded to the floor and disappeared under a nearby table.

"—fifteen bodies?" Remo finished.

"Yes," the Master of Sinanju replied.

Remo frowned. "But there's sixteen. Smitty said sixteen bodies were found at the commercial shoot."

Chiun's face was bland. "Put his head back on his shoulders so that we might ask him if he can count."

Before Remo could reply, the morgue doors swung open.

"Hey, Magic Fingers," the upstairs receptionist said. "It's been ten—" Her eyes fell to the bodies, and she screamed a scream to wake the dead.

"You want to handle this one, Little Father?" said Remo.

The elderly Asian turned his back. "I have told you, I am a disinterested bystander. Do what you must quietly."

Remo sighed. "Work, work, work."

7

Harold Smith was behind his desk sorting through
Folcroft cafeteria invoices.

The work of CURE did not occupy all of Smith's time. He
was director of Folcroft Sanitarium as well as director of
CURE, and so devoted several hours a week to sanitarium
business. It was a point of pride for Smith that in an age of
escalating medical costs and government meddling, Folcroft
continued to see a yearly profit.

There had been a time a few months before when Smith
discovered that one of the cafeteria workers had been ordering extra cans of condiments and sneaking off with the ex-
cess. The amounts were so small, just a can or two a month,
that someone without Smith's eagle eye for the bottom line
would doubtless have missed it. Smith had ordered the employee in question fired and reprimanded the cafeteria director for not discovering the theft herself.

And so Smith was at his desk, studying the blue carbon
copies of the cafeteria invoices and paying particularly close
attention to the ketchup and mayonnaise order when the blue

contact phone at his elbow buzzed to life. Smith answered on the first ring.

"Smith," the lemony voice of the CURE director said with crisp efficiency.

"It's no serial killer, Smitty," Remo's voice said. "But I'm guessing now that you pretty much knew that. They're not Sinanju, if that's what you were worried about. Chiun and I still have that market cornered."

Smith leaned back in his chair, a hint of worry on his gaunt face.

"The descriptions of the forehead blows were so similar," Smith said. "That's why the CURE mainframes flagged the deaths in the first place."

"Well, in this case your computers aren't on the fritz. These guys are moshuh nanren."

Smith frowned at the unfamiliar term. "Moshuh nanren?"

"Think ninjas, only better. They're one step back from ninjas, which makes them one step closer to Sinanju."

"So they are Japanese?"

"No," Remo said. "Chinese. The Japanese ninja actually stole most of their techniques from the moshuh nanren. There was some big-time turmoil with the House of Sinanju back then. Basically, a Chinese emperor tricked an elderly Master into showing them some moves. When the Japanese got wind that Sinanju was being stolen, they wanted a taste. They stole from the moshuh nanren who had stolen from us, and they became ninja, even though it's written in the scrolls that they stole straight from us, 'cause that's more or less what they did, once removed. Everybody was stealing all over the place. Believe me, there was hell to pay over that. Bodies stacked up like cordwood all over the Orient for about a hundred years. It's not nice to steal from Sinanju. Anyway, they were extinct as far as I knew. Supposedly Master Pook got rid of them all, or so he claimed. Chiun probably has a story to tell about that."

"No, I do not," the squeaky singsong of the Master of Sinanju chimed in from the background. "These thieves were thought to have been eradicated four hundred years ago in the time of Master Pook, who will be hereafter known in the Sinanju scrolls as Pook the Incompetent."

"So there you have it, Smitty," Remo said. "Pook didn't finish the job, so we have to."

Smith placed a flat palm on his desk. "So these moshuh nanren you encountered. They are Chinese?"

"Were," Remo corrected. "And yes, they were. They don't train outside the race. At least that was the way they were in Pook's time. Gotta keep that racial purity. There's a couple of levels up to their master. Unfortunately these guys didn't know squat about who or where he is, or even what they were doing here, so we're still at square one."

"I might be able to shed some light on that," Smith said. Pushing the cafeteria invoices aside, the CURE director tapped a few commands on his keyboard. A file popped up on his computer screen. "I had Mark do some research on the murdered men."

Mark Howard was Smith's assistant at Folcroft Sanitarium and with CURE. Smith's flint-gray eyes scanned the list his assistant had compiled for him.

"Randall Bruce, Pacific marketing division, Yuma Cigarettes, Inc. Joseph Meehan, senior vice president, Greybull Tobacco. John Feathers, research scientist for Cheyenne Tobacco, Inc. Christopher Ingman, Asia-Pacific director of distribution, Transglobal Pesticides, a division of Silver Bow Tobacco, Inc." Smith stopped reading the list. "You get the idea. All of the dead men found in Manhattan were in some way associated with one of the big American tobacco companies. Except for one, they were all part of the Asian divisions of their respective companies."

"What about the one that wasn't?"

"That would be Dr. John Feathers. He was a research scientist for Cheyenne Tobacco in West Virginia."

"Okay, so they're all tobacco guys. What was that name again? The jokers who were filming the commercial here?"

"The Campaign for a Smoke-Free World," Smith said. "We have researched their group. Much of their funding comes from tobacco companies. You'll recall that the big tobacco companies agreed to fund anti-smoking campaigns as part of a court settlement years ago. It appears that the CSFW may have taken their anti-tobacco message a step too far."

"I'll check them out next. Where's their HQ?"

Smith gave him an address in Connecticut that was not too far from Remo and Chiun's condominium.

"Got it," Remo said. "Talk to you soon, Smitty."

"Remo," Smith said. "About these moshuh nanren. Is Master Chiun concerned about them?"

A few miles from where Smith sat at his gleaming onyx desk, in an empty office in the New York Morgue, Remo glanced across the room.

Against an exterior wall was a row of metal file cabinets. Stretched across the top of them and snoring contentedly was the purple-fingernailed receptionist. Beside the woman's slumbering form was the Master of Sinanju. Chiun was standing at a window, hands clenched behind his back. The old Korean was in a staring contest with a white pigeon that was perched outside on the windowsill. The contest had been going on for five minutes and the pigeon was becoming agitated. It flapped its wings and bobbed its head. Chiun remained as motionless as any stone statue sentry.

"I don't think he's sweating them too much, Smitty," Remo said. "They're competition, so they're stealing food from those deadbeats that we support back in Sinanju. But if the ones we saw today are the best they've got, they're not much more dangerous than your everyday contract killers."

"So you won't be requiring assistance?"

"If we needed it, who'd give it?" Remo asked reasonably. The silence on the other end of the line made clear that Smith was at a loss. "Don't sweat it, Smitty. As far as I could see, they're just karate dancers in S&M pajamas. They're still covering their faces like they were ordered to by us hundreds of years ago, 'cause we told them they had to mask their shame for being thieves. They're nothing."

At the window, the Master of Sinanju wheeled. The sudden movement startled the pigeon, and it fluttered away in a flurry of panicked feathers. The sleeping receptionist snorted and rolled over against the wall. Her snoring resumed, louder than before.

"Do not tell him that," Chiun hissed. Flouncing over to Remo's side, he called loudly, "We thank you for your kind offer, Emperor, but would never dream of exposing you to such grave personal danger. Though we face great peril and may not return alive, we gladly depart to our almost certain doom with hearts ever soaring, comforted by the knowledge that, although we risk life and limb against these fearsome Chinese assassins, you remain safely in your fortress, away from all harm." His voice dropped once more so that only Remo could hear. "Let the ghost-face think we are risking our necks against these masked nincompoops. The only thing moshuh nanren are good for is raising our rates for those who think them genuine threats. Let them at least do that job right."

"Is your Scam-O-Meter ever off, Little Father?" Remo asked. "Even mini-vacs have to recharge their batteries."

"Hush, Remo," Chiun whispered. Loudly, so that Smith would hear, he called. "Remind me, Remo, to contact my attorney to update our wills, lest we do not return from this dangerous mission on behalf of our beloved emperor."

"Remo, this sounds more dangerous than you think," Smith said. "Are you sure you're both going to be all right?"

"I must dig out my funeral robes," Chiun called.

"Yeah," Remo said to Smith. "We'll be fine." He tried to shoo Chiun away, but the old Asian had a shell-like ear glued to the receiver.

"Are you sure?" Smith asked. "It sounds like these moshuh nanren are more dangerous than you claim."

Chiun nodded sharply for Remo to agree that they were.

Remo sighed. "I guess, Smitty. I mean, they could be." Chiun nodded approval. "I mean, we've never met them before today and they *are* supposed to be extinct. I guess they could have some tricks up their sleeves we don't know about." Chiun shook his head violently. Remo held out the phone. "Well, what the damn hell lie am I supposed to tell him?" he asked, peeved. Chiun snatched the phone from him.

"Of course, while very dangerous, the moshuh nanren know nothing that is not already known to Sinanju, Emperor Smith. The danger comes from the fact that their skills are our skills. Stolen, diluted, and removed from the Sun Source, yes, but still closer than others we have encountered, which is why the danger we now face is so great. Yet face them we must. Farewell, Smith the Wise. If we do not meet again in this life, know that your humble servants were honored to have died in service to your crown. Pax vobiscum!"

Chiun dropped the phone into the cradle. "Don't ever tell them that others know things we do not know."

"I thought you wanted me to oversell these mooshie-mooshies."

"I wanted you to learn how to properly deal with an emperor," Chiun said. "However, that craft set sail many years ago and is at the bottom of the ocean now, sunk with all the other hopes of my youth by Hurricane Remo, which is why I find myself tethered to you when I should be retired and spending my waning days mending fishing nets and watching the gulls dip over my beloved West Korean Bay."

"Tell you what. If I get everything wrong all the time, why don't you do the talking from now on?"

"That is the smartest thing you have said since the first day I met you eight hundred years ago."

Turning on a sandaled heel, the elderly Korean marched from the office.

Remo turned to the blissfully slumbering receptionist. "You were a big help in all of this, you know that?"

The woman purred and snored and rolled off the file cabinets, thudding to a heap on the office floor where she continued to snore, blissfully unaware of anything and everything beyond her own rapturous contentment.

8

Aphrodite Janise of the Campaign for a Smoke-Free World scanned the front-page story in the *New Haven Register* and threw the paper down in disgust.

"Front page. We even got the goddamn local front page," Aphrodite snapped.

The young woman at the front desk of the CSFW office gathered up and smoothed out the crumpled newspaper. She was a pretty young thing, a sophomore at the University of Connecticut, with bright eyes, long blond hair and an eager-to-please expression that rarely left her smooth, flawless face. She hated smoking, smokers, Republicans, Republican smokers, Big Tobacco, midterms and lacrosse players.

"I don't think it's so bad," the girl said. "It's not like a headline-headline. Like, you know, a really bad war or something would, like, get a big banner headline at the top. We didn't get that. At least it's below the fold."

Aphrodite glared down at the seated girl. "Am I paying you to think?"

"You're not paying me anything," the girl said. "I'm a volunteer."

"Then volunteer," Aphrodite snapped. "Do some filing, answer the phones, open the mail." She snatched the paper from the girl's hands. "And keep your opinions to yourself." Crumpled newspaper under her arm, she marched to her private office and slammed the door.

Aphrodite wanted the building to shake when she slammed the door. Unfortunately the building owned by the Campaign for a Smoke-Free World was over one hundred years old and of solid Victorian construction. It would have taken a direct bazooka blast to rattle the shutters of the pretty blue and green converted three-story house with its wrought-iron fence, widow's walk and big clay flowerpots on the front porch overflowing with purple and white petunias.

Aphrodite paced her big office which in another age, when the building had been a home, had been a family's library. It had been stripped of books and in place of the greatest literature of the Western world were now neatly stacked pamphlets, lush green ferns and posters that read "Say No To Tobacco" and "Lungs for the Memories."

Sixteen bodies. One would have been okay. One could have been sold as a secret attack by Big Tobacco to discredit the CSFW. The CSFW could absolutely have spun it that way, with Aphrodite Janise leading the charge on all networks, and the media would have lapped it up. "Big Tobacco Kills Own To Stop Anti-Smoking Message." One body would have been absolutely perfect. Okay, two bodies, maybe. Three would certainly have been pushing it. But sixteen? Sixteen was insanity, and just the sort of demented zealousness that detractors always ascribed to the Campaign for a Smoke-Free World. Whoever had dumped all those bodies on the CSFW ad shoot had really been out to get the anti-smoking group.

"Dammit," Aphrodite said to the empty room.

Prowling the perimeter of the room, she closed all the blinds on the ceiling-to-floor windows.

Aphrodite marched over to her gleaming pine desk and plunked into the soft nylon chair. With a key from the top drawer, she unlocked a bottom drawer. Inside were a dozen long red-and-white boxes. Aphrodite tore the top box open and dumped out a little box, smaller than her hand. Ripping off the top, she shook out a slender white tube.

She stuffed the cigarette between her lips and fished angrily in her purse for a lighter.

The first drag was deeply unsatisfying. Scowling, she tore off the filtered end and threw it in the trash barrel under her desk. The next pull flooded her lungs with a warm, gratifying glow, like a hug except from the inside.

Leaning over, she blew the smoke up the chimney behind her desk. She felt the familiar tingle in her fingertips. Her rattled nerves began to steady.

Amazing thing, nicotine, she thought. It's killing you a little more with every puff, but it beats Valium all to hell.

She was still puffing away when her office door opened a moment later. Panicked, Aphrodite threw her cigarette into an open desk drawer and slammed it shut.

The little college know-it-all who thought a front-page catastrophe only mattered if it was a banner headline stuck her pretty little blond head in the door.

"Ms. Janise, two gentlemen are here to see you."

Aphrodite nodded and waved the girl to let the visitors in. As soon as the girl's back was turned, Aphrodite ducked down and blew her last lungful of smoke up the chimney. She was smoothing wrinkles in her blouse and straightening her hair when the two guests entered her office.

One appeared to be in his thirties, with cruel but handsome features. The other was an ancient Asian who looked as if he'd been old when the CSFW building had been built during Queen Victoria's reign. The men were arguing.

"So sue me, I just don't think it's necessary to always be running the long con on Smith," the young one was saying.

"Is it a confidence game that I labor to keep the poor and elderly of my village fed and clothed?" the old one asked.

"Is it a con that the crippled and dying have a roof over their heads and wood for the fire? Tell me, is it a con that I sustain a village that would starve without me? Is that a con, Remo?"

"Can I help you?" Aphrodite asked.

Remo held up a staying finger to Aphrodite. "Just a second, babe." To Chiun, he said, "I'm just saying you could give it a rest for five seconds. Give Smitty a break. He did us a favor this time, even though he didn't know it. And you were the one who said on the way to New York that he was just giving me busy work because of Virginia."

"I would have been foolish if I did not think that Smith was wasting our time, for why would this day be any different from every day we have spent in his employ?"

"Excuse me," Aphrodite interjected.

This time Remo seemed grateful for the interruption. He turned from Chiun to Aphrodite.

"Okay, let's get this out of the way," he sighed. "Farrah Fawcett out front said you were the top guy."

She offered a frosty smile that barely curled the corners of her full lips. "Aphrodite Janise, president of the Campaign for a Smoke-Free World."

Remo shook her offered hand. Chiun looked at it as if it were a sack of moist garbage, then turned away.

"Don't mind Emily Post here," Remo said. "Aphrodite? The goddess of love."

Aphrodite shrugged, as cool as glacial ice. "What can I say? My parents were literature professors at a small New England college."

"Well, goddess of love," Remo said, "did you know your desk is on fire?"

Turning, Aphrodite saw the black smoke billowing from her closed desk drawer and lunged for a little red fire extinguisher that was hanging on the wall next to the mantel.

"No problem," she said, squirting high pressure carbon dioxide into her desk. "Not a problem." A long, sustained squirt. "Happens all the time," she reassured them. A final squirt and the desk was out. "See? All better. It's a paper shredder. Mice get into the wiring. Wires get chewed." She put the fire extinguisher down behind the desk. "What can I do for you gentlemen?"

Remo had already used pleasure once today, but that was before their encounter with the moshuh nanren. It was a whole new ball game now. Reaching over, he took Aphrodite's elbow between his thumb and forefinger.

He had moved faster than a striking cobra. Before she could pull away, she felt a pain like nothing she had ever experienced in her life. She had no idea how the younger man had snuck a pot of molten metal into her office since his hands had been empty when he came into the room, but he had obviously torn open her arm and poured liquid metal into her elbow joint. The furious pain raced into her bloodstream in a horrible burning rush that exploded in white-hot agony in her shoulder. Then he was asking questions, and she found that she was eager to answer truthfully.

"What do you know about Chinese assassins?" Remo asked.

"Nothing!" Aphrodite gasped.

"Who hired the moshuh nanren? Did you?"

"The what? I don't know what you mean. Please."

"Who dumped all those bodies at your commercial?"

"All? I don't know. It's just like the news says. They found them after we were finished."

The old one was talking. Aphrodite could scarcely hear him over the screaming pain in her brain.

"She speaks the truth," Chiun said.

Grunting agreement, Remo released Aphrodite's elbow. "I thought sure you were the brains behind this. Why can't anything ever be neat and tidy for us?" he complained.

Aphrodite was no longer listening. Her elbow was shredded. Her arm had been ripped off at the joint. It had to have been for a pain that great. But when she examined it, she found that the arm was as perfect as it had ever been, skin and bone unbroken. In fact, the pain was gone. She wiggled her fingers to make sure.

"Sorry," Remo said.

He and Chiun turned to go.

"That's it?" Aphrodite asked. "You break in here like a couple of maniacs, assault me, ask a couple of questions, then just turn around and go?"

"That's the general idea."

"Who is a maniac?" Chiun asked. He glanced around, looking for someone who might be standing behind him.

"You didn't even ask me if I thought I knew who was behind the frame-up," Aphrodite said.

Remo stopped at the door. "Did too."

"No, you asked me if I'd dumped all the bodies. My parents were real sticklers over language. You never asked me if I knew who'd actually done it."

Chiun had determined that they were, in fact, alone. "Did this female with the yellow teeth just lump me in with maniac you?" the Master of Sinanju asked.

"You want to wait in the car, Little Father?" Remo said.

"I want to be able to go somewhere in this nation where I am not insulted."

Shaking his head in disgust, he offered Aphrodite and Remo his back. He opened the blinds over the big window near his elbow and stared out at a small rear garden.

Remo turned back to Aphrodite. "So who did it?"

She leaned forward, knuckles resting on the pale and shining surface of her tidy desk. She beckoned Remo toward her with a conspiratorial nod of her head.

Remo stayed rooted to the carpet near the door. "I'm trying to cut down on wear and tear on my shoes. Tell me from over here."

She straightened up and frowned, irritated that her great moment of intrigue had been ruined.

"Big Tobacco," she said.

"That's it?" Remo asked. "Lady, I've seen your commercials. You blame Big Tobacco if the cat gets run over or the toilet overflows. Besides, I don't think you're really solid on whose side you're on."

"What do you mean?"

Leaving the Master of Sinanju at the window, Remo

strolled back across the room. Aphrodite grabbed each of her elbows protectively in opposing hands. But Remo was not going for her elbows. He skirted the desk. When he reached for the bottom drawer Aphrodite jumped forward to stop him, but was too late. Remo pulled the drawer open and upended the contents on the surface of her desk.

"Stop that!" she commanded.

Blocking her with his body, Remo pulled out the next drawer, then the next. Six deep drawers he dumped out onto her desk. Dozens of cigarette cartons, several charred from the fire, spilled off the surface onto the floor.

For a moment Aphrodite Janise was like a cornered animal, eyes wide, seemingly ready to bolt. Then a look of reluctant acceptance seeped across her face. With a heavy sigh, she dropped down in her chair.

"Okay, so you know. Big deal." There was no pretense now. She grabbed up an open pack and lit a new cigarette. "This doesn't make me a hypocrite," she insisted, blowing a plume of smoke from the corner of her mouth.

"No, it makes you a dummy," Remo said.

Across the room, Chiun grunted disapproval. One long fingernail snaked out and seemed barely to touch the window latch. The big window shot open, panes rattling.

"Probably," Aphrodite said. "But it also gives me the perspective these punk kids in the movement can't ever have. Take Miss October out there." She blew a cloud of smoke toward the closed office door. "There was no smoking at the top of the human pyramid in the high school pep squad, so she dodged a nicotine bullet there. She's in college now, so she figures she has to take up a cause. Smoking is 'all icky.' Can you believe it? The ditz told me that her first day here, so that's why we got her. Her other choices were 'that icky war' and 'nuclear power which is so, like, icky.' I feel so lucky to have won her, I think I'll go play the lottery."

"Still doesn't explain why you think the tobacco industry would be behind this," Remo said.

She leaned back in her chair, thoroughly relaxed. "It's a frame, plain and simple," Aphrodite said. "Those guys pay lip service to anti-smoking campaigns but they know what side their bread is buttered on. They're evil to the core but they're not idiots. They need smokers, or else no new BMW, junior is out of private school and the bank takes the house. You hear the latest news? It was just on NPR. All the guys killed were involved in the tobacco business. Would they want to kill their own? No way. So that leads an investigator to ask who would? And, of course, the answer is us. They make us look like radicals and murderers, and suddenly our cause is in the ashtray of history. Big Tobacco is setting us up. You can take that to the bank."

"How do I know you're not radicals out killing people yourself?"

"First off, I would have admitted it while you were questioning me. Second, just like Big Tobacco, we're not idiots. We start killing tons of tobacco people, we might as well paint an arrow straight to our front door. It looks too much like us for it to be us. Frame-up." She smiled yellow teeth in a pretty face and blew a cloud of smoke ceilingward.

Remo could not argue with her logic. Still, he doubted that the entire tobacco industry would be behind a plot to mass-murder its own, and he said so.

"I didn't say the whole industry necessarily," Aphrodite explained. "Could be just a couple of companies united, or maybe just one acting alone. If you want my educated guess, I wouldn't put it past those SOBs at Cheyenne Tobacco."

"Why them?"

"They're on the verge of the biggest rollout in the industry since cigarettes were passed out in the trenches in World War I. Our sources have found out they've got a new tobacco they've developed in their labs. There was apparently some superaddictive variety of the plant that went extinct hundreds of years ago. They got hold of some old preserved leaves and have managed to bring it back."

The Master of Sinanju turned. Bored expression fleeing, he was suddenly interested in Aphrodite's words.

"This plant," he demanded, "was it from the province of the Virgin Queen?"

She looked to Remo for help. "Virgin Queen?"

"He means Virginia."

"Yes, yes," Chiun snapped. "These leaves you mentioned, were they discovered there?"

"No. Montana. They were saved by a Native American tribe, the Chowok."

Chiun wheeled on Remo. "We are leaving."

"We're almost through here, Little Father."

"Now," Chiun insisted. His tone would brook no disagreement. Kimono hems swirling urgently, the old Asian marched from the room.

Remo threw up his arms. "I guess we're leaving."

Aphrodite had hustled to a closet in the corner of the room. She was lugging out a blue nylon backpack.

"I'm going with you," she insisted, too busy to even glance at him. At her desk, she jammed as many cartons of cigarettes as she could manage inside the backpack.

Remo could see the firm set of her jaw as she hustled past him and out the door. The young girl at the desk out front watched in helpless confusion as her boss hurried out the front door.

"I think I have a say in the matter," Remo said, following Aphrodite down the front porch steps. Chiun was waiting impatiently by Remo's car.

Aphrodite adjusted the backpack on her shoulder as she turned on Remo. "It's my neck on the line here. They got me hooked on their product and now they're trying to ruin us for telling the world the truth. You're here to stop them? Well so am I. So no, you don't have a say."

"Yeah, I do," Remo said. He jangled his keys in her face. "You're not coming. You've got another elbow, you know."

He danced around her and headed for the car. Chiun got in the backseat.

"I can help," Aphrodite said. "I've been in the anti-smoking business for almost a decade. Do you know the names and addresses of every tobacco bigshot in this country? I do. Do you know every product every one of them puts out, and every country where they're sold? Do you know where all the factories and fields and offices are?"

Remo rolled his eyes heavenward. "You're not smoking in my car," he said with a sigh.

"I'll crack a window," Aphrodite promised, pulling open the passenger side door.

Remo was at the driver's door. "He'll crack your skull," he warned over the roof.

Aphrodite looked at Chiun. Seated in the center of the back seat, the old Korean appeared frail. But there was a glint in his hazel eyes that promised sudden, violent death to any who refused to obey the invisible no-smoking cordon he'd set up around himself.

"Maybe I can sneak a few in the airport parking lot," Aphrodite said. She dropped her backpack to the floor and hopped in the front seat next to Remo.

9

He had decided a long time ago that the one thing he could not stand more than anything else in this business was the bastards. The bastards were everywhere. They would stab you in the back, sell you up the river, order everything on the menu and stick you with the bill.

The bastards were all those who tried to slip their greasy hands in your pocket, and that was pretty much everyone. Business rivals stole your bottom line, layabout employees stole your time, the government stole your profits with fines and taxes and court settlements, and worst of all were the consumers, who were doing the worst bastard thing of all. By dying left and right and six ways to Sunday, they stole from your future revenues, which was stealing meat from the table of Cheyenne Tobacco, Inc.

"Bastards to a man," announced Edgar Rawly, CEO of Cheyenne Tobacco.

The corporate world headquarters of the tobacco giant was a steel and glass tower that rose like a gleaming silver jewel from three hundred private acres of forests and fields in rural West Virginia. Much of the eighth floor of the ultra-modern building was given over to Edgar Rawly's office suite. A rolling wall blocked off the conference room where once a month for more than half a century Mr. Rawly had met with the bastards from the board of directors.

Mr. Rawly was sure to schedule meetings early in the morning. At his age he was in bed by six o'clock most nights and up most mornings before the cock crowed. The board members would be sitting around the huge table yawning and sucking down coffee like it was mother's milk while Rawly was being wheeled up to the head of the conference table, the spotless eastern glass walls to his back. As the meeting commenced, the sun would slowly rise over the hills behind him and the blinding orange sunlight would burn around him as if he were Lucifer risen in full glory from the depths of perdition, and all the doughnut-gobbling bastards before him would wince and cower from his mighty silhouette.

Of course, that worked a lot better back in the days when his legs worked more of the time, and he wasn't stuck in this goddamned infernal wheelchair. The bastards.

Rawly rarely walked these days. His will was as strong as it had ever been, but his body was weak. And that, he said a dozen times a day, had everything to do with bastard doctors and absolutely nothing to do with smoking.

Today was not a board meeting day. Today was for an all-new print commercial for the Asian markets, and Mr. Rawly was in the midst of a maelstrom of lighting, makeup and camera people. High-level Cheyenne executives mingled with the ad people, along with marketing strategists and men and women from one of Cheyenne's public relations firms.

Shuffling around among the men was a frail old woman who looked as if she had fished her clothes from a Goodwill donation box. She had spent most of her time peeking around equipment and poking at buttons. She wore a "Rape Is Violence" button, and an expression that dared anyone to challenge her button's assertion. The men seemed as used to her presence as they were to ignoring her.

Edgar Rawly was at the center of the whirlwind, head lolling to one side as he tried desperately to stay awake.

He must have dozed for a little while, for when he woke the lights on their poles had been repositioned and someone had wheeled him behind his broad desk.

Above him was a large portrait surrounded by a fat mahogany frame. At a glance one would not recognize the robust young man with the dark hair striking the heroic pose in the painting as the same withered shell of a man who sat mildewing in a wheelchair beneath it.

The portrait had been duplicated millions of times throughout the years, and over the course of five decades had appeared in hundreds of Cheyenne Tobacco pamphlets and press releases. Copies of the painting hung in every hallway in every corner of the Cheyenne Tobacco complex.

Edgar Rawly glanced up at the idealized version of himself, with its chiselled cheekbones, healthy glowing skin and fingers that were not stained yellow from an eight-decade-long smoking habit. The sagging cheeks of the real-life Rawly bunched into an angry frown.

"I look like a goddamn fink," Rawly snarled. Sucking a glob of mucus down his throat, he turned to the room. "Light me up!" the tobacco CEO demanded.

A cigarette appeared between his dry lips, then a flicking lighter held in a young, certain hand lit the tip.

Rawly sucked in the soothing, warm smoke.

The instant smoke kissed alveoli he was bent double, racked with a coughing spasm that lasted nearly two full minutes, which caused many heads in the room to turn in frightened concern.

"Sweet merciful Jesus, smoking is a beautiful thing," Rawly gasped when he was finally able to come up for air, his voice a phlegmy rasp. "Clears everything out as clean and new as a baby's first breath. Pail!"

A shiny silver bucket was brought forward, into which Rawly hacked a greenish black ball of mucus as big as a small turtle. It struck with a satisfying clang.

"Nobody these days appreciates how great smoking is for

dealing with the bad humors. Hell, they don't appreciate anything we've done for them. No appreciation even for something as simple as how manly smoking makes them look. How else is a ninety-pound weakling gonna look like John Wayne, for Christ's sake? Tell me how. Go on."

Most of the men in the room, so concerned for the old man a moment before, suddenly pretended that the question was rhetorical and continued working.

Everyone at the corporate headquarters of Cheyenne Tobacco in West Virginia knew that Mr. Rawly never asked rhetorical questions. When Mr. Rawly asked a question, even a rhetorical one, he expected to be answered. Fortunately, it was someone else's responsibility to talk directly to Mr. Rawly. Mr. Rawly did not like to talk much to people, a situation that was fine with most people since most people did not like being called a "no good bastard," something which invariably happened within two minutes of any conversation with Mr. Edgar Rawly.

The man whose responsibility it was to engage in direct conversation with Mr. Rawly was the same man who lit his employer's cigarettes and carried Mr. Rawly's spit bucket. The young man had been cleaning the bucket across the room when the not-quite-rhetorical question was asked. He hurried back to his employer's side.

"Sir?" asked David Merkel, personal assistant to Cheyenne Tobacco's chief executive officer.

"Squeeze the bee's wax out of your ears, Merkel, you stupid bastard," Rawly snarled. "I said my product makes little sissy finks like you into the kind of real men the ladies'll kill for. Tell me what else can do that?"

Confidence, gym membership, fancy car, no gut, good teeth, fame, money, hair.

Merkel ran down the obvious list in his head, then selected something that was as far removed from modern reality as a hula hoop but which he knew, with Mr. Edgar Rawly, was the right answer.

"One of those Charles Atlas ads they have in the backs of the funnybooks, Mr. Rawly?" Merkel asked.

"Charles Atlas?" Rawly demanded, delighted to be appalled. His jaundiced, bloodshot eyes bugged out of his ancient skull. "You think Bogie bagged Lauren Bacall thanks to Mr. Charles Atlas? Hah!" He shook his head so violently he got dizzy, and Merkel had to grab his arm to keep him from falling out of his chair. "Bogie was a Cheyenne Chum back in the Forties. We had all the big names, Merkel. Bogie, Gable, Tracy, Cagney. Did you know I met Bogie twice?"

Rawly aimed a liver-spotted hand at a framed picture on his office wall behind his desk.

Merkel had seen the photograph before. Mr. Rawly pointed it out to him at least five times every day. In the photograph a much younger Edgar Rawly had his arm wrapped around a young and uncomfortable-looking Humphrey Bogart. Curling smoke rose from the cigarettes in each man's hand.

"Ah, those were the days, Merkel," Rawly said, a wistful glint in his rheumy eyes. "Nobody came running after us with this balderdash about cancer. Maybe Great Aunt Tillie or Old Uncle Joe got it, but they hadn't yet invented that fairy tale about it coming from smoking, that's for damn sure." A tear came to his eye as he stared out the window at the West Virginia hills. "Bastards," he sniffled.

There was a time when Edgar Rawly would have sawed off his own feet rather than get all weepy sentimental in front of the help. But the more decades and cash one piled up, the less one cared. Edgar Rawly was north of nine decades, and with a personal fortune in the billions, he was long past a time when he gave a damn what the bastard proles thought. If he wanted to get sloppy maudlin over the way things were back in the old days then, dammit, he was rich and old enough to stare out his eighth-floor window and remember how good things used to be.

Not that the tobacco business had ever been perfection. There had always been bastard vultures circling, gumming up the works, causing their bastard trouble. This was true even way back in the halcyon days when life was great, tobacco was king, and everyone smoked, from president to peon.

When he had first gotten into tobacco eighty years ago, Rawly's name had been Edgar Coffin. By the time he was twenty-two, Coffin Cigarettes had become one of the more successful brands, its market share expanding rapidly in the years between the two world wars. Then the cancer lie started to creep into the public consciousness, even though it was never spoken about much back then. But at some point some smartass had started calling a perfectly clean, healthy and only slightly addictive product "coffin nails."

"You've got to change that name," one of his early public relations flacks had insisted.

Rawly was a young man in those days, but he had the same go-to-hell attitude that would carry him through a long life as well as the ups and downs that came hand in glove with the persecuted product he peddled.

"We're not changing the name from Coffin Cigarettes, and that's that," Rawly had said all those years ago. "I worked like a dog getting my name on those packs. I worked the tobacco fields as a boy. I picked it, baled it, stacked it and rode it to market. My blood is in each and every one of those packs. No way we're calling them nothing else."

"You don't understand, Mr. Coffin," the PR man had said. "There was already a negative reaction among consumers to the 'Coffin' name. But now that the term 'coffin nails' is catching on among the public—"

"If I ever catch the bastard who started that slur I'll wring his scrawny neck."

"Be that as it may, the name has stuck. The negative connotation has stuck. You're going to have to change it."

"I'll change my name before I change the name of my product," the young Mr. Rawly né Coffin had insisted.

"Actually, according to my research it would be wise if you changed both," the bastard PR man said.

Rawly resisted the idea for a few years, but the term "coffin nails" refused to die. As bigger names in cigarettes rose up from the tobacco fields, eating into more and more of his market share, he was forced to reconsider.

"How about I change my name to 'America'?" he growled

furiously three years and millions of dollars in losses later. " 'Edgar America' sounds good to me. We can call our new product 'America's Candy.' The kids'll eat that up. And if my name's America, the next time the bastards come after me they'll be saying they hate America. We can nail their Nazi fascist hides to the wall over that."

The marketing people thought the name was a bit of a stretch. "Maybe there's someone in your life you respect whose name you wouldn't mind taking? A favorite uncle, or perhaps your mother's maiden name?"

"My uncles were all scrounging, lowlife bastards, and my mother doesn't even smoke, the no-good tramp, even though I sent her a dozen cases when I first started Coffin Cigarettes. She donated them to the local orphanage. At least we got some business out of those little buggers."

"It doesn't have to be a family member. Is there someone else, someone you respect?"

Edgar Coffin could not think of one single living person for whom he had so much as one ounce of respect. But there was one historical figure that he admired. Sir Walter Raleigh, the man who had introduced tobacco to Europe, was a much beloved figure to the young tobacco industry leader. So much did he idolize his hero that he refused to sully the great man's name by taking it for his own. The spelling "Raleigh" became "Rawly," and "Edgar Rawly" was born.

Renaming his line of cigarettes was even easier. By this time the romanticized image of the American West had long taken hold throughout the country. The rugged cowboy on his noble steed was the crystallization of the American spirit. Every kid wanted to be a cowboy, and Edgar Rawly wanted every kid to be a smoker.

Rawly took out an atlas, poked his finger around a few Western states, and before lunch had become founder of Cheyenne Tobacco, Inc., which would go on to be the most successful tobacco company in the history of the world.

But all was not as it had been in the great days of the industry. A lot of young people were refusing to smoke, and a lot of the old-timers were catching cancer for some reason.

It was an amazing coincidence, one that baffled Edgar Rawly, that so many smokers caught cancer. He had a theory that it might have something to do with sugar.

"You know how sugar causes cancer, Merkel?" the old man in the wheelchair asked. He tore his eyes from the Virginia hills, the same hills he had watched turn green, then brown, then green again for almost a century.

"Yes, Mr. Rawly," David Merkel said, parroting the unorthodox theory he had heard hundreds of times since coming to work for Cheyenne Tobacco six years ago. "Studies show that most smokers are also coffee drinkers. Most coffee drinkers use sugar in their coffee. A lifetime of sugar usage can increase the risk of lung cancer."

Across the room, a voice hissed, "Not so loud."

There was an argument going on between the ad people and the Cheyenne executives about how to make the current Mr. Rawly appear as healthy as the Mr. Rawly framed in the painting on the wall. Apparently the photographer, a temperamental fellow who was not being paid enough to accomplish the impossible, had suggested they embalm the current Mr. Rawly, which caused much angry whispering among the Cheyenne Tobacco executives.

"And emphysema," Rawly said, to Merkel, oblivious to the chatter across the room. "Sugar also has been known to cause emphysema in some laboratory animals."

This was a study commissioned by Mr. Rawly himself. The lab animals had been rats which, in addition to a force-fed diet of sugar, also happened to be kept in airtight containers that happened to be kept filled with tobacco smoke. In Rawly's mind, exposure to the sugar had eventually given one hundred percent of the rats emphysema.

"It could also be the coffee itself," Rawly mused. "We can't rule that out. But the bastards make us put on the warning labels, while Juan Valdez struts around like a sailor on leave. Ridiculous. But we're going to have the last laugh, Merkel."

Dry lip curling into a deformed smile, he flashed a row of dingy brown teeth with yellow tips.

The argument across the room suddenly resolved itself when a raised voice issued from the throng in the center of the room.

"Watch out, damn you, you horrible old fool!"

Merkel's stomach turned to water. For a moment he thought that someone was talking to Mr. Rawly. When he looked over, he realized that it was almost as bad.

The elderly woman who had spent most of the morning shuffling around the lighting and camera people had snagged a thread from her sleeve on a lighting tripod. She had nearly pulled the tower over as she tried to yank herself free. Flapping his wrists and hissing angrily, the photographer grabbed the tripod and snapped the thread.

"You stupid old thing," he cried, as he set the tripod upright. "Who let you in here to torment me?"

It took the photographer a moment to realize the room had fallen silent. Puzzled, he followed dozens of frightened eyes. Everyone was staring at the old man in the wheelchair.

Eyes low, staring from underneath shaggy eyebrows, Edgar Rawly gritted his yellowed molars. "Tell that fruit the score, or he's gone," he growled, his voice suddenly stronger than his years and laced with cold menace.

Grown men gulped. A crowd hastily formed around the photographer, words were whispered. The man accepted a scolding with a histrionic sigh and resumed his work.

The old woman continued to shuffle around amid the Sturm und Drang, seemingly baffled by all the excitement.

"Maybe I could ask her to leave, Mr. Rawly," Merkel suggested.

"You'll go before she will," Rawly growled. "She knows where all the bodies are buried. That is, if she remembers. Besides, how many men can boast they've had the same secretary through twelve presidential administrations?"

How many would want to boast about that? Merkel wondered.

The woman had been at Rawly's side long before David Merkel had taken his position as Mr. Rawly's assistant, and it looked very much to Merkel as if she would be there long after. Merkel assumed she had been young at one point, but he dared not venture a guess when. He was, however, reasonably certain that lightbulbs had probably already been invented.

Rawly's secretary wore a tweed skirt that had gone out of style fifty years ago. Judging from the placement of the zipper, she had put it on backwards. A pair of baggy nylons and white sneakers protected bony legs and feet. Her hair was dyed jet black and styled in a pageboy fashion, with sharp points that jutted out like black horns on either side of her pale, drawn face. She wore a pair of glasses as big as ski goggles that wrapped around either side of her face. A cigarette dangled from her lip and she left a trail of smoke wherever she walked.

The woman was a joke among the staff. She was older even than Edgar Rawly himself, and should have been put out to pasture years ago. But Rawly kept her on, despite the fact that she didn't seem to do much but smoke, carry papers around, and yell at anyone who tried to enter the CEO's office.

As she walked among the ad people, a thick manila folder tucked under the arm of her threadbare sweater, she stared at the lights and nearly tripped over some cables. A marketing executive caught her by the elbow and set her right.

"Are you all right, Mrs. Z?"

"Who are all these people?" she demanded loudly.

"It's for the new rollout. The Cheyenne Smooths?" The marketing man offered a hopeful smile, like someone asking a nursing home patient directions to the men's room.

"I know all about them. I'm not senile, you know," she snapped. "And get your mitts off me. I'm not a slab of meat." She pulled her elbow from his hand and shuffled over to her employer. "Sign here," she demanded, swatting open the folder and pointing at the topmost sheet.

Rawly dutifully accepted the pen and did as he was told. As he autographed, she kept a suspicious eye trained on his hands. When he was finished, she snatched up the folder and shuffled from the room, shaking her head and muttering.

Merkel was glad to see her go. There was always an uncomfortable tension when she and Rawly were close. Rawly had hinted once about an affair during the Second World War.

Merkel cleared his throat. "About the Cheyenne Smooths, Mr. Rawly—" he said, a nervous twitch flickering at the corner of his eye.

"Great product," Rawly interrupted. "The Cheyenne Smooths are gonna pull my bony ass out of the fire, even with that contract I signed with those Injun bastards. I'm gonna put all the competition out of business. And America will be back to what she oughta be. The smoking capital of the world. Ridiculous, just ridiculous that we've been having to rely on the European and Asian markets these last few years. France and the godless yellow Chinese keeping us afloat. Disgraceful. No more, Merkel."

Merkel pitched his voice low and leaned in to his employer. "We've gotten word from New York. You remember I told you about the ad the Campaign for a Smoke-Free World was filming, the one where they found the bodies afterward?"

"'Course I remember," Rawly snapped. "I remember every penny I've sent to them. You know we have to finance those bastards? Part of our settlement with the government. Imagine it. Tobacco companies paying to tell people smoking's bad for them. And these pissants at the other companies all caved, Merkel. Left me dangling in the wind. If I'd've fought it, I'd've been alone. Serves 'em right I'm going to drive them all out of business. They probably see nothing wrong with funding ads that oppose their own damned product. Does Arby's fund anti-beef messages? Does Hershey fund anti-chocolate messages?"

"Of course not, sir," Merkel said, steering the conversation back on track. "About the bodies in New York. I've confirmed that one of the murdered men was one of ours. Dr. John Feathers, the Native American who brought the new tobacco to our attention."

Rawly scowled. "Native American. Bullshit. He's an Injun. Light me up!"

Merkel slipped a cigarette between his employer's arid lips and lit it. After the hacking and spitting had subsided, Rawly chewed on a glob of mucus thoughtfully.

"We had an Injun for a while in our print ads. Chief Running Elk? Chief Running Deer? Something running."

"Runs with Antelope," Merkel said. "He wasn't actually a chief. You just claimed that in the ads."

"Wasn't he?"

"No, sir."

"Well, dammit, whatever happened to him? Maybe we can get him for this new ad blitz."

"Dead, sir," Merkel replied. "He died of throat cancer back in 1981."

"Was Running Wolf a coffee drinker?" Rawly asked.

"I, um, don't know, sir. That was before my time."

"It's the sugar, Merkel. Mark my words, they're going to admit one day that it's the sugar and we'll be vindicated." He placed a crooked finger beside his nose and winked at his assistant.

"I'm sure you're right, sir," Merkel said. "About John Feathers, sir, the . . . Injun who brought the new tobacco to our attention. He was not alone. All of the sixteen murdered men worked for the major tobacco companies."

"A conspiracy?"

"It looks that way, Mr. Rawly. And Feathers was last seen alive at the Chowok reservation in Montana."

A spark came to the eyes of the tired old man in the wheelchair, a glint of the fiery, driven young man who had fought his way out of poverty, who had built an empire, a hint of youth that age and infirmity could not eradicate.

"They're trying to stop us, Merkel."

Across the room, the photographer clapped his hands. He had decided the best lighting in which to photograph his subject. He had shut off most of his own lights, as well as the room lights and draped black velvet over the windows.

"We're ready," the photographer trilled.

An executive hustled over to collect Rawly's wheelchair. As the old CEO was being wheeled away, he reached up and grabbed Merkel's necktie, reeling the younger man in like a mackerel. The old man's breath was a moist ashtray.

"Call Wollrich," Rawly commanded in a hoarse whisper. The look of fear on his assistant's face brought a wicked grin to the ancient tobacco CEO's face. "I didn't get where I am by pussyfooting around, Merkel. And tell me what good it is having a certifiable maniac on retainer if you're never gonna use him?" He released Merkel's tie. "Call him. Tell him to get out to that reservation. In the meantime, Miss DeMille over there is ready for my close-up."

Cackling evil joy, the old man allowed himself to be wheeled over to the waiting crowd.

10

Chiun would not allow Remo to go directly to the airport from the offices of the Campaign for a Smoke-Free World. The Master of Sinanju had insisted that they first stop by their condominium. Remo had wanted to refuse but Chiun was wearing that face. The face that said that he would make Remo's life miserable from now until two weeks after doomsday if Remo even dared think about refusing the old Korean's demand. Not being a masochist in this life, and not wanting to put up with an eternity of kvetching in the next, Remo had submitted to the will of his teacher and done as he was told.

The trick was Aphrodite, who had insisted on tagging along. In the old days, Remo had been forced to change addresses on nearly a weekly basis. He was sick of bouncing from hotel to motel and had gotten used to living at the same address, almost like a normal person. But for that to work he had to keep his business and private lives separate. No one he came into contact with on CURE missions could know where he lived and that made Aphrodite a problem.

Dumping her out on the highway might kill her, and since they had just met her he thought it would be rude to knock her out cold, so instead he just made her blind a little.

As they drove, he reached out and touched her temple with two fingertips. "How's that?" Remo asked.

"I'm blind," Aphrodite cried, panicked.

"Just a little," said Remo.

Aphrodite screamed.

"Is she going to do that the whole way?" Chiun asked from the backseat.

"It'll come back," Remo promised.

"Aaaahh," Aphrodite screamed again.

"You don't take pressure well, do you?" Remo asked, and knocked her out.

Unconscious, Aphrodite missed the short trip to Remo's condo and slept through Chiun's foraging through his collection of steamer trunks. She snored all the way to the airport, where a little pressure at the base of her spine brought her back to the land of the living.

"Voilá," Remo said with a little flourish.

"I'm still blind," Aphrodite screamed.

"Oopsie, my bad," Remo said, and returned her vision to her.

The sun was blinding, and Aphrodite found that she was walking through a parking lot at LaGuardia Airport, her backpack slung once more over her shoulder.

"That thing is as heavy as lead," Remo said.

"I've got self-help books on how to quit smoking in it," Aphrodite said. Hesitantly, she touched her temples where Remo's fingers had pressed.

"Along with about a hundred cartons of cigarettes," Remo pointed out.

Aphrodite waved her hands in the air, erasing his words as irrelevant. "How did you do that thing with the eyes?" she asked, amazed. "Is it like acupressure?"

"Clean lungs, clean soul," Remo said, and sauntered off to buy their plane tickets.

The Master of Sinanju refused to wait for a scheduled

flight. Remo said a plane was leaving in an hour. Chiun said that was too long and told Remo to hire a private plane. Remo suggested that as long as they were at it, they could hire a juggler, a brass band and Luciano Pavarotti to entertain them on the flight. Chiun told him that after he rented a plane he could hire whoever he wanted, provided they didn't mind being thrown out a door at twenty thousand feet. Aphrodite was finally able to get a word in edgewise and told them that the CSFW had its own private jet.

"I love you nonprofits," Remo said. "You always know how to travel in style."

On the jet to Montana, the Master of Sinanju took his usual seat over the left wing. American engineering had performed a miracle by being able to get a plane in the air, and since he felt Americans could get nothing right, Chiun assumed something would inevitably go wrong with their airplane design. The left wing had over the years become the focus of this lack of confidence in American engineering.

Remo sat beside his teacher. In the seat behind Remo, Aphrodite was afraid to blink for fear of losing her vision once more.

"What is with you and this private plane business?" Remo asked Chiun. "Commercial has always been good enough before."

"It was called a favor, Remo. I have heard that some people who appreciate the many things that others have done for them have been known to grant them from time to time. But why would you want to do me a favor? It is not like I have ever done anything for you."

Remo only grunted and waited for takeoff.

"Care to tell me what you fished out of your trunks back home?" Remo asked once they were airborne.

He was forced to address the back of the Master of Sinanju's age-speckled head, since Chiun's eyes were locked on the shuddering wing. "You have the title of Reigning Master, yet you have no interest in the little things that make our business work."

"I'm more of a big picture kind of guy."

"Which is why I, in my declining years, must hold your hand through the first stumbling steps of what, without my daily assistance, would surely be a doomed Masterhood."

Remo folded his arms across his chest and smiled. "Doomed shmoomed. You just like my company."

At this the old man cackled. He turned from the wing, which had not fallen off during takeoff. "Like your company. Heh-heh-heh. Yes, Remo, that is the reason I do all that I do. Because I cannot bear to be parted from you. Heh-heh-heh. Please, Remo, never give excuse for me to leave you. Continue to bumble into the furniture so that I can forever be tethered to your side." He returned his attention to the quivering wing. "Like your company. Heh-heh-heh."

Remo felt the smile melt from his face. "Okay, Henny Youngman, so what did you get from your trunks? And what got you so worked up back at that no-smoker place?"

They were at cruising altitude. Chiun was satisfied that the wing would stay fastened to the fuselage. The old man turned from the window, fussing with the robes in his lap. "Tell me, Remo, what you know of Master To-Un."

Remo frowned. "Not a whole lot. You made me memorize his name along with all the other past Masters. He's remembered as To-Un the Disgraced, but there are a couple of Masters with that title. I assumed he got stiffed on a bill at some point and got struck from the official record."

"No, my son, To-Un never failed to receive payment. In fact, To-Un might have been remembered for one of our more clever assassinations, had it been his last. During To-Un's time an Englishman, much like your Aesop before him, stole some of our best stories and turned them into plays. To-Un could have simply removed him, but first he shrewdly collected a fee from the writer's jealous peers to do a job he would have done anyway. A neat and skillfully plotted assassination, worthy of the greatest Masters in our history." As he contemplated the notion of To-Un receiving payment for a task that would have been performed whether or not money was received, there was a glint of admiration in the Master of Sinanju's hazel eyes.

"So why isn't he remembered for that?"

"Because, my son, his masterhood did not end there," Chiun said, shaking his head. His voice took on the familiar cadence of instruction. "To-Un's was a time of new opportunities. For most of our history, the House of Sinanju found employment in Asia, the Middle East, and sometimes Africa. Rome had been good to the House for many centuries, of course, but much of Europe was still young for us, these barbarians only having dragged themselves up out of the mud and into their castles a few centuries before. Spain and Portugal were favored clients, France less so, but still adequate when need compelled us. But we recognized most of all that England would be the power in Europe in the coming centuries. As her fortunes rose, so too would ours.

"Sinanju had already spent much time in England even before the masterhood of To-Un, and so the skills of the Masters of Sinanju were well known to England's elite.

"Now there was a knight who had found favor with Queen Elizabeth I, a pirate by the name of Walter Raleigh. If he was not showing off by dropping his cloak in mud puddles for the Virgin Queen to walk on, he was passing out moldy potatoes to underage schoolchildren. The man was a grandstander and a menace. It was only a matter of time before someone hired us to puncture that swelled head of his.

"Now Raleigh had been charged by Queen Elizabeth to establish a colony in the New World, which was what the backwards English called this land at that time. The colony was founded on Roanoke Island, off the shore of what is now called North Carolina. Another knight of Elizabeth's court, jealous of the attention showered on Raleigh by the Virgin Queen, hired To-Un to remove the entire colony, hoping to embarrass this showoff before his mistress.

"And Master To-Un did travel on a special boat called a 'turtle ship' to the wilds of this new land. He was accompanied by several trusted servants, for the Master traveled with an entourage in those days, men who would carry the Master's trunks and sail the Master's boat. And there did he remove this colony so that scarcely any evidence of its existence remained. When the English returned they found the colonists gone, one hundred and twenty-two persons in all."

"I've heard this before," Remo said. "That's the story of the Lost Colony. I learned about it in grammar school. So you're saying we wiped out the Lost Colony just to embarrass Sir Walter Raleigh?"

"I am saying nothing of the sort," Chiun sniffed. "Sinanju does not 'wipe out.' Earthquakes wipe out. Typhoons wipe out. Tidal waves wipe out. Sinanju is a precise instrument, not some continent-leveling nuclear boom." Long-nailed hands fluttered angrily at the air. "And besides, that Raleigh person was incapable of embarrassment. The showoff even ruined his own execution. Who wants to see someone joking with his executioner? Certainly not anyone who paid for good seats up front. Walter Raleigh was a showoff to the end. Whoever thought he would be shamed by losing an entire settlement did not know Raleigh."

"So what really happened to the Lost Colony? Did To-Un kill them all?"

"Kill?" Chiun said. His wrinkled face puckered like a bunched fist. "Women and children, killed? Really, Remo, we are not savages."

"Oh," said Remo. "That's good."

"We sold them," said Chiun.

"That's not much better, Little Father."

"It is better than death, for that was the only alternative. Even if To-Un had never ventured to these shores, the savages who lived in this land would have killed the settlers eventually. To-Un was contracted to remove the colony, but if he failed to do so the enemies of Walter Raleigh would have sent others to finish the task. So death was coming for these colonists one way or another.

"So here was a problem," Chiun continued. "To-Un knew that he could not slaughter innocents, but he was a clever man, and did think of a cunning solution. To-Un did meet with the savages, who were called Indians, even though they knew naught of Brahma or Bombay and would have been lost in the great palaces of the rajahs, and he did claim ownership of the white colony. To-Un conveyed to the chief of the tribe that he was displeased with his settlers. A difficult task, for these wild men spoke no civilized tongue, not even French. And a deal was struck that these Indians-who-were-not-from-India would purchase To-Un's unwanted colonists for a few worthless trinkets. Now see you the true cleverness of To-Un. By making the Indians think they had purchased the colonists of Roanoke, he had ensured their survival. No longer were they in danger, for they were accepted as members of the tribe and thus their lives were spared.

"Before they were taken off, the Englishmen carved something in a tree. 'Croatoan.' Some have thought it was a clue to where they had gone, but it was not. The careful eye would see that the first half is 'Korea.'"

"Croa?" Remo said. "Chiun, Croa doesn't look anything like Korea."

"Why are you surprised? None of those Englishmen could spell right, especially in their own language. For years they did not even know the difference between an F and an S and were forever writing ridiculous things like 'juftice fhall not be fold.' But in their defense, how could those people on that island be expected to correctly spell the name of a country they had never heard of? For at this time Korea had yet to officially discover England, so they spelled it as it sounded to their uneducated ears. The second half of the word carved into the tree was of the Master from that land who had saved their lives."

"To-Un became 'toan'," Remo said.

The Master of Sinanju nodded.

"So that's the story of the Lost Colony," Remo said. "I still don't know why To-Un was disgraced. It sounds to me like he did exactly what he was supposed to do."

"If the tale had ended there, To-Un would have returned to Sinanju in glory. Sadly, that was not the end for To-Un, but it was nearly the end for Sinanju." He resumed the story, his tone more sorrowful than before.

"As part of the ritual of departing, the Indians brought forth a pipe from which they instructed To-Un to smoke.

These Indians were a sickly lot, coughing and unable to take in full breath. There were no men over the age of forty. This illness affected even the women and children of the tribe. They were clearly a dying people, yet none displayed symptoms consistent with any disease known to Sinanju. To-Un concluded that the illness must be in the smoke, which all of this tribe ritualistically inhaled. Now Sinanju is about breathing at its most basic, and To-Un would never willingly take smoke into his lungs. But he also knew enough not to insult potential clients, for all of Europe had once been backwards tribes like this, and one never knew where the next great civilization would arise. So To-Un pretended to accept the smoke into his body, but blocked it from entering his lungs, and so all were happy and To-Un was able to go on his way.

"Alas, not very far into his journey he felt a stirring in his very soul, one that overwhelmed his will. To-Un felt a craving for the smoke of the Indians. For although he had thought he had kept his body free of the vile smoke, a little of it had managed to find its way in. Three days at sea, To-Un ordered his craft to turn around and return him to shore. There did he find the Indians, living peacefully with the whites he had pretended to sell to them. They were tending the fields of this plant which when burned produced upon those exposed an overwhelming desire to burn more. To-Un arranged to purchase some of the leaves of the Indians. For these leaves he traded back the trinkets he had bartered from the Indians for the colonists of Roanoke Island.

"And To-Un did return to his boat, but ten days out his supply of leaves ran low and he ordered the craft to return once more. With nothing left to offer for the leaves, To-Un did turn over his vessel and servants to the tribe.

"It did not take long for the skills of Sinanju to leave him, for with breath gone so too did the Sun Source leave him. And when his powers ebbed, To-Un fell into a deep sleep from which none of his servants could awaken him.

"Now it happened that To-Un's apprentice had been nearly ready to assume Reigning Masterhood, and when after several years his teacher failed to return to Sinanju, the younger Master did travel to England to discover the fate of To-Un. Learned he about the plot to remove the Roanoke colony, and since an expedition was about to depart for the New World, this apprentice to To-Un did go along with it.

"And the ruins of the colony were discovered as had been To-Un's plan, along with the strange carving 'Croatoan' in the tree. None but the young Master of Sinanju understood its meaning, and so as the English poked around the remnants of the colony, the young Master struck out in search of his teacher. He found the tribe that To-Un had encountered, as well as the English colonists and To-Un's servants. By now the Englishmen were already breeding with the indigenous tribe, and there were many white babies to be found. And when he found his teacher lying on the floor of a squalid hut, the young Master of Sinanju's heart tore in two.

"The old Master had once radiated strength, but here was a creature that was a withered husk of a man. Life had not left him, but breath had failed him. The thing that kept this tribe in perpetual sickness had attacked To-Un more viciously than the Indians, for our lives in Sinanju rely on the perfection of breathing. And when he learned how the old Master had been brought to this condition, the young Master of Sinanju did feel the anger swell within him.

"Now you might think that this was tobacco, but it was not. This plant was similar to that other plant but far more addictive and, therefore, far more deadly. Not only was the smoking of it dangerous, but merely touching a leaf produced a rash on the skin. This plant had nearly died out many years before, but careful tending kept a few plants alive in a few small acres. And each growing season the plant grew more deadly, as endless inbreeding produced plants that amplified its worst characteristics, until it had nearly obliterated the tribe that worshiped it. The young Master of Sinanju did demand that the fields be burned so that this poison could not be visited on any others.

"But the Indians did not want to part with their special plant, for they had saved it from extinction for generations, and consequently generations of their people had come to crave this weed. And so when the wind was right, they set a small fire and directed the smoke so that it would engulf the hut where the young Master was tending To-Un."

"You're talking about secondhand smoke," a voice chimed in from the aisle.

Aphrodite had been listening to the story, and was leaning around Remo to hear more.

"Remember that thing I did to your eyes?" Remo asked. "Want to make it permanent?"

"No kidding, Remo," Aphrodite said. "Your old friend is talking about secondhand smoke. And by the sounds of it, he knows about the Cheyenne Smooths. That's why you're in such a hurry to get to Montana, isn't it?" she asked Chiun.

"Cheyenne Smooths?" Remo asked.

"I told you, that's the new product Cheyenne Tobacco's working on that's supposed to be horribly addictive," she explained. "According to our informants, the secondhand smoke is incredibly dangerous. Minimal exposure to it is supposed to get a nonsmoker hooked. If that's right, there's billions to be made off these things worldwide. They're producing them with the help of some Indian tribe. That's the tribe you're talking about, isn't it, Chiun? They're growing the same stuff from your story. But how did your tribe get from the East Coast all the way to Montana?"

"I am used, Remo, to your incessant interruptions when I am trying to tell you a story from our history," Chiun said, eyes leveled on Aphrodite. "But my tolerance does not extend to whatever scarlet women you happen to pick up along the side of the road."

"Aphrodite, why don't you do us all a favor and sit this one out?" Remo suggested.

She was prepared to argue, but then she remembered waking up blind in an airport parking lot and decided against it. Frowning, she disappeared back behind Remo's seat.

"So what happened to To-Un and his apprentice?"

"There is not much more to tell. The young Master knew that the Indians would not want to part with their addictive weed, but he had wanted to first give them the chance to re-move it themselves. It is better, Remo, to willingly give up a bad habit than to be forced to do so. To-Un's apprentice had already spirited his teacher from the hut, so the smoke never came to him. He eventually burned the fields himself and salted the earth so that nothing more would grow there. For their own good in case any of the plants survived, he ban-ished the tribe to the farthest reaches of this dark continent, where it was assumed they would never be heard from again. He retrieved To-Un's turtle boat and, along with his Master's servants, set sail for home. To-Un never regained conscious-ness and died during the long journey at sea. This land would remain officially undiscovered by Sinanju for many years after."

Shaking his head, the old Korean stared sadly at the back of the seat in front of him, his thoughts a million miles and four centuries away.

"So you think Aphrodite is right?" Remo asked. "You think the plant from your story is the same one Cheyenne Tobacco is growing in Montana?"

"The woman mentioned the Chowok tribe. These are the same people encountered by To-Un. It is the same plant. A plant that killed a Master of Sinanju, a plant that the tribe was forbidden ever to cultivate again." Turning from his pupil, Chiun stared at the blanket of clouds below blue sky.

"So what did you have to get from home? You never told me what you had to go fish out of your trunks."

"No, I did not," Chiun replied, and was silent.

"Oh, well. If history's any indication, I assume you'll spring it on me soon enough," Remo said. He crossed his arms and slumped back in his seat. He was silent for only a moment when a thought suddenly occurred to him. "Wait a minute. That writer you mentioned, the one you said stole our best stories and turned them into plays. This was around the time of Queen Elizabeth. Did To-Un ice Shakespeare?"

"That might have been his name," Chiun said, stroking his thread of beard. "Pear, apple, orange. I believe there was a fruit in it somewhere. See now why To-Un's story is so tragic. If he had but ended his masterhood with the elimination of that page-ruiner he would have been remembered as To-Un the Good. Instead, he is disgraced. There is a lesson there for us all."

Remo considered the tale of Master To-Un. Until now he had been just a name on a list, with no exploits attributed to him. Now he was a tragic figure.

"That's unfair, Little Father. The guy made one mistake in an otherwise decent Masterhood. And that end is just plain sad. It's not fair one screw-up should reduce him in the histories to 'To-Un the Disgraced.' That's almost as bad as—" He stopped dead. "Hold on. To-Un was succeeded by Master Pook. The guy you want to call Pook the Incompetent, because he failed to wipe out the moshuh nanren like he claimed he did in the scrolls. Pook is the Master who burned the fields and sent the Lost Colony Indians into exile?"

"The teacher died in disgrace at sea and in undiscovered land, the pupil failed the great test of his age." The Master of Sinanju turned from the window. Wisdom deepened by sadness lengthened the furrows of age in his leathery skin. "When history comes to judge us, my son, pray we fare better."

"No one will judge you harshly, Little Father," Remo said with a smile. "Who would dare?"

Reaching out one bony hand, the old Korean patted the back of his pupil's hand. He did not return Remo's smile.

Turning back to the window, he studied the clouds. He did not speak for the remainder of the flight.

11

The black limousine with the tinted windows sped along a raised road that cut through fields of freshly tilled black soil. The fields had once been rice paddies but the water had been drained and diverted to the river or to pools that would eventually feed the new irrigation system.

Men and women in peasant trousers and blouses, many with straw hats as shields from the unforgiving sun, worked the fields by hand. Some wore shoes but most did not. Oxen yoked to plows lounged in the mud next to the peasant field hands.

The entire tableau could have been lifted from a large feudal farm hundreds of years in the past. Except, of course, for the greenhouses. The shimmering glass structures were a modern contrast to the ancient farming techniques. The greenhouses were vacant now, but inside rows upon rows of empty wooden boxes sitting beneath a modern sprinkler system would soon be nursing thousands of seedlings, all growing in climate-controlled comfort. Once transplanted, the plants would quickly grow to maturity. From those simple little seeds, a billion-dollar empire would be grown.

In the rear of the speeding limo, Zhii Zaw sat on soft leather seats and watched the peasants toil. Their hard work made him sweat and he jiggled with the air conditioning. A blast of cold hit his jowly face. Zhii did not smile.

Ordinarily the old man with the heavy jowls would have delighted in the scene outside his limo window. Most days he loved to watch his peasants work. And despite all the high talk of shared communist goals, there was no doubt that he owned each and every one of them. Like a great lord of old, Zhii Zaw could do whatever he wanted with them.

His peasants. His land.

It was by special arrangement with the government in Beijing that he was master of all he surveyed. The arrangement was a simple one: Zhii Zaw did not bother Beijing and Beijing did not bother Zhii Zaw.

It was a strange time to live in the People's Republic of China. Not quite the dictatorship it had once been but certainly not yet free. Caught somewhere between total oppression and the first hints of freedom. A place where until very recently a disgraced general would certainly meet with death or exile, but now a nation where a disgraced general like Zhii Zaw could find a new life and great wealth at home.

Zaw often tried to recall what it was like to be a general in the People's Army. It was not so long ago that he had served and scarcely five years had passed since he had surrendered his commission. Yet in so little time it already seemed that his earlier career had existed in the life of another, a story read as a child and now barely remembered.

Zaw was an old man of sixty-five when he left the service, disgraced for a reason he would never speak of. He had assumed he would die in squalor, but he found an unlikely savior in his older brother Qian.

Qian had been the shame of his family, a petty thief who had disappeared in his twenties. Once he had vanished, none spoke of Qian. It was as if he had never existed. For fifty years Zaw assumed his brother was dead.

But then came Zaw's trouble with the government and his forced resignation. And at his lowest point, when all hope was lost and all Zhii Zaw wished for was a speedy and painless death, a ghost from his past reappeared.

Zaw had been living for three months in a squalid boarding house in Bengbu. Built by the British over a century before, the home was run by a toothless old crone and was so dirty the local prostitutes would not use it. Amid the garbage and rats, Zhii Zaw had an unexpected visitor.

"How the great people's general has fallen," said the well-dressed older gentleman with the white hair. "Aren't you thrilled how Mao Tse-Tung and his little book which explained everything took care of all of you?"

Zaw did not recognize the man, yet there was something familiar to the jolly glint in his narrow, pouchy eyes.

And then his guest had laughed, and Zaw was struck with the sudden shock of ancient memory.

"Qian?" he asked.

Zaw's older brother smiled. "I have followed your career with interest, brother general. You have done all they have commanded, and this is how they repay you."

Qian was carrying a British-made umbrella, which he used to gesture around the filthy room. The silver tip of the umbrella startled a large gray rat which had been feasting on a rotting piece of fruit on the wobbly table. The animal scurried to the shadows.

"It is not my place to question the decisions of the people's government," Zaw replied.

"Really?" Qian said with an impish grin. "Even after all the people's government has done for you? My brother, you mouth their words but your tone tells me you do not believe them. Come with me. You have come to this awful place thinking that it is your end. I will not permit it. Come, Zhii. Come and see what life exists outside the government that you served and which has betrayed you."

It was a choice between dying with the rats or leaving with a long-lost brother who appeared clean and well fed. In his first year as a criminal, Zhii Zaw told himself that no man would have chosen to live with the rats.

His brother, he soon learned, had not remained a petty thief. In the years since their separation, Qian had moved up the criminal hierarchy until now, at seventy years of age, he was one of the most powerful crime lords in Asia.

Zhii Zaw, the former proud people's general, took on the responsibilities of Qian's second in command.

"Who else could I trust in this position but my flesh and blood?" Qian asked.

It was not so difficult a transition as Zaw had imagined. In his position he dealt with underlings, handled government bureaucrats, and saw to it that his brother's organization was run with ruthless efficiency. Except for a lack of uniforms, it was almost exactly as if Zaw were back in the People's Army. Better, in fact, since he no longer had to deal with the government in Beijing. Beijing was aware of Qian and Zhii's activities, but because of their political influence chose to ignore the two lawless brothers.

Zaw had once thought that the communist government of China forced necessary order on a disorderly world. Thanks to Qian, his eyes were opened. The government existed only to oppress the people and perpetuate its own power. When it encountered an organization within its own borders that was doing precisely the same thing but which could not be controlled or eradicated, it turned a blind eye.

A lifetime of patriotism for Zhii Zaw had in a matter of a few short months turned to revulsion and contempt. *Mao Tse-Tung was a liar. And a fool.*

Zaw remained his older brother's loyal second for four years. On the day that Qian died of a heart attack, Zaw assumed the reins of his brother's organization.

The transition had been a peaceful one, and Zaw was on the verge of brokering a deal that would forge a thousand-year criminal empire. Yet even the most carefully laid plans did not come off without minor annoyances. The first of these

Zhii Zaw had experienced that morning, which was why he could not smile while watching his peasants work his fields.

On a low mountain amid the tilled farmland a home like a palace rose from the rock, more a modern fortress than the house of a former peasant thief. A visitor would first notice the screens and wood and bamboo, but these were mere window dressing, decoration for the thick granite walls and iron gates that kept away all but the invited.

The house had been Qian's and was now Zhii's.

Through the guarded gates and up the gravel drive, and then his limousine dropped Zaw off at the main entrance.

A servant opened the door to the car. Another opened the door to the house. A third waited inside to hand him his messages. Another asked if there were any special requests for dinner. A fifth asked about Zaw's trip to the United States. A sixth opened the door to his private study.

Zaw dismissed them all without a word. Shutting the door for privacy, he hustled over to his desk and booted up his computer.

He was not used to typing. Stubby fingers searched out the proper keys one by one. He found the latest English-language news stories out of the United States. He had checked the articles about the Manhattan massacre several times that morning.

When Zaw read the latest updates, his mouth formed a shocked O. "What is this?" he said to the empty room.

He was startled when the room replied.

"They are all dead."

Zaw jumped at the voice.

He had not even been aware that the man was in the room. But then, he never knew when this man was close.

When his brother died, Zhii Zaw, the loyal former people's general, had inherited everything that had belonged to Qian. This included the quiet assassin with the black fighting costume, bare arms and the dark purple mask who was now standing in the shadows near the walls of bookcases in the study of the Chongqing estate. Powerful forearms crossed over his chest, the small man stepped forward.

The costumed killer did not so much as walk as glide across the floor. Feet wrapped in black cloth made not a sound.

"You have failed," Zaw accused.

"I have failed them," the slight man said simply, in a reed thin, almost feminine voice.

Zaw knew the man only as Jian. He had never heard the man's full name. Like the masked man, his followers were moshuh nanren, deadly assassins, but were lesser acolytes of the greater master, Jian, whose blood could be traced back hundreds of years to the last moshuh nanren of that ancient age.

"So you know of this?" Zaw demanded, waving a fat hand at his computer screen.

The story of the dead Chinese killers at the New York City morgue had just broken on the Web. It was a new story so few details were given. Two photographs accompanied the story. The first was the outside of the morgue, the second was of a gleaming silver disk with razor-sharp fins.

"The first wave has failed," Jian said. "They appear to have encountered a force that exceeded their capabilities."

"What force?" Zaw demanded.

"At the moment I do not know. But there is always one greater, for even the mountain must give way to the river."

"Do not speak in riddles to me," Zaw snapped. "I am on the verge of an undertaking greater than any my brother could have hoped to imagine. My contact in the United States is about to deliver to my scientists a plant more valuable than the poppy or the coca leaf. Your followers were supposed to cause chaos in the Asian tobacco distribution network while simultaneously discrediting Cheyenne Tobacco."

"And so they did. The men you wanted dead are dead."

Zaw spluttered furiously. "Yes, but your foolish followers did not even get that right. They killed one from Cheyenne Tobacco." Zaw consulted his computer, pulling up the story he had read earlier that day, before he had left home. "See? A scientist called John Feathers is dead."

The masked man shook his head. "My men removed fifteen, and fifteen did they leave just as you instructed. The sixteenth was not killed by them."

Zhii Zaw snorted. "So he came to be there by accident. Is that what you are saying? You and your men have been stupid."

He expected a protest but none came. "Everyone knows the contempt Edgar Rawly has for the anti-tobacco groups whose lunacy he is forced to finance. He would have been the perfect scapegoat if all the men who were killed worked for his competitors. Everyone would think he had tried to blame the murders on the anti-smoking groups he detests so much. My plan was brilliant. And now it is lost because one of Rawly's own employees was killed along with the rest. And you say. . . ."

"Not by my men," Jian interrupted . . .

"Gah!" Zaw snapped, fanning the air with a fat, angry hand. "These men you trust so much. Are they the same ones who foolishly left one of their own weapons in a body and had to return to retrieve it?"

On his computer, Zaw closed the last window he had opened. The story of the dead Chinese appeared once more. For the first time, the masked man saw the photograph of the silver moshuh nanren weapon. Etched into the disk were the traditional characters for honor, sacrifice and duty. But in an act of graffiti, another character had been cut above them. A trapezoid bisected by a vertical line.

Above the purple mask, the brown eyes widened.

It was the closest Zaw had ever seen his personal assassin come to surprise. He glanced at the photograph again but saw nothing startling. "What is wrong?" Zaw asked.

"The danger to your enterprise may be greater than you imagined," the masked man said. "That is the symbol of a very old enemy of my discipline."

"That?" Zaw asked, waving to the etching. "It is the symbol for 'China' or 'center.' What does it mean?"

"It is more than you think, and it is not discussed with outsiders," Jian said. He paused, gathering his thoughts. "Young men are fools. The younger the man, the greater the fool. I will go to the United States at once."

"What?" Zaw scoffed. "No, you will not. You are supposed to be the best. That is what I pay you to be. My contact will make the delivery any day now. You will stay with me until that time, and when I go to America you will accompany me as my bodyguard. If you believe there is a danger that affects me, send in your next wave. That is how you people operate, is it not?"

There was hesitation in the eyes above the purple mask. It was something Zaw had never before seen from this man, whose code of honor pledged unwavering loyalty to his employer. At last, the masked man bowed.

"As you command," Jian said, "I obey."

Zaw turned his attention back to his computer screen.

The old general did not like surprises. The fact that the first wave of moshuh nanren had been eradicated was precisely the sort of surprise he detested the most.

They had been vicious young men. Their skills were not as great as those of their master, yet they were greater than any Zhii Zaw had ever seen.

Almost any.

A flutter of fear touched the pit of Zaw's stomach.

"Do you really know what killed them?"

"Something greater than they," Jian replied.

The masked man's voice spoke like a fading memory. When Zhii Zaw turned to find him, the man in black had been swallowed by shadow and was gone.

12

Their plane touched down in Great Falls, Montana, in late afternoon. Remo rented a car at the airport, bought a few maps at a gas station, tried to read them, gave up, tried to fold them, gave that up too, and stuffed them in a crumpled wad in Aphrodite's hands.

"I'll give you an Indian Head nickel if you can figure out where the hell we are," he said.

Aphrodite smoothed the maps on the dashboard and, telling Remo exactly where to turn left and right, managed to get them to the Chowok reservation before nightfall.

Amid the sad squalor of the rundown reservation, they found themselves driving on a modern highway that was lined on either side with fields of green leaves.

Remo stopped the car and the three of them climbed out.

"Thank God," Aphrodite said. With shaking hands she lit up a cigarette. Before she had taken a single good puff, Chiun flicked it from between her lips. It exploded orange ash on the pavement. "Hey, I did as you wanted. I didn't smoke in the car back in Connecticut which, I admit, wasn't so hard because I was unconscious. I didn't smoke on the plane or in two airports, and I got all the way out here without lighting up, even though I haven't gone this long without a recharge since college. But we're in open air now, so cut me a break, okay?" Angrily, she tried to light another cigarette. It was Remo who stopped her this time. "That's about as tolerant as he gets," he warned her. "If you light up in his presence again, the next thing that bounces across the road won't be a cigarette."

"I should put him to work for the CSFW," Aphrodite muttered. Scowling at the old Korean, she stuffed her pack of cigarettes back inside her backpack.

Remo and Chiun turned their attention to the fields.

In the distance a row of greenhouses glinted orange in the dying light. The two Masters of Sinanju could feel the pressure waves from distant security cameras. They had been rotating automatically, but moments after Remo parked the car, one camera stopped moving and locked its eye on their little group. A moment later, a second camera from the other corner of the field stopped its slow rotation, its unblinking lens fixed squarely on Remo and the others.

Remo and Chiun ignored the cameras.

It appeared that Cheyenne Tobacco had spared no expense on its valuable crop. There were no hoses or traditional sprinklers scattered around this farm in Great Falls, Montana. Structures that looked like hollow metal scaffolding rolled slowly over the far reaches of the tobacco fields. The pipes extended over the fields and the supporting structure was attached to wheels which automatically carried the modern watering system slowly forward. Water continuously sprayed from nozzles that were spaced along the metal tubes.

"We've come a long way from a leaky bucket," Remo said. "So is this the stuff or what? I'm no expert, but it looks like regular tobacco leaves to me."

"You," Chiun commanded, pointing to Aphrodite. "Examine the plants. My son and I will wait here."

"Don't be so worried, Chiun. I'll be careful." Remo tried

to step forward, but a firm hand gripping his forearm held him in place.

"Let the female go," the old Korean insisted.

Remo sighed. "Okay. Fine. Aphrodite?"

Nodding, Aphrodite slid down the shoulder of the paved road to the little dirt service road that ran parallel to the field. She took the tip of one of the leaves between her thumb and forefinger and gave the gentlest rub.

"This is it," she announced. She held up her hand. The tips of her two fingers were already breaking out in tiny red bumps. "Our sources said this is one of the side effects. It's like walking through a cloud of burning poison oak."

"Okay, this is the stuff," Remo said. "If it's so bad let's get rid of it right now. I'll go pick up some matches and gas. We'll roast some weenies. It'll be fun."

"No," Chiun said. "It is too dangerous."

"Pook burned the crops and he survived, Chiun. You said so yourself. We should be okay."

"We did these people a favor once, even if they did not appreciate it at the time. They were warned of the consequences if they started this madness again. Sinanju is done risking our lives for these scalp collectors. They will clean up their own mess this time."

"I don't think they're going to follow orders so easily," Aphrodite warned. "They've got a lot invested in this. Cheyenne Tobacco must have built this road and these farms, and I hear the Native Americans are getting a good chunk of change for bringing the leaf to old Edgar Rawly's attention."

"Rawly?" Remo asked.

"Bigshot Big Tobacco goon," Aphrodite explained. "You really are out of it. Anyway, Rawly and the Chowok are thick as purveyors of poison can be. They're not going to let you burn this stuff without putting up a fight."

Remo nodded to the road. "Let's ask them."

Actually, Remo was surprised by how quickly they had responded to the security cameras. Remo and Chiun had both heard the sound long before Aphrodite. When she looked down the road, fear blossomed full on her beautiful face.

A line of Indians in war paint and feather headdresses was thundering down the highway on horseback.

Aphrodite grabbed Remo's arm and hid behind him as the horses pounded down on them, surrounding their small party.

When Remo saw the Indians close up, he could barely contain a laugh. Remo had encountered some Montana Indians many years before. Those were the Apowa, and they looked as he would have expected them to. These Chowok, on the other hand, reminded him of Indians in an old black-and-white Western, when anyone who happened to be walking across the studio lot had been stuck in buckskin and feathers in order to fill out the background. Some of the braves had faint features almost consistent with other tribes of American Indians, but most looked as if they had been recruited from the ranks of Her Majesty's palace guard. A very pale brave with exceedingly big teeth trotted to the front of the others.

"What are you people doing here?" the pale Indian asked.

Remo had expected the Indian to sound like he was addressing the House of Lords, but his accent was that of any other American Indian Remo had ever encountered.

Before Remo could reply, the Master of Sinanju strode forward. From the folds of his kimono, the old Korean produced two small objects, which he held high in the air.

Remo saw that the two objects were actually two halves of the same arrow. The shaft appeared to be wooden, but the arrowhead appeared to be chipped from copper. The feathers too were of the same ornamental metal.

And Remo now knew what the Master of Sinanju had collected from his trunks back in Connecticut.

The Indians on horseback seemed surprised by the broken arrow. Their surprise turned to awe when the ancient Asian shouted out a few short sentences in what could only be Chowok. The Master of Sinanju made a show of holding the arrow halves together, reforming the shaft. He held the arrow up to the dark eastern sky and made a snapping motion.

"You speak Chowok?" Remo asked, impressed.

"Pook was with them for a little while," Chiun explained. "And To-Un had scratched down a few phrases before succumbing to their evil smoke. Chowok is easy, learning to speak American is hard."

A few more harsh words and two of the braves hurriedly dismounted and offered their ponies to Chiun and Remo.

"What about Aphrodite?" Remo asked.

"Do not embarrass me in front of the savages," Chiun said as he slid up onto his horse. "Females walk. It is their tradition. Besides, she should use her lungs for something other than inhaling filth."

Remo shrugged to Aphrodite. "Sorry, toots. Who am I to fight tradition?" He mounted his own horse.

The braves on foot took the reins and walked Remo's and Chiun's horses down the road. The other horsemen thundered off, Remo assumed, to warn of their coming. Aphrodite fell in behind the entourage, grumbling all the way.

"And thus would it be written of the exalted manner in which the Reigning Master Emeritus of the House of Sinanju and his apprentice, the young Reigning Master, returned to the land of the Sickly Breath, the place of the savage men once of red skin, saved from death by Sinanju and known as the Chowok," Chiun announced from the lead pony.

"I need a smoke," Aphrodite whined.

"Light a horse flop," said Remo.

13

The twenty-year-old Technics stereo with the half-
blown left speaker blared "Eve of Destruction" in all its
warped, scratchy LP glory. Although the noise rattled windows throughout the apartment complex, the bulky black
telephone on the pressboard coffee table did not ring.

Once, a new neighbor in the apartment three doors down
had complained to the landlord about the loud music blast-
ing from the apartment at the end of the hall. The neighbor
was cautioned that people did not complain about Mr. Wollrich or his music. But after being awakened at five a.m. for
the seventh day in a row, the unwise new neighbor had
spurned the landlord's advice and called the police. His
body was discovered in a Dumpster five days later, a single
bullet wound to the forehead.

The police never solved the crime, but the rest of the
neighbors had gotten a clear message. One did nothing to
get on the bad side of Mr. Wollrich.

Even though the parking spaces were clearly labelled, one

resident and one guest per unit, Mr. Wollrich was allowed to park his 1977 Buick wherever his whims guided him.

Unlike the other tenants, Mr. Wollrich was not charged for gas or electric. Mr. Wollrich merely had to drop his trash bags off the balcony and others collected them and threw them away for him. When it was found that Mr. Wollrich was stealing cable television from a neighboring apartment, the neighbors pitched in to cover the fees and fines.

Mr. Arvin Wollrich lived as charmed a life as was possible for a homicidal maniac and it was all thanks to one remarkable individual. Edgar Rawly.

Mr. Rawly had spotted Wollrich's potential thirty-five years before, when Wollrich was a young former soldier just returned from the jungles of Vietnam.

In the early seventies, Wollrich had taken a temporary job loading cases of cigarettes on trucks in a Cheyenne Tobacco warehouse in West Virginia. During his first week on the job, a young high school punk, only a couple years younger than Arvin Wollrich, filched an apple from Wollrich's bagged lunch. The kid wound up in the hospital with multiple stab wounds and two missing front teeth, and Wollrich was on his way to a sure stint in prison. Then a miracle happened that changed Wollrich's life.

The charges were mysteriously dropped and Wollrich was freed. A Rolls-Royce was waiting for him outside the jail building.

"Mr. Wollrich?" the driver said, more politely than anyone had ever spoken to Arvin Wollrich in his life.

So taken aback was he by the politeness of the man in chauffeur's livery, Arvin Wollrich completely failed to beat the snot out of him for the crime of being British and, therefore, more than likely a faggot.

Wollrich accepted a ride in the yellow Rolls, and was surprised when he was taken back to Cheyenne Tobacco.

An old woman in gigantic glasses that looked like goggles ushered him into the offices of the CEO of Cheyenne Tobacco, Inc., Mr. Edgar Rawly.

Feeling uncomfortable for the first time in his young life, Arvin Wollrich had quietly taken a seat.

"Don't sit down, Wollrich, you dummy," Rawly snapped. "You're not going to be here that long."

The tobacco giant was sitting behind a gleaming desk that was as big as Wollrich's entire kitchen. His secretary had placed some papers before him which Rawly signed without even reading. The old woman merely pointed and Rawly dutifully signed. A cigarette dangled from her lower lip as if it had been fastened with epoxy.

"You're a crazy bastard, aren't you?" Mr. Rawly said as he signed. "Cost me a bundle to make that mess of yours go away. How'd you like to put that psych-ward nutso insanity of yours to good use?"

This was all happening so fast, Wollrich could not help but be overwhelmed. As was his nature, however, he hid his confusion behind a veil of hostility. "Who do I have to kill?" he said with a nonchalant chuckle.

"Depends on who I decide needs killing," Rawly said.

It took a moment for Wollrich to realize that Rawly was not joking. Wollrich shot a furtive glance at the tobacco man's secretary, a move not lost on Rawly.

"Hell, Wollrich, Mrs. Z. knows everything that goes on around here, except for the stuff she's forgotten. Been with me for nearly forty years now. The rate she's going, I expect she'll be here another forty. You wouldn't know it to look at her, but she was quite the looker back in the dark ages." Rawly gave the elderly woman a hearty swat on her bony rear.

The secretary must either have had nerve damage in her bottom or had become used to frequent rump swatting over the course of her forty years at Cheyenne, for she did not seem even to feel his touch. She merely gathered up the paperwork he had signed and strode from the room.

"Okay, Wollrich, here's the deal," Rawly said once the woman had left the office. "You're a loon. And I need a loon on my payroll. But not for stabbing kids on my loading docks. You keep the genie in the bottle until I tell you who to release it on and you're set for life. You in?"

Wollrich accepted the offer with a handshake, a smile and without a second thought. The truth was Wollrich had never had much of an idea what to do with his life. Lousy parents set him on the wrong path early on. But in that office, for the first time in his life, he felt a connection with someone that was as close to a parental bond as he had ever experienced. Wollrich would kill for Mr. Rawly. In fact, over the next thirty-five years he did so on many, many occasions. And the next time was warming up in the bullpen.

The call had come an hour ago. The message was short but had been sweet music to Wollrich's ears.

"Almost time to clean the ashtrays."

The line went dead in his sweaty hand.

Wollrich had recognized the voice of Mr. Rawly's personal assistant, David Merkel. Wollrich didn't like the young man. No one but Wollrich respected Mr. Rawly like a father.

Almost time to clean the ashtrays.

It was part of a code Wollrich and Rawly had devised. In the past, Mr. Rawly's hits had been simple point-and-shoots, but this time would be multiple targets, hence the plural on "ashtrays." Wollrich would do his employer proud. After all, the Formica table with the one short leg, the Mark McGwire bobblehead, the used Swanks purchased on eBay . . . Arvin Wollrich owed them all to Mr. Rawly.

Wollrich slipped his Australian machete bayonet into a special pouch down the back of his jacket and shimmied into a two-sided shoulder holster, an automatic pistol under each armpit.

There would be specific instructions in a post office box two towns over. That was the arrangement and it had worked each time.

In the corner of the room, the record skipped and began repeating the same line over and over. Wollrich didn't even notice. The sound was white noise to the thrill of death that pounded in his ears.

Leaving the stereo to skip eternally over the same three words, Arvin Wollrich hurried from his apartment.

* * *

For most of the walk to the Chowok village, Aphrodite Janise lagged behind the others. She had been edgy since the airport back east and, far from Chiun and with the wind blowing in the right direction, was finally able to light a cigarette she had retrieved from her backpack. She sucked down a deep lungful of smoke and exhaled a soft plume into the Montana twilight.

As she smoked, she found a horse plodding beside her. Remo had fallen back and was keeping pace with Aphrodite.

"You know a gentleman would give up his horse for me," she said without looking up at him.

"Tell you what, Pilgrim. I'll let you know if one moseys up," Remo said. He nodded to a bumper sticker that was pasted to Aphrodite's backpack. " 'Lungs for the Memories'?"

"What's wrong with it?" Aphrodite snapped. As soon as the words were out, her angry expression collapsed and she nodded. "Okay, it's crap, I know. Not one of my best efforts. We were trying to reach an older demographic with that one. Our ads have worked okay for hitting the younger crowd but we're not very good at cracking the older market."

"Have you tried backing away from the usual sanctimonious stuff and just tried telling people the truth?"

"The truth?" she scoffed. "This is the twenty-first century. The truth is for crap."

"Didn't you used to be Dee Dee Myers?" Remo asked.

"Hah-hah," she said. "Let me give you an example. Remember that old ad, the one with the eggs frying and the narrator saying that was your brain on drugs? Big-time effective back in its day. Then there was 'Just say no to drugs.' People mocked it, but you know what? It worked. Understated worked great before the MTV generation came of age. Problem is society got louder and attention spans got shorter. That ad with the frying eggs became an ad with some woman beating the hell out of her kitchen with the frying pan. That's what we're dealing with now. You don't like our ads? You don't have to, you're not a smoker. We reach the audience any way we know how."

"Aphrodite, that is the smartest thing you've said all day," Remo said. "And for the record, I used to smoke."

Aphrodite took a long drag and blew the smoke to the stars. "How'd you quit?"

Remo nodded up to Chiun. The wizened Korean was like a fragile porcelain doll perched on the back of his plodding horse. The horse rose and fell with each footfall, yet the Master of Sinanju remained perfectly parallel to the ground, as if he were gliding along without a sixteen-hundred-pound beast between him and earth.

"I quit because of him," Remo said.

"What, did he get you on the patch or something?"

"Imagine every one of your nerve endings dipped in acid. Burning acid. Like fire. He can do that with a touch. The pain he inflicted was worse than any nicotine cravings. One day I woke up and didn't want to smoke anymore. I can no longer imagine willingly accepting pollutants into my body."

"Sounds like New Age voodoo to me," Aphrodite said.

"More like Old Age. Five thousand years and counting."

Aphrodite took out a fresh cigarette and lit it with the stub of the old one. She ground the used butt under her toe.

"So it's aversion therapy. Do you know how to do that?"

"Yup."

"Can you use it on me, like that thing you did with my elbow back at CSFW headquarters?"

"Sorry, Aphrodite," Remo said. "That's only for training. Only one lucky stiff per century is charmed enough to get the crap kicked out of him like that."

"How about that acupressure stuff you used to make me lose my vision? Can you use that to make me quit?"

For the briefest moment her tough veneer melted and her face became desperately optimistic.

He shook his head. "You'd have to really want to quit."

"You think I don't want to quit?" Aphrodite said. "I hate this rotten habit. It smells. It costs me a fortune. And one day I know it's going to kill me."

Remo suddenly understood. "How long have you got?"

Aphrodite looked up, startled. Tearing her eyes away from his, she sucked down a lungful of smoke. "Doctors don't know everything. I went through their treatments. Made me feel sicker than these things, I lost my hair, couldn't eat. I finally told them no more. I feel fine now, but it won't last. They say less than a year, but to hell with that. If you can make me quit, maybe I can turn it all around. Then I can devote all my energy to the CSFW. We really do do good work, Remo, despite what you say. So can you help me quit?"

Remo offered her a sad smile. "If you wanted to quit, Aphrodite, you'd quit. Yes, I could get you to give it up for a little while. But it would be a temporary fix. The reason something like hypnosis works is because those people that it actually works on really want to quit, and they've taken an active step to do it. The fact that you're standing there puffing away tells me you don't want to quit."

Aphrodite's brow dropped. She chewed the filter of her cigarette as she considered his words. "So what you're saying is the only way you can make me quit is if I quit?"

"Afraid so."

"You're worthless, you know that, Remo?"

A singsong voice chimed in from up ahead. "Welcome to my life," called the Master of Sinanju.

The Montana road outside Great Falls led to a small town of new wooden buildings. It was apparent that the Chowok had recently come into money. Wooden frames of a dozen new civic buildings had been built at the edge of the existing village. A new two-story town hall rose, nearly complete, in the center.

The two Indians led Remo's and Chiun's horses to the big building. Aphrodite trudged up between them as the two Masters of Sinanju slid lightly off their horses.

"What . . . are . . . we . . . doing . . . here?" she panted. She watched, breathless, as the two Indians hustled inside.

"See that look on his face?" Remo said, nodding to the Master of Sinanju, whose expression as he padded up the steps to the town hall was carved in stone. "That look means we're giving them an ultimatum."

"No, we're wasting time," she said, catching her breath. "We should go after Rawly. He's the one behind all this."

"Maybe," Remo said. "But that look on his face tells me I'll miss a lot of headaches if I just go along with him."

Remo followed his teacher into the new building. Tossing up her hands in frustration, Aphrodite clomped up the wooden stairs and trailed them inside.

The building smelled of freshly cut lumber. The unfinished floors were sheets of plywood. Framed walls offered views into future offices. High above, tarps on the roof crackled in the soft breeze.

An emergency council meeting had been called in the auditorium of the town hall. Members of the Chowok had been summoned from all over the reservation. Many stood around the edges of the room, others sat on toolboxes and stacks of lumber.

The men had pale skin and all appeared edgy, shifting anxiously from foot to foot. Many did not seem to know what to do with their hands. Although their skin was broken out in the red rash of the Cheyenne Smooths, none smoked.

A few long planks had been set up across sawhorses to act as a table, behind which a group of older men sat on folding chairs. The Indians who had led Remo and Chiun to this place, as well as the others who had ridden back before them, were in heated discussion with the seated men. They were arguing and gesturing toward the door. When Remo's party entered, the men around the plywood table fell silent.

All eyes were on the wizened Asian who marched across the floor. As he passed by, eager conversation broke out and the men whispered anxiously to one another.

Aphrodite was uncomfortable with the attention they were drawing. She repositioned her heavy backpack on her shoulder and tried to melt into Remo's side.

They stopped before the makeshift table.

At the center of the table was a man in his sixties. He had a large, crooked nose, a fleshy face and skin as pale as a Montana summer cloud. For this meeting Chief Soaring Eagle had hastily donned a large ceremonial feather headdress.

Remo appraised the seated man skeptically. "Don't tell me he's an Indian too," he said softly to Chiun. "He looks like Sir Anthony Cecil Hogmanay Melchett, for crying out loud."

"He is their chief," the Master of Sinanju explained in Korean. "Now be silent while I do your job for you."

Turning to the Chowok, the old Asian spoke a few words in the Indian language. Men who had doubted the claims of the braves who had ridden out to confront the intruders at the tobacco fields were startled to hear their own tongue issuing from the tiny old foreigner with skin like a walnut shell. The whispering around the room ceased. When Chiun held aloft the broken arrow, audible gasps issued from the main table and gathered multitude.

Once Chiun was finished with his ceremonial greeting, he said in English, "For the benefit of my son, I will continue now in the language of your forebears."

"You speak the language of the White Man," said the white man at the table, "not that of our ancestors."

"I cannot help if you are blind to the evidence of your own mirrors," the Master of Sinanju proclaimed, "for one merely needs eyes to see that the blood of the Celts, Angles, Saxons, Jutes, Danes and Normans flows in your veins. I come to you now, descendant of him you tried to murder, a son of Pook, a son of To-Un, to save you once more from yourselves."

"We are not in need of saving, old one," Chief Soaring Eagle said. He began to say more, but the words caught in his throat.

The chief suddenly pressed his lips tightly together, as if holding in that which he dared not say. But it quickly became evident that it was not words he feared to release.

His face turned red, teeth clenched, eyes watered. For a few moments he held it in. Then all at once the chief's mouth burst open and he coughed, loud and long. The coughing fit seemed as if it would never end. The Indian beside him patted Soaring Eagle on the back while another fished in his pocket for a cough suppressing lozenge.

Through it all, Chiun remained mute, and when the chief was through and wiping tears from his eyes and sucking on a Sucrets, the Master of Sinanju shook his head.

"Not in need of saving? Fools. If it were only you committing slow suicide, I might leave you to your fate. But as before, you inflict your folly on others. The world is smaller than it was in the days of To-Un. A few hours and your poison can reach the most distant shores."

"We have heard the legend of this To-Un and of the great migration west," the chief said, coughing a few times into his balled fist. His throat was raw. "But they are only stories, the same as the silly tales of the whites he is supposed to have traded into our tribe long ago."

Remo raised his hand. "Yeah, see, the thing is, Chief Hacks Up Lung, I'd have an easier time with your position if you weren't as white as Michael Jackson."

"If the skin of some of us is pale, that is because of the whites who came later, who raped our women and chased our braves from the land of our ancestors."

"It is clear you know the histories of your people," the Master of Sinanju said. "Yet you pick and choose what to believe. It is To-Un's heir who banished you from the east, not the whites who came later. Your tribe was dying and the English whites who became Chowok saved you from extinction. Therefore To-Un saved your people. But as enemies of truth, this clearly has no meaning to you." He held aloft once more the broken arrow. "Nonetheless I am here to tell you now that even though you choose to ignore your true history, there are those who hold it sacred, but only where it intersects with our own. And the Master of Sinanju has returned to you now to tell you that you will destroy forever this evil you have brought back from destruction."

Standing a few feet back from Chiun, Aphrodite caught movement from the corner of her eye. When she glanced over, she saw rifles being handed up through a gap in the floor. The braves were quietly passing the guns out to the crowd. Urgently, she tugged the back of Remo's T-shirt.

"Psst, Remo!" she hissed.

"Careful who you're pssting on," Remo said, annoyed. "You're like a nicotine sprinkler."

She tugged harder, twisting the cotton fabric. She tried to pinch his skin, but his skin seemed to pinch back. "They have guns," she said.

Remo glanced blandly over his shoulder. The leading edge of the semicircle of braves around them all held rifles in their hands. The weapons were trained on Remo's small group of three.

"Don't be culturally insensitive, Aphrodite," Remo said. "They prefer to call them 'fire sticks.'" He turned his attention back to the action in the front of the hall.

The chief's pale skin had reddened. "You dare come to the land of the Chowok and make demands of us?" Soaring Eagle said to the Master of Sinanju. "Fire destroyed this most sacred plant hundreds of years ago. We thought it was lost forever. But thanks to one of our own who learned your white man's science we have had it returned to us. And you think that you can come here and order us to destroy it?"

Clapping his hands, the chief shouted an angry order in the Chowok language to the braves around the room.

The braves were only supposed to escort Remo, Chiun and Aphrodite off the reservation. But an anxious finger somewhere in the group clenched too tight on a trigger.

A single shot cracked the air.

The bullet had been aimed at Remo's back. It zinged through the empty space where a moment before had stood solid flesh and bone. The bullet struck a support beam with a heavy thwack, splintering pine.

The hall erupted in pandemonium. Taking the accidental shot as a cue, the other braves opened fire. Gun barrels exploded, bullets flying like angry hornets through the air. The chief and council dove under their makeshift table.

Aphrodite had a split second to scream. Swirling through the hail of bullets, Remo grabbed a clump of her backpack, pivoted on one heel and bowled her across the room. Sliding on her rear end, she knocked over a dozen shooting braves on her way out the door to safety.

Dodging bullets all the way, Remo raced left, Chiun flounced right.

Remo danced up the line, splintering rifles and slapping the sides of Indian heads. "Tum-tum-tum-tum, beat the drum-drum," he sang, with a "tum" for each smacked head.

Across the room, Chiun attacked the line in a furious blur. Hands lashed down, severing rifle barrels which clanged hollow on the unfinished plywood floor.

It took less than fifteen seconds to disarm the entire Chowok Nation. When the guns finally fell silent and the chief and elders peeked over their sawhorse table, they saw a sight that chilled them to their marrow.

Around the room, smoke curled from split stocks and severed barrels. Many braves still held fragments of shattered weapons, expressions of fear and confusion on their faces. Still others had dropped their broken rifles and were rubbing stinging hands and heads. The walls were riddled with holes, the black of the Montana night visible beyond. The acrid smell of gunpowder filled the room.

And in the center of the hall, unharmed and immovable, stood Remo and Chiun. The Master of Sinanju's hands were folded inside his voluminous kimono sleeves. His expression was hard. Remo appeared more irritated than angry.

"Prepare quarters for us," the Master of Sinanju announced. "We will accept your hospitality for the night. When the first light of dawn breaks, you will destroy your crops and end this madness forever."

Not permitting room for argument, the Master of Sinanju turned and, Remo in tow, marched from the room.

Dawn was kissing the treetops of West Virginia and the birds were singing a chorus to greet the new day as the small crowd assembled in the little landscaped park next to the Cheyenne Tobacco administrative building. Three men struggled to hoist Edgar Rawly into a leather saddle.

"Careful, you snotnoses," Rawly snarled. "I'm not a sack of potatoes, you know." In punctuation, he swatted the nearest young man on the top of the head with a riding crop.

David Merkel accepted the abuse with a resigned grunt.

The magazine ad photo shoot had taken most of the previous day and had not ended well. A new firm had been hastily hired and, at Mr. Rawly's command, a new direction was being taken.

The photographer and his crew were due in ten minutes. Mr. Rawly preferred it when people arrived early. Merkel knew that heaven would not help this new crew if they were late.

"Okay, careful, careful," Rawly said. "Now balance me off. You there—" He struck an accounting vice president on the head. "—nudge me back to the right."

Although the center of activity, the horse on which Rawly was perched remained perfectly still. The animal was several decades beyond skittishness. It had been rolled out into the new day sunshine from a glass display case in the lobby of the main building.

Merkel noticed that the stuffed horse had a few missing patches of fur. This ad was for the Asian markets, and even though it would not hit for several months, it was of crucial importance. The overseas markets were vital to the future of the tobacco industry. It was bad enough that Mr. Rawly was insisting that his face be used in the newest rollout, but an elderly man on a balding stuffed horse was not exactly the image of vitality Cheyenne should be projecting. Merkel hoped the photography people would be able to Photoshop in some fur to cover the horse's mangy areas.

"Great gal, Misty," Rawly said, stroking the stuffed horse's shaggy mane. "We used her in a hundred and eight TV spots back in the fifties, not counting the live spots she did for the *Cheyenne All-Star Theater Featuring Morey Amsterdam and the Alison Dickering Dancers*. That was in the good old days, when the bastards hadn't kicked us off TV. Misty here was partnered with Ramblin' Bob DeLucca. They did print ads, too. Wonder where Bob got himself off to?"

"Pinegreen Cemetery, across town," Merkel replied. "Died of lung cancer back in 1968."

"The bastard," Rawly complained. "Would've sold us through the roof to have him back in this saddle. No one could push smokes like Bob and Misty."

Merkel hoped the photographers would arrive soon. Mr. Rawly was waxing nostalgic and was in a rare moment of good humor. That would change in a heartbeat if the new ad people failed to arrive on time.

Merkel suddenly heard the sound of an automobile engine and turned an optimistic eye to the parking lot.

It was not the photographer.

A big red Cadillac Fleetwood Seventy-Five with bald tires and broken fins had just driven into view. Although the lot was virtually empty, the car still managed to scrape along two light poles on its way to its reserved space. Merkel held his breath as the gigantic car passed his own parked Saturn. The Cadillac hit a curb and buried its bumper in some azaleas before it finally chugged to a smoky stop.

The elderly driver took five minutes to sort through scraps of paper and bits of twine on the front seat and another three to climb out of her behemoth car.

Rawly's secretary looked around, then wandered in from her special parking space, her omnipresent cigarette glued to her lower lip. Her great goggle-like glasses took in the scene of Rawly on the stuffed horse, attended to by executives in suits. Scowling, she shuffled wordlessly past the group and disappeared inside the great glass and steel headquarters.

A few other early risers had begun to arrive. Two men had parked far across the lot at the research and development building. They were watching with interest the spectacle of their employer straddling the ratty stuffed horse.

"Get to work, you bastards," Rawly bellowed at them.

Turning rapidly away, the men hustled into the building across the big parking lot.

"You ever meet John Huston, Merkel?" Rawly asked. He didn't wait for an answer. "Didn't think so. I met him through Bogie. Big rough-and-tumble guy. Great director. He was a Cheyenne Chum for a time. Bastards start letting us on TV again, maybe we could get him for our new spots. We can use Misty here and get us a new Ramblin' Bob."

"I don't think so, Mr. Rawly," Merkel said, distracted by a sudden vibration in his pocket. "Emphysema in the Eighties. He cut an anti-smoking spot before he died."

As his employer cursed the memory of the late, great director, Merkel fished his cell phone from his pocket and scanned the text message he had just received.

"We'll do it without Huston," Rawly grunted. "Wish we could get old Bogie for the new Ramblin' Bob. What about that young whippersnapper? What's his name? Steve McQueen?"

Merkel had read the message and was in the middle of dialing. "Sir?" he said, distracted. "No. He's gone, too."

"Dead, huh? What got him? And if you value your job, Merkel, it won't be cancer."

Merkel was pressing the phone to his ear. "Ah, um, a motorcycle accident in the Seventies. Please, sir, I have to make this call. It's about the Smooths."

Rawly scrutinized his subordinate's face, but Merkel was already in deep conversation. Eventually the old man accepted the lie, nodding. "Motorcycles, huh? Those contraptions should be banned. Cracked his skull open, did he? No one ever cracked his skull open on a Cheyenne cigarette, Merkel. But we're the ones who have to put on the warning labels. Bastards."

Merkel finished his call and quickly chased away the other Cheyenne executives. Once they were alone, he handed his phone up to Rawly.

"That was Chief Soaring Eagle," Merkel whispered.

On his horse, the Cheyenne Tobacco CEO squinted at the phone. There was a small image on the tiny screen. It showed two men and a woman near a field of tobacco. Rawly recognized instantly the farm his people had constructed on the Chowok reservation. The picture had been taken with a surveillance camera. But something was wrong. The woman's face was as clear as day, but the faces of the two men were blurry. It was almost as if they had some way of making themselves unrecognizable to cameras. But that was ludicrous, of course.

Rawly scowled down at his assistant. "When the hell was this taken?" he demanded.

"Last night. The men have apparently put the fear of God into the Native Americans, sir. Some sort of Chowok legend come to life. I couldn't really get it all, but there was something about a great migration, and the Chowok tobacco plant and something called a 'Croatoan.' These people are ordering the Chowok to destroy the fields."

Rawly nearly fell off his stuffed horse. Merkel had to grab a bony leg and arm to hold him in place.

"What!" the tobacco CEO bellowed. "Get me that Chief Soaring Shit on this thing." He shoved the cell phone into

Merkel's hand. "Those Chowok bastards are already costing me a fortune in royalties for that damned plant of theirs. If he thinks he can screw with the billions I have tied up in this, I'll shove his damn peace pipe up his goddamn ass."

Merkel had pressed only three numbers before he felt the lash of a riding crop on his scalp.

"Hold the phone, Merkel," Rawly said. The rage of an instant before was gone, replaced with a yellow-toothed grin. "Is Wollrich on the ground in Montana?"

Merkel's eyes widened. "Yes, sir, Mr. Rawly. You had me send him there after Dr. Feathers was killed."

Rawly smacked Merkel with his riding crop. "I don't need to be reminded where I sent him. I'm not senile you know. Have Wollrich take care of them."

Merkel gulped. "Both of them?" he asked.

"All of them," Edgar Rawly replied. "The woman, those two, and whatever goddamned Injuns are in the immediate vicinity. Make it look like those CSFW no-smoking crazies did it. They already did all those guys in New York. Won't be a stretch to have them go on the warpath in Montana."

"Sir—" Merkel was frightened of the sound of his own voice. "Sir," he repeated, whispering, "it's still not certain that the CSFW was responsible for those deaths."

"Course it was," Rawly snapped. "Now hurry up and get on that whoozitz to Wollrich."

"Are you sure that's a wise course of action?"

The withering look his employer shot him caused David Merkel to wince worse than any lash of a riding crop.

"The Chowok were going to cost me a fortune," Rawly said. "I'm paying a percentage per head on the net. The fewer of them there are, the less out of pocket for me. Chief Soaring Sissy wants to cut and run on me, I say screw the bastard. I don't need their fields anymore anyway. Call Wollrich. Tell him he's off his leash. Any and all means."

For emphasis, Rawly kicked his assistant in the ribs with the toe of his cowboy boot. The action nearly toppled him off the horse in the opposite direction, and the other two executives on hand had to race forward and reset their employer in the saddle.

Merkel did not even feel the pain in his side. He was considering the ramifications to being an accessory to mass murder, imagining how long it would take his boss to send Wollrich after him if ever he were to betray Cheyenne Tobacco, wondering if Death Row could possibly be any worse than working for Edgar Rawly, and thinking he maybe should have gone to veterinary rather than business school after all.

Merkel took a few steps away from the tobacco CEO, the mangy stuffed horse Misty and the other Cheyenne executives. Hands shaking as he dialed, he placed a call to Edgar Rawly's terrifying hired killer. And prayed for his own black soul.

When the bright sun of the new day at last broke yellow and hot over the Chowok Indian reservation, it revealed a trudging line of very pale braves making their reluctant way along the new black strip of highway to the tobacco fields.

On foot, shoulders slumped as they walked, the Chowok resembled the dispossessed villagers of Anatevka, forced from their homes by the cruel Tsar.

Only one vehicle moved along the road.

Chiun had commandeered a jeep from a driveway. The owner had witnessed Chiun's and Remo's performance at the new town hall the previous evening and rather than drive had offered to sign the title over to the frightening old Korean.

Remo was only glad Chiun had not heard the man or else he'd be schlepping the jeep all the way back to Connecticut, probably strapped to his back the way things were going. "He's got enough toys," Remo had whispered. "Just give me the damned keys."

Remo drove, Aphrodite sat in the passenger's seat and standing on the backseat was the Master of Sinanju.

Chief Soaring Eagle remained back at the main village

along with the women and children of the tribe. The Chowok chief was still making phone calls and knocking on doors, rousing every able-bodied brave across the big reservation for the forced harvest.

The elderly Korean had taken along for the ride several strings of the beads Chowok women sold to tourists. Whenever he spied a brave dogging it along the trail, Chiun would send a bead zinging into the back of his head. Like a bee sting, it caused no permanent injury but was enough to motivate the Indians forward. Dozens of men were rubbing their heads and muttering to one another as the jeep, at Chiun's direction, rode back and forth along the line.

"It would have been quicker if you let them drive," Remo said as Chiun slipped another bead from a necklace.

The bead rolled onto a leathery fingertip and, with the flick of a lightning fast thumb, zipped through air. It hit with an audible smack just behind the ear of a lollygagging brave. The brave yelped and quickened his pace.

"No," the Master of Sinanju replied sternly. "They must learn the lesson of their ancestors. Although, frankly, Remo, they are getting off easy. The Chowok of old walked thousands of miles. But they were true Indians, not these pasty English things. For these lazy white descendants of Sir Raleigh's folly, a stroll of a few miles from their television sets may as well be a forced march to the moon."

Aphrodite was rummaging inside her omnipresent backpack. "Do you mind if I smoke?" she asked hopefully.

"You may inhale your poisons only on the day I neglect to bring my healthy lungs with me," the old Asian said. Distracted by a brave who had stopped to tie a shoelace, he slipped another bead off a necklace.

"Is that a no?" she grumbled. Zipping up her backpack, she stuffed it back down between her ankles.

"You really should give a shot at quitting, Aphrodite. You've gone mostly for a day already," Remo said.

Sighing and staring out at the scenery, Aphrodite shook her head. "That ship's already sailed. I just have to make the best use of the time I've got left." Behind her, Chiun let another bead fly, and another Chowok yelped. She turned back, fixing Remo with a gimlet eye. "In case you were wondering, this doesn't count as best use of my time."

An hour's slow drive brought them to the tobacco fields.

At Chief Soaring Eagle's order the sprinkler system had been deactivated. With no morning misting, the big leaves were dry and were already curling in the rising sunlight.

Remo parked at the road's shoulder. Waving bony arms high in the air, Chiun directed the gathering Indians down into the fields on either side of the road.

Scratching blossoming red rashes and complaining all the way, the Chowok began the arduous task of uprooting and stacking plants in piles for burning.

Chiun marched along the side of the road, supervising the work. Much of the time he stood watching disdainfully, head held high, arms folded across his chest.

Remo had seen that pose before. With a pair of aviator's sunglasses and a shotgun in the crook of his elbow, the Master of Sinanju could have been a southern deputy supervising a chain gang on highway duty.

"Got a harmonica?" Remo asked Aphrodite.

He had remained in the jeep and was drumming bored fingers on the dashboard.

"You shouldn't make fun. Your old friend may be an anti-smoking zealot, but that's not so bad. I wish I'd had someone like him keeping me honest when I could have used him. He's certainly doing the right thing here."

"So do you think free will should enter into anything you do or do you want everything that's bad for you destroyed for your own good? Or maybe you'd rather other people pick and choose stuff you shouldn't do at random. They can rotate banned stuff in and out. Maybe decide by spinning a big wheel. We can sell tickets. It'll be fun."

"You don't agree with him?"

"I believe that people should be able to make their own stupid choices for themselves. On the other hand, if this stuff is as bad as you and he say it is, maybe it's not a bad idea we're getting rid of it." He shrugged. "I don't know. I just work here." He leaned his arms down around the steering wheel and set his nose on his interlocking fingers.

"This is all pointless if we don't get to Rawly. He'll just start this up somewhere else."

"One catastrophe at a time, lady."

"Really, Remo," Aphrodite insisted. "Rawly is the driving force behind this. That old man would get the whole world hooked if it would fatten his wallet just one dollar more. Did I tell you that the first cigarette I ever smoked was a Cheyenne Slim? I was a freshman in high school. All my friends were trying it, so I figured I would, too. You know every single one of them has quit? No kidding. Years ago. I was the last one to try it, and I'm the only one of them still puffing away. Rawly needs to pay for that."

For an instant it was apparent that she thought she had said too much, but when Remo did not reply, she glanced over.

Remo was no longer leaning on the steering wheel. Eyes narrowed, he was looking east, into the sun.

"What is it?" she asked. She had just heard the sound of something over the breeze. She squinted, but could not see a thing in the blinding sunlight.

The sound grew louder. A plane engine.

Remo got out of the jeep and walked over to the Master of Sinanju. Aphrodite scurried down after him.

The old Korean's gaze was directed heavenward. Wattled neck stretching from his kimono collar, Chiun was looking to the eastern sky and the approaching aircraft.

"We've got company," Remo said.

Chiun nodded. "This craft did not take off from Chowok land."

"How can you know that?" said Aphrodite, who had yet to see the approaching airplane. She squinted into the sun.

"We heard it," Remo told her. To Chiun, he said, "Whoever he is, Little Father, he's not friendly."

"Wait, you can tell whether or not a plane is friendly just from hearing the engine?" Aphrodite asked.

But Remo was no longer listening to her. "We better get

the Chowok out of these fields," he said to Chiun. A sharp nod of agreement from his teacher and Remo ran to the edge of the road. "Okay, let's go!" he shouted. "Move it! Everybody back up on the road!"

The Indians were sweating and scratching in the midmorning sun. They looked up, confused, from their piles of plants, underarms stained dark and faces glistening wet.

"Come on!" Remo yelled more urgently, glancing up at the ever louder approaching plane. "Out of the fields now!"

A ripple of confusion passed through the fields on both sides of the road. None of the Chowok wanted to disobey the Master of Sinanju, but when they looked to the old Korean for guidance they saw that he was nodding stern agreement. Remo's urgency seemed to thrill through them. Throwing down the plants in their hands, they stumbled toward the road. As they ran, many glanced at the sky.

Aphrodite finally saw the plane. It was a large craft, bigger than the small jet that had brought them to Montana. It looked like it might have been military at one point, but the color was wrong. Instead of drab greens or blues, the plane was painted bright red. Black tiger stripes decorated both sides. The nose had been painted to look like an open mouth, with two rows of razor teeth around the cockpit.

As soon as she saw the plane, she saw something fall from its belly.

No, not just one object. A few small, dark somethings. At first she thought they were skydivers, but the plane was too low to the ground. Then she realized that the objects, which were far too small to be human beings, were whistling as they fell. Aphrodite had heard that sound before, but only in movies, and before she could reconcile with the real world her Hollywood conceptions of the whistling sound of falling bombs, the distant greenhouses suddenly shattered into a million pieces in brilliant bursts of fire and scattering glass.

The sound from the explosions rolled in a split second after the blasts, swallowing all other sound. In the fields, panicked Chowok began running for the road.

"Damn," Aphrodite screamed. "Are they dropping bombs?"

Remo was running toward her. "Here," he said, slapping the keys to the jeep into her hand. "Go."

The shock from the sudden closeness of the next explosion knocked her backwards onto the road.

A brilliant orange cloud erupted behind Remo.

Aphrodite realized even as she fell that it was not an explosion, at least not like the ones that had taken out the greenhouses. There was no whistling, no blasts. Just eruptions of fire across the tobacco fields.

And then she saw it.

Liquid poured from sprinkler heads stretched across both wings of the attacking plane. The plane passed low over the fields and wherever the sprayed substance fell, plumes of soot-capped orange flame vomited into the sky.

The air was fire. A single breath and her throat was raw. A cloud worse than anything that could be produced by a mere tobacco plant, a cloud that smelled of ammonia flames, burned mouth and nose.

Aphrodite could hear men screaming. Through the smoke and fire she saw charred bodies scattered around the fields. Many of the men who had not been able to outrun the attack had been killed instantly in the chemical downpour. Those were the lucky ones. Others who had been burned on the plane's first pass tried to crawl to safety, only to be engulfed by flames or sprayed a second time.

A group of Indians that had survived two passovers were caught between parallel rows of fire. As she watched, the far ends of the lines joined in fire, trapping the men.

Strong hands pulled her from the ground. Remo's face was forged in steel. "Go," he commanded.

She was still clutching the keys. Aphrodite covered her mouth with the sleeve of her blouse. Hoisting her backpack higher onto her shoulder, she staggered to the jeep.

Indians ran all around. Some piled into the jeep around Aphrodite, but she could not take them all.

The plane passed over the road, a great shadow of death across the lone jeep. Aphrodite turned the jeep around and floored it back in the direction of the Chowok village. The last she saw of Remo was in her rearview mirror.

Despite Chiun's concerns about his exposure to the Chowok tobacco smoke, Remo had turned on his heel and was racing down to the access road that ran parallel to the main highway toward the group of trapped Chowok. Straight into the burning fires of hell.

The paved road pitched down to a narrow drainage
ditch. Remo hit the furrow in a single leap. With another
bound he was halfway across the dirt access road.

Walls of fire raced across the fields. Touched off by
falling chemicals, the infernos took on a life of their own,
catching nearer tobacco plants and raging into an unstoppable prairie fire. Many of the Indians had fled the fields on
both sides of the road. There was an exodus in both highway
directions. Every minute more heads appeared at the roadside as men scrambled up out of the culverts.

Even before he had handed off his keys to Aphrodite,
Remo had spotted a dozen Indians cut off from the rest.
They had been running for the highway when the plane
passed between them and the road. Fire erupted beneath its
wings, blocking the men from reaching safety.

The edge of the field near Remo had not yet gone up in
flame. As he raced across the access road, the Master of
Sinanju spied his pupil flying toward the burning field.

"Remo, no!" Chiun cried, flouncing to the highway's edge.

But Remo was already darting toward the wall of flames and the trapped Chowok.

"I'm okay, Chiun," he shouted over his shoulder. "Be ready."

Remo could function for extended periods of time without oxygen, but fire was tricky to deal with and offered a half-dozen dangers beyond the fact that it sucked the oxygen from the air. And if this dippy plant was as bad as everyone kept saying it was, the smoke was something to watch out for.

The trick would be speed.

"Help us."

"Over here."

Remo forced his body to shut down all pores so that no smoke could enter his system. Mindful that the ancestors of the Chowok had attempted to kill two Masters of Sinanju with a burning field of their sacred tobacco, Remo dived through the wall of flame. He landed among the panicked Chowok. Desperate hands grabbed at his clothes.

Remo snatched the collars of two shirts and snapped his arms back. The men lifted off the ground so fast they left their smoking boots behind. He made sure they were traveling too fast to get singed by the flames.

Quickly, he launched another pair the same way, trusting that the Master of Sinanju would pluck them safely from the air once they reached the road.

The next pair and he could sense his strength ebbing.

The effort to repel the tobacco smoke was taking a toll. He felt the oxygen leeching from his body. As it fled, a great numbing fatigue settled into his limbs.

A voice called somewhere behind him.

"Guard your breath, my son," he heard Chiun cry.

He grabbed another Indian. The man panicked, and struggled in Remo's hands. Remo had neither time nor voice to argue. Knocking the man unconscious with a blow to the temple, he flung him back toward the road.

One at a time now, he grabbed another, then another.

The circle of flame was closing in around the Indians.

Remo's arms were sluggish, as if he were carrying a sack of wet concrete mix in each hand.

The field around his feet was nearly gone. Flames scorched the hair on his arms. Despite his body's need to do so, he fought to keep from perspiring, not wanting to open up any avenue for the tobacco poison to seep into his system.

He could feel himself growing progressively weaker as he hurled the final three Chowoks up to the road.

Once the men were safe, Remo crouched low to the ground and uncoiled his legs like a spring. A hurled human javelin, he shot through the wall of blinding flame. The back of his T-shirt caught fire, and he hit the dirt road and rolled, smothering the flames. Up at a sprint, he bounded back up to the main road, landing flat on the smoking soles of his loafers beside the Master of Sinanju.

"Tah-da," Remo called, throwing out his hands like an Olympic gymnast.

Chiun was not in the mood for jokes. Face furious, the old Korean used long, wickedly sharp fingernails to tear off Remo's still-smoking T-shirt. He flung the cotton strips down to the dirt access road. Long-nailed fingers pressed Remo's chest, feeling heart, examining lungs. Finally, he examined Remo's skin, poking at flesh as if he were examining a sickly infant.

"Knock it off, Little Father," Remo said, pulling his arm from his teacher's vise-like grip.

"I will knock nothing, save your fool head," Chiun said, face a puckered fist of fury. "You are lucky to be alive. Come. We must hie from this place before the wind changes."

Chiun turned, but Remo remained rooted to the road.

"No," Remo said, turning his gaze to the smoke-streaked sky. "One more thing first."

If Arvin Wollrich had been the sort of mincing little nancy boy who kept a diary, this day would have had a special notation as the happiest day in all the five-plus decades of miserable days he had spent on this godforsaken planet. In fact, he decided that on his way home after slaughtering the

Chowok, he would stop by the dollar store in the strip mall near the corner laundromat and pick up a diary just so he could make a special notation about this day. This day would get five stars and a dozen exclamation points, and every word would be underlined in bright red ink.

As he buzzed the burning Chowok tobacco fields, he watched the Indians scatter like terrified mice. In the cockpit of his plane, Arvin whooped a delighted war cry.

Roaring down over the thickest concentration of running men, Wollrich cranked the lever at his ankle. The sprayer on the underside of the plane opened up once more. The hiss of chemical spray issued from the tanks beneath his feet. More plants burst into orange flame.

Wollrich was so close to the ground that even the whine of his own engine could not blot out the screams of humans in agony. For others the great music was Mozart, but for Arvin Wollrich the music of pain brought tears of joy to his eyes.

Banking right, Wollrich came back around for another pass. The orange smoke was beginning to clear. In an area where the fire had already receded, he saw a number of Indians scattered on the ground. Pale flesh peeled back red and raw. A few bodies still quivered in the last throes of agonizing death. One had managed to escape the cloud and was running along the dirt access road toward the annihilated greenhouses. A flip of his thumb and Wollrich aimed a nose-mounted machine gun at the fleeing man. Bullets screamed from the barrel, tearing through a torso and leaving holes as wide open as the Montana prairies. The Indian fell into the burning field, a bloodied scarecrow of twisted arms and legs.

Wollrich screamed low over the corpse then pulled skyward. The plane hummed on the ascent.

The plane was a loaner from Manny Boleyn, an old Vietnam buddy who lived in Montana. Boleyn was still licking his wounds over the war in East Asia, and was constantly e-mailing Wollrich about the upgrades he had made to the plane. Boleyn had spent thirty years juicing it up, tinkering with it, adding tanks and guns. He had never flown it. God only knew what revenge he had planned to use it for if he ever got it in the air. Wollrich made a note to ask God if he ever met Him. He could not find out from his old war buddy. When Wollrich showed up at his door in the middle of the night urgently asking to borrow the plane, Boleyn had not wanted to lend it. Wollrich had asked to use the bathroom and, when his friend was not looking, crept up behind him and stuck a knife in Boleyn's spine.

He had not put up much of a fight, but Wollrich had to admit it. The crazy pilot had built one hell of a plane.

Up—high up—then down again. The engine whined on the upswing, then howled on the descent. Below the belly of the aircraft, tobacco fields burned like the plains of Dis. Satan's realm blazed below him.

Wollrich wanted to kick open the windshield, wanted to feel the exhilaration of burning wind whipping his face. Movement on the main road. The highway was a black strip that ran between the two main fields. It made sense that the Indians would race for the road. The fields were ablaze, the greenhouses destroyed. There was no place else safe for them to go. And in a moment, they would find no safety there.

Wollrich grinned. With his thumb he wiped a bit of frothy spittle from the corner of his mouth.

Bringing the plane down parallel to the road, he raced along scarcely twenty feet above the ground. The fires to left and right tore past his wings in an orange blur.

The Indians who had survived the fire were running in both directions along the road. Up ahead were dozens of fleeing men.

As he sped toward the little stick figures, Wollrich noticed that two of them were not fleeing. In defiance of all logic, of all instincts of self-preservation, the two men stood rooted to the road, facing down the incoming plane.

Wollrich felt a little jump in his heart.

How dare they? Arvin Wollrich lived for the terror he inspired in his fellow human beings. Yet here were these two, not running, evidently not fearing, standing up to him like the white hats in some wild west shootout.

Anger flashed to hatred. He hated these two men who would not give him the satisfaction of chasing them down the road and murdering them from the back.

Furiously, Wollrich flicked the toggle on the machine gun. As he screamed at the two men, bullets shrieked rat-a-tat from the nose of the plane. Heat from sun and fire had turned the asphalt gummy. He watched the bullets tear tiny bursts of scattering black around the two unmoving figures.

Wollrich fired two hundred rounds, and when he was finished his big gun was empty and the two men were standing unharmed exactly where they had been before he'd opened fire.

Fury flickered into fear.

Impossible. He was coming up on point-blank range. There was no way he could have missed.

Fumbling with one hand, Wollrich opened up the wing-mounted guns. Even as the smaller machine guns blazed to life, he suddenly recognized one of the targets. It was the old gook in the bathrobe, one of the three main targets that Mr. Rawly had sent him to Montana to kill.

Wollrich was nearly on them when he realized the second man must be the other from the picture he had been forwarded by Mr. Rawly's assistant. The face had been blurry in the photograph, but the build was the same.

Dead eyes, as deep and black as the darkest depths of space, stared out from behind high cheekbones. And as the world crawled down to that slow motion that sometimes comes in the moments before one's own death, Arvin Wollrich realized that he was staring into the eyes of a killer.

This was a real killer, not a maniac who murdered for fun.

Wollrich continued to fire at the thin white with the thick wrists. And the slow time bubble that seemed to have formed around his cockpit allowed Arvin Wollrich to finally see that his aim had not in fact been poor. Twisting, turning, the target was everywhere the bullets were not. Blurs of motion, flickering ghosts on Wollrich's retinas, indicated where the man had been.

And then the faces of the two men disappeared as the

plane passed over them. Clicking off the guns, Wollrich tried to pull up. He did not see what was happening on the road beneath the plane's belly.

Twisting on one ankle, Remo shot high into the air. Across the road, Chiun tensed his calves and rocketed into a somersault. And in midair, the very movable object of Arvin Wollrich's plane met the unstoppable force of two Masters of Sinanju trained to the very limits of human perfection.

The plane's own momentum brought Remo's and Chiun's hands neatly through fiberglass and metal. Wollrich had a brief glimpse of the two very close men. He thought the young white one was saying something. It looked as if he was mouthing the words, "You lose. That's the biz, sweetheart."

And then the wings came off Arvin Wollrich's plane and the aircraft did a spinning, whining, fatal bellyflop straight into the newly constructed Chowok highway.

16

The chemical fires burned hot but died quickly. The recently constructed service roads and irrigation trenches prevented the flames from skipping over to the prairie that surrounded the tobacco fields. The Chowok had called for help from outside the reservation. The overwhelmed Chowok sheriff was accepting assistance from the Montana state police. Fire trucks and rescue vehicles from a dozen communities were on hand when Remo and Chiun returned to the scene.

Remo had wanted to come sooner, but Chiun insisted that they wait until all danger of inhaling the smoke had passed. As it was, they barely escaped. The wind had shifted after they crippled Wollrich's plane, and they had been forced to race from the scene ahead of the angry black cloud.

Chiun had been giving Remo the modified silent treatment. Modified because, unlike the normal silent treatment where the old Korean frequently broke in to remind Remo that he was giving him the silent treatment, this time the Master of Sinanju had scarcely spoken two words to his pupil since their escape from the burning fields.

It was concern for Remo that had silenced the Master of Sinanju. For a moment Chiun had been afraid he might lose his son and, Remo had to admit, his teacher was right to be worried. Remo had had minimal exposure to the smoke, prepared himself as best he could beforehand, yet still felt a strange weakening effect from the dangerous plant.

Mindful every moment of the sad tale as well as the lesson of Master To-Un, Remo strolled to the police cordon. He and Chiun were ducking under the yellow police tape when a horn honked behind him. Turning, they saw Aphrodite Janise hopping down from their borrowed jeep.

"You're all right!" she called. Suddenly aware of the cigarette in her mouth, she tossed it to the pavement and ground it out with her toe. She hitched her backpack up over her shoulder and hustled over to them.

"Where have you been?" Remo asked.

She looked at him as if he were demented. "You nuts? This place was going up like Hiroshima. I've been hiding." She peered up the road. "Holy smoke," she said, shaking her head.

The wings of the plane were two hundred yards back, on either side of the road. There was a deep gouge in the asphalt for a few dozen yards where the plane had first hit, followed by a black stripe where the main body of the craft had skidded to a stop. It had come to rest with its nose peering over the edge of the road.

"I don't know how you did it, but I have a feeling a lot of people owe you two a lot," Aphrodite said.

But Remo knew that out there were smoldering black lumps that only a few short hours before had been human beings, as well as the sheet-draped corpses that were being carted up from the fields. He was in no mood to accept congratulations. Just more deaths. The story of his life.

Flashing NTSB identification, Remo got the three of them over to the downed plane. Most of the activity still centered on the fields, allowing them to inspect the crash without interference. Chiun remained on the road with Aphrodite while Remo clambered up the wreckage.

Arvin Wollrich had survived the initial impact, but a section of windshield had broken off and impaled him through the chest, securing his body to the pilot's seat. But it was not the condition of the body that caught Remo's attention.

"Get a load of this," he called down.

Chiun turned and walked away.

"What's wrong with him?" Aphrodite asked.

"Nothing. He'll come around. He always does."

But when Chiun failed to call back a sarcastic jibe, Remo just shrugged and helped Aphrodite up onto the crushed nose of the plane. She did not flinch at the grisly sight of Wollrich's body.

Instead, she stabbed a finger so hard at Wollrich Remo had to grab the strap of her backpack to keep her from falling off the plane.

"I told you," she said triumphantly. "It's Rawly. Him and his damned Cheyenne Tobacco. He's the guy you should be going after."

Remo looked down at Wollrich's corpse and had to admit that it was hard to argue with Aphrodite.

Edgar Rawly's hitman was wearing a Cheyenne Tobacco baseball cap, available from the official Cheyenne Tobacco Catalogue for only four hundred proofs of purchase. The official mock-leather Cheyenne Tobacco driving gloves were another five hundred and fifty proofs of purchase. Wollrich's Cheyenne Tobacco belt buckle was a collector's item no longer available to the general public, but while it had been a catalogue item, it sold for five hundred UPC labels. His Cheyenne Tobacco Henley shirt cost six hundred proofs of purchase. The big ticket item was the leather Cheyenne Tobacco bomber jacket, which was available exclusively through the official Cheyenne Tobacco catalogue for ten thousand proofs of purchase.

"That's all promo stuff," Aphrodite said. "Either he's the biggest smoker who ever lived or somebody gave him this stuff for free. It's Rawly."

"Why would he torch his own crops?"

"I heard some of the Chowok talking. The tribe made a

deal with Rawly over this plant and got a lot of money from him. This was probably just his way of reducing some of his overhead. Remo, he kills his own customers with his product. He wouldn't blink twice over killing a few Native Americans if it helped the bottom line."

"Maybe," Remo said. He was rummaging in Wollrich's pockets. He stuffed the dead man's wallet in the pocket of his chinos.

"No maybe," she insisted. "He's working for Cheyenne."

Remo noticed something pinned to the dead man's shirt. The round disk was peeking out from behind the zipper of Wollrich's leather Cheyenne Tobacco jacket. He pushed open the jacket to reveal the object.

"You sure about whose side he's on?" Remo asked.

"What do you mean?" Aphrodite asked. When she leaned over to get a better look at the body, her eyes widened.

A big white button was pinned to Wollrich's shirt. On it, a picture of a grinning monkey holding a lollipop appeared under bright letters which read, "Eye QUIT, U Kan 2." Smaller letters printed at the bottom of the button read, "Campaign for a Smoke-Free World."

Aphrodite shook her head. "He's not one of ours, if that's what you're thinking," she insisted. "Remo, we hand those buttons out all over the place. This is obviously a pathetic trick by Cheyenne to throw people off their trail."

She reached for the button, but Remo stopped her.

"Sorry, Aphrodite, that stays. It's evidence."

"But you just took his wallet," she sputtered.

"Yeah, but when I do it it's cute," Remo said. He hopped to the ground and helped a furious Aphrodite down to the road.

"This is a frame," she insisted. "What's more, it's an insulting frame. It goes right along with what they did in New York. Cheyenne knows we're their greatest threat. They don't want us to get the word out, so they're trying to knock the CSFW out of the game preemptively. It's Rawly, Remo. That crazy old fossil is murdering people left and right. We've got to go after him."

Up the road, Remo saw the Master of Sinanju watching the rescue crews, his back still to Remo. The old Korean's hands were clasped behind his back as he stared off toward the setting sun.

"Rawly can keep," Remo said. "If nothing else he's set himself back a few months before he can grow another crop of this stuff. Right now, I have bigger worries than the whole world becoming addicted to some new weed."

Leaving a frustrated Aphrodite near Arvin Wollrich's crashed plane, Remo trudged up the road toward his teacher.

In a small office in the executive wing of Folcroft Sanitarium, a set of sharp, youthful green eyes scanned the latest reports from the Chowok Indian reservation.

The CURE mainframes had automatically flagged the story and dumped it into the regular update cycle. The article was bounced to the top and had received a red pushpin icon, indicating relevance to a current CURE crisis.

Mark Howard, assistant director of CURE, read the story with growing concern.

According to the article, the Chowok reservation was in flames. Dozens were dead. The chief had been murdered. Calls for aid had gone out to many neighboring communities.

An Indian spokesman in Washington was already blaming the current presidential administration for the attack. The chairman of one of the major political parties had picked up the thread and was quoted as saying, "While we don't yet know the level of involvement of the president in this tragedy, questions have been brought up about him and the vice president that at the very least should give Congress grounds for beginning impeachment hearings." Left unmentioned was the fact that the same party chairman had blamed the same president for orchestrating the 9/11 attacks, sabotaging the chairman's own failed presidential run, for three years of bad weather and for strong-arming the NBC television network into canceling *The West Wing*.

Mark quickly checked the clock in the corner of his computer screen. The time read 5:02.

"Five o'clock, shut off computer," Mark said, shutting down his own computer and shooting to his feet.

Racing to his office door, he flew down the hallway, muttering as he ran.

"Five o'clock and thirty seconds, 'good night, Mrs. Mikulka. Five o'clock and forty, stairwell door. Twenty seconds down the stairs. Walk to parking lot. One minute, thirty seconds after five, unlock car door."

Mark burst through the fire doors at the end of the hallway and raced into the stairwell. The big stairwell window offered a partial view of the employee parking lot. A familiar porkpie hat was disappearing inside a battered station wagon. The car door shut.

Mark took the stairs two at a time, bursting out the side door. Running full out, he intercepted the station wagon before it could leave the parking lot.

Behind the wheel, Dr. Harold W. Smith frowned at his assistant. He rolled down the window with the old-fashioned door crank. "What's wrong?" Smith asked.

In the wide open of the Folcroft parking lot, where any ears could be listening, Howard hesitated. "It's a patient, Dr. Smith. A problem with some family members in Montana. I hate to stop you on your way home, but I figured you'd want to know."

Nodding understanding, Smith returned his car to his reserved parking space.

When Smith and Howard returned to the CURE director's office, Smith's matronly secretary was placing the freshly washed coffeepot in its tidy little spot inside the coffeemaker and was about to shut off her office lights.

Eileen Mikulka glanced up, surprised. "Dr. Smith. Oh. You left for home."

So confused was she, she said it as a statement of fact, as if her employer could possibly have forgotten where he was supposed to be at 5:04 on a Tuesday afternoon.

"I know, Mrs. Mikulka," Smith replied. "But Mark brought a matter concerning one of our patients to my attention. I thought it would be best to deal with it today rather than push it off until tomorrow."

Mrs. Mikulka seemed uncertain what to do. She was accustomed to her employer keeping to a rigid schedule. Eileen Mikulka had often told people that she could set her watch to Dr. Smith's comings and goings. For others that would be hyperbole, but for Harold W. Smith it was a literal truth. There had been several times during Eileen Mikulka's nearly forty years at Folcroft that Dr. Smith's arrival or departure had signaled that her watch was wrong, causing her to reset it.

"Do you want me to stay, Dr. Smith?" Mrs. Mikulka asked as her employer and his assistant passed hurriedly through to Smith's private office.

"That isn't necessary," Smith said crisply. "But before you go, could you please phone my wife and inform her that I will be late for dinner this evening? Thank you."

Smith shut the door on Mrs. Mikulka's confused face.

Placing his hat on the coatrack inside the door, Smith hustled over to his desk.

Settling in his comfortable leather chair, Smith tucked his battered leather briefcase at his ankle and booted up his computer. Mark took a sentry position at Smith's side. As they waited for the startup routine to finish, Howard gave the CURE director a rough rundown of the report the mainframes had flagged.

Remo had phoned Smith from the CSFW jet just before they landed in Montana and had given the CURE director a quick report of Master To-Un's encounter with the Chowok and the connection to the new Cheyenne tobacco. With news of trouble on the Chowok reservation coming in so soon after their arrival, it was likely that Remo and Chiun were in the thick of it.

Smith read the story for himself. It was brief, but there was enough to cause concern, particularly the fire in the tobacco fields. Remo had mentioned that in the past the smoke had been too much even for a Master of Sinanju.

"I'm sure they're all right," Howard said.

In his long career, Smith had seen sudden death arrive unexpectedly on what had been the most pleasant of days. Any moment could bring the worst possible news. He exhaled a sigh of relief when the blue contact phone abruptly rang and he did not have to inform his assistant of yet another ugly reality of their chosen profession.

"Smith," the CURE director said.

"Hey, Smitty," Remo's voice replied. "Before you blame us, we didn't do it."

Smith glanced at the news story on his computer screen. "The story I have says that there was an aerial attack on the Chowok reservation. The story focuses on the dead, and mentions only in passing that some crops were burned. I assume Cheyenne's tobacco was the target?"

"That's the understatement of the decade."

Remo rehashed the events of the previous few hours for the CURE director. When CURE's enforcement arm was finished, Smith was frowning deeply and shaking his head in concern.

"This must be related to the deaths in New York. The Cheyenne Tobacco scientist killed was a Chowok. What about those Chinese assassins you encountered at the morgue in Manhattan? Were they the same ones responsible for the attack on the Chowok reservation?"

"No," Remo said. "The pilot absolutely wasn't a moshuh nanren. He was as Chinese as me. Besides, they're into stealth and hiding and all that jazz, not dumping Agent Orange cocktails out of a plane in broad daylight. This isn't their M.O., Smitty. I'm starting to think that maybe the ones we met in New York are an isolated group."

"No," Chiun's voice chimed in from very nearby. "The moshuh nanren exist in three levels. What we encountered in that dirty city was the lowest level. There is another level in between, better trained and more deadly. Then is their master at the highest. There will be two more levels."

"That's a comfort," Remo said. "Since we still have no idea who they're working for."

"Until now I still thought it was possible that it was Rawly," Smith said, "since virtually all of the Manhattan dead worked for his competition. However, the events at the reservation put Cheyenne Tobacco on the target list now, too."

"Maybe," Remo said. "But no matter what, this guy was no moshuh nanren. Wait a sec. I've got his license right here. Guy by the name of Arvin Wollrich."

Smith's fingers were already poised over his keyboard. "Is that Wollrich with one or two L's?"

"Two, as in 'loonball' times two. And don't be so quick to let Rawly off the hook, Smitty. The guy here went on this killing spree decked out in about a million boxtops' worth of Cheyenne Tobacco swag. If Rawly is behind this, his henchman did a piss poor job hiding his tracks. His clothes alone finger Cheyenne Tobacco as mass murderers."

"This Rawly is more dangerous than his namesake," Chiun said, "for our histories have it that this plant is far more evil than that which Sir Walter Raleigh brought to Europe."

"And Edgar Rawly is already a mass murderer," a female voice called out from the background. "He and his partners in Big Tobacco have killed millions over the past century. Now they're trying to frame my group to stop us from getting the truth out about their killer product."

Smith stopped typing. "Who was that?"

"Just some busybody we picked up along the way," Remo explained. "She can't quit smoking herself, so she thinks the government should ban it for her own good."

"That was the woman from the Campaign for a Smoke-Free World?" Smith said. "Remo, please, we cannot have this conversation while she is within earshot."

"Yeah, okay, hold on a minute," Remo said. "Beat it, Aphrodite." Smith could hear the woman arguing, although he could not make out what she was saying. "Listen," Remo insisted, "this is private, honey. You know private. Like people who want to smoke in their own homes? No, wait. You guys want to ban everybody from doing that, too, don't you?" The woman snapped at Remo and offered a few choice curse words that Smith could clearly make out before her voice faded in the distance. Remo returned to the phone. "She's gone, Smitty. Probably to smoke. And to protest herself for smoking too near herself. She leads a complicated life."

"Just don't get her involved in ours," Smith said. "Hold on. I've found some information on Wollrich." He adjusted his glasses and scanned the data the CURE mainframes had collected on the dead pilot. "Arvin Wollrich. Served in the Army in Vietnam. Dishonorable discharge. Hmm."

"What 'hmm'?" Remo asked.

"Mr. Wollrich has apparently not worked in the past thirty-five years. He has not filed a single tax return, yet has not received any government assistance."

"Good for him on both counts," Remo said.

"No, Remo," Smith explained. "He has to eat, so he is obviously getting money from somewhere, yet there is no record of employment of any kind. One moment, Remo. Mark, could you take this?"

Smith handed off the phone to his assistant and, with practiced fingers, began delving deeper into the life of the late Arvin Wollrich. The money trail was not easy to follow, since the dollar amounts were so small. Still, by knowing what he was looking for, it took Smith only a few minutes to discover the likely source of Wollrich's allowance.

"Remo, Mark," Howard said, reading the information as it appeared on Smith's computer screen. "The entire block Wollrich lived on is owned by Cheyenne. It's right near one of their major warehouses. In fact, they own most of the town near there. So he's living rent-free in a Cheyenne-owned building. His stipend was small, so it's easy to lose in a budget as massive as Cheyenne's, but Wollrich's bank deposits are consistent with Cheyenne's pay schedule. It's all cash deposits, not one check in the lot of them. Wait. Dr. Smith is just pulling up his criminal record."

Finished typing, Smith reached for the phone. "Remo," the CURE director said in a level voice, "you're right. It is

Rawly. Wollrich was arrested for assault in the early Seventies. Rawly made the charges go away. More recently, Wollrich was the primary suspect in the death of one of his neighbors. It never went to trial due to lack of evidence, but in that instance Wollrich's lawyer is one that also represents Cheyenne in small local matters."

Mark Howard was leaning his knuckles on the edge of the desk as he read the information on the computer screen.

"It doesn't make sense, Dr. Smith," Howard said. "If this guy was some kind of hired muscle for Rawly, what was he doing burning his own boss's crops?" Frowning, he pointed to the computer keyboard and mouthed the words, "May I?"

Smith rolled his chair back, allowing his assistant access to his computer.

"I agree with the kid, Smitty," Remo said as the assistant CURE director typed. "The only thing we've heard on this end is that Rawly's deal with the Chowok was going to cost him too much, so maybe he was just cutting down the number of people he was going to have to pay off."

"Money is a strong enough motivation," Smith said. "If the Chowok were shrewd, over time Rawly's agreement with them could cost Cheyenne Tobacco billions."

"But who knows?" Remo said. "Maybe this was just some kind of cheap labor dispute. Maybe Rawly doesn't give his psycho hired killers free dental. By the way, if it is Rawly, he tried to pin all of this on the CSFW. The killer was wearing one of their buttons."

"That would be consistent with what we know," Smith said. "Rawly despises the anti-smoking campaigns he is required to sponsor, and has made no secret of his attitude."

"So he's our bad guy," Remo said. "We go after Rawly."

"Yes," the Master of Sinanju's determined voice announced.

"Yes," Aphrodite Janise's resolved voice echoed.

"Get the hell out of here, Aphrodite," Remo's annoyed voice said.

"Bingo," Mark Howard said triumphantly.

Feeling as if he had lost control of the situation, Smith

glanced at his assistant. Mark was still at Smith's keyboard, and was pointing excitedly at the screen. Smith rolled his chair forward to see what Howard had discovered.

"Apparently Rawly was not destroying his only source for the genetically engineered tobacco plant after all," Smith said once he had cast a rapid eye over the screen. "In the past eighteen months, Cheyenne Tobacco has purchased several farms in Canada. Since they own enough tobacco farmland to meet normal demand here in the United States, we can assume that these new purchases have been turned over to their newest crop. It makes sense. Our northern border is porous. Even before they get FDA approval here, they will already have an illegal leg up on the domestic market."

"They've already got it," Remo said. "They've been selling them on the reservation. There are signs up all over the place hawking Cheyenne Smooths."

"You did not tell me that. Are you certain?"

"Saw the signs with my own eyes. And the rashes. This stuff has got to be powerfully addictive for what people seem to go through to smoke them, Smitty."

"If they are selling them already, that means they have already grown some crops to maturity. And they would have to have a place where they are being manufactured. They would not be permitted to do so in the United States. It's got to be Canada."

"Then we will make haste to Canadia," Chiun called. "That nation of goose wranglers has crossed the Master of Sinanju one time too many. We will tear up these evil plants by the roots wherever they are being grown."

Smith was surprised by the old Korean's passion. "No," he said to Remo. "Tell Master Chiun the next step should be Rawly. If he is behind this, we can stop it all by stopping him."

"I don't know, Smitty," Remo said. "Chiun is pretty fired up about this. The Chowok were already screwing with Sinanju when they started growing this stuff again."

"Please tell Master Chiun that destroying the crops will be difficult." He glanced at his computer monitor. "According to the information Mark found, there are five locations in Canada where the plant is being grown."

"You get that, Little Father?" Remo asked.

"Ask where is the nearest," Chiun demanded.

"It is not too far from where you are now," Smith said. "Across the border in a town called Macatchawa. If you have personal business to deal with, you may do so after you take care of Rawly. However, as it stands now, the Canadian end of this is not a CURE concern. This plant will be treated like any unregulated product entering the country."

"And we all know what a whizbang job the FBI and ATF and whoever-the-hell else does intercepting drug shipments."

"Again, that is not our problem," Smith said. "We need to focus our attention on Rawly. Go to West Virginia im—"

"Macatchawa you say?" Chiun's impatient voice broke in.

"That is correct, Master Chiun, but—"

Before he could finish, the phone went dead in Smith's ear. Smith listened for a few seconds, hoping against hope that it was a malfunction on the line. Finally, with a sigh, he replaced the blue phone in its cradle.

Mark Howard had only heard Smith's end of the conversation, but that was enough. "So I take it we're about to invade Canada?" the assistant CURE director said.

Smith said not a word. He climbed wearily to his feet, picked up his briefcase, and stepped past his assistant. Gathering his hat from the coatrack, he turned at the door.

"I will be back after dinner," Harold W. Smith said. Every minute of the bone-wearying eight decades he had spent on the planet pressed down on his tired shoulders. "While I am gone, please do your best to keep the world from crashing down around all our ears."

Remo looked at the severed phone cord in his hand, and then to the Master of Sinanju's retreating hand. The old Korean's sharpened fingernails vanished inside the billowing sleeves of his silk kimono.

They were in the small parking lot beside a Chowok reservation package store. The elderly proprietor, a very white

Indian with a very red rash, was tossing a We Have Cheyenne
Smooths! sandwich board sign into a nearby trash bin. As he
passed back inside the store, he grunted disapproval at the broken pay phone in Remo's hand.

"What the hell did you do that for?" Remo asked. He
dropped the useless receiver back in the pay phone cradle.

"You were wasting time," Chiun said, arms crossed and
jaw firmly set. "We know where we are going."

"Chiun, we can't run off and invade Canada. Smitty wants
us to go after Rawly."

"That's right," Aphrodite said. "Rawly first."

"What are you even doing here?" Remo snapped at her. "I
told you this was a private call. Besides, shouldn't you be off
suing the company that sold you your lighter?"

"I have a stake in this too," she said fiercely. "It's my life
they've stolen. I think it should be Rawly first. He's the one
who bought this plant from the Chowok. He's the one who's
responsible for everything that's happened. We should get
him first."

Chiun glanced around, as if searching for a voice among
the many buzzing flies that swirled around the small parking
lot. "Forgive me, perhaps at my advanced years I heard in-
correctly, but is it possible that some wench is deluded
enough to believe that her opinion matters to the Master of
Sinanju?" To Remo, he said. "We are going to Canadia."

The final word on the subject delivered, the aged Korean
turned and marched over to Remo's rental car.

"If you're going to declare war on it, you should at least
learn its name," Remo shouted after him.

He started to walk to the car, but Aphrodite grabbed his
wrist. "Remo, you can't let him do this," she pleaded.
"We're going to go to West Virginia, right?"

She was a tough girl, but for the first time Remo saw the
frightened frailty in her eyes and the specter of death that,
despite an outward appearance of health, was creeping rapidly up on Aphrodite Janise.

Remo glanced over to the Master of Sinanju. The old Korean had not waited for someone to open his car door. He

was already sitting in the middle of the back seat, wrinkled face turned determinedly northward.

Remo sighed. "No we're not. I'm sorry, Aphrodite, but he's on the snot. And not doing what he wants to do will just put him more on the snot. And since you don't have to live with him and I do, we do what he wants us to do first. Then we can go after Edgar Rawly."

When Remo headed for the car, Aphrodite hesitated near the broken phone, as if considering letting them go off on their own. "Dammit," she muttered and with visible reluctance hitched up her backpack and, breathing an impatient sigh, hustled to the waiting car.

17

In the age of the twenty-four-hour news channels, where even the smallest story could be turned into a weeks-long sensation if played right, the call had gone out the previous day for all news workers to keep their eyes open for the next big story. The Traci Rydel drama had ended and, unfortunately from a ratings standpoint, done so with mostly a happy finale, and so cable and network news directors in New York and Washington were scrambling to find the next disaster of the week, determined that whatever it was would highlight human suffering and not end with some boring kid found sleeping in her own boring bed. For TV news people with a constant eye on the Nielsen's, the attack on the Chowok reservation was a heaven-sent tragedy.

The charred fields and the shattered greenhouses formed a backdrop of TV news beauty. The tribal chief having been found dead after the attack with two nails in his heart, the same end met by one of his own people in Manhattan earlier in the week, added a welcome touch of mystery. And the hint of tantalizing gore as sheet-draped bodies were carted out of the ruined tobacco fields was a news voyeur's delight.

As background to the main story, mention was made of the special tobacco that had been growing on the reservation and of the apparent highly addictive quality it possessed.

"It is, of course, very dangerous, Kittie," was the mantra spoken in serious tones by reporters on the scene, "and the FDA spokesman I talked to early today told me that it could be years before the Cheyenne Smooths are cleared for sale in this country, if ever."

Cheyenne Tobacco could not have bought better advertising. Without government approval, Cheyenne Smooths had the cachet of Cuban cigars; a banned product, exciting specifically because of the danger of illegality.

With the instantaneous communication allowed by e-mail, fax and cell phone, there was not a corner of the nation that was not aware of the Cheyenne Smooths by suppertime. And in the era of overnight deliveries, the dawn of a new day found packages, the contents of which could be traced north of the border, turning up in mailboxes all across the contiguous United States. The greatest concentration winged westward, to a state where vice was so often embraced as virtue that few there could tell the difference.

And so it was that a FedEx package ended up on the desk of the secretary to the governor of California.

"Good morning, Governor Scheissenhauser," the woman said as she brought the mail in and set it on the governor's desk.

Governor Konrad Scheissenhauser was trotting on a treadmill in a corner of the big office. His green Nike sweatshirt was stained with perspiration.

"Thank you, Marie," Scheissenhauser panted. "Would you please toss me that towel?"

His secretary brought a clean white towel from the back of Scheissenhauser's office chair and handed it to the sweating governor. "Is there anything else, governor?"

"No, thank you," he said. The words came out "tonk you."

Scheissenhauser had been born in Germany to Austrian parents and had emigrated to the United States while still a teenager. A professional bodybuilder who spoke no English, Scheissenhauser had taught himself the language of his adopted country. Working hard and squeezing every penny, he had made a small fortune investing in a small restaurant chain that was about to go national before parlaying his minor bodybuilding celebrity into a career in B-movies.

Despite his thick accent and odd appearance, the future governor of California eventually became one of the biggest stars in the history of motion pictures, and for two decades the name Scheissenhauser was synonymous with action.

But age had begun to catch up with him and in recent years his box office appeal had begun to wane. Before allowing himself to suffer the humiliation of too many flops in a row, one of the greatest modern American success stories transformed himself once more, this time into a politician. Scheissenhauser had run for governor of California and won.

Many thought it was appropriate that the movie capital of the world should have one of its own in charge, and Scheissenhauser had thrown himself into his new vocation with the same energy and excitement he brought to every endeavor. But his time in Sacramento was taking a toll.

His once great physique had lately turned to flab. The demands of political office made it difficult to stick to his old exercise regimen. In truth, Governor Scheissenhauser didn't mind all that much. He had enjoyed a long and successful career thanks to that physique, but he was nearly sixty now and had grown tired of the strict routine that had got him where he was today. The only time it bothered him was when the tabloids got a picture of him in a bathing suit with his protruding belly and sagging chest. It had happened again last week, and as a result Scheissenhauser was back on the treadmill six days a week and pumping iron every other day.

Switching off the treadmill, Scheissenhauser stepped down to the floor on wobbly legs.

"What do you expect?" he told his creaking knees. "We are not thirty-five any longer." Hobbling over to his desk, he collapsed into his chair.

It took him five minutes to catch his breath. Once the chorus line of white spots had stopped dancing before his eyes, he dropped his sopped towel to the carpet and dragged the morning mail into his lap.

Governor Scheissenhauser's mail was screened by security at several levels, but there were a few people who still had direct mail access to the former star.

Scheissenhauser tore open the sealed FedEx mail envelope and shook the smaller manila envelope that was inside into his mighty hand.

The package was from an old director friend. The man had won an Academy Award for turning one of the most thrilling and tragic maritime disasters in human history into a hackneyed story about an effeminate boy's love for a slightly less effeminate girl. A bigger tragedy than the ship sinking was that the movie had made six hundred million dollars at the box office. The famous filmmaker had also directed Governor Scheissenhauser in his breakout film role as *The Killbot,* an unstoppable android that could form weapons from his hands, assume different shapes, and mimic human beings perfectly.

There was a Post-it note stuck to the outside of the envelope that read, "Konrad: Forget those smelly Havanas, these are cutting edge—Bill."

Despite a lifetime devoted to physical fitness, Konrad Scheissenhauser was an avid cigar smoker, but he had given up the habit a week before at the start of his latest health kick. He had ordered his staff at work and at home to collect every cigar, lighter and book of matches they could find and destroy them. Glancing longingly at the empty humidor on his desk, he ripped open the manila envelope.

A small rectangular box plopped out on his desk.

Scheissenhauser picked up the pack of cigarettes, flipping them over in his big hand.

It had been ten days since he'd had his last cigar. He had

been battling the craving for nicotine by throwing himself into exercise. But ten days was a long time, and it wasn't like he was breaking his diet or anything.

Tearing at the plastic wrapper, he slipped a single cigarette from the box.

His staff had been thorough in removing all matches from the office, but they had not thought of everything. Scheissenhauser got a light from the butane wand used to light the big gas office fireplace.

Drawing a deep, satisfying lungful of smoke, Konrad Scheissenhauser leaned back in his chair.

In less than two minutes he had finished the first cigarette. They seemed to burn fast and, in only half an hour, he had gone through half the pack. His hands and face were broken out in tiny red pimples. Itching with one hand, the governor smoked with the other. In an hour the entire pack was nearly gone and he was on the phone with his old director friend.

"Aren't they great?" the director asked.

"I am itchy," Scheissenhauser boomed, in a voice that had terrified many a celluloid villain.

"That's common," the director assured him. "So what do you think?" He did not wait for a reply. "They're the greatest, aren't they? I knew you'd love them, Konrad. Only dinosaurs smoke cigars now. Sure, they stink like shit and give you Elephant Man hide, but they're what's in. I'm waiting on a new shipment from Canada. Of course, it's not quite legal so we've got to keep it all hush-hush. Do you want me to give you a call when they show up?"

Diet and exercise was forgotten. Hunching down behind his desk, the governor of California sucked the last glowing orange life out of his final Cheyenne Smooth. When he spoke, his accent was thick, his voice a hoarse command.

"Call me back," Killbot Konrad Scheissenhauser demanded.

Maryann Hammelfarb placed her cup of quarters on her favorite lucky slot machine at Coyote Cove Casino, nestled in the woods on the Mattawantam Indian reservation in Connecticut and wondered for the hundredth time that morning where her husband Bernie had gotten himself lost.

Maryann decided that the fact that he was missing was actually a stroke of luck. Bernie was a terrible jinx. It was clearly his fault that her lucky slot machine had not paid out in two years. Her three-hundred-dollar windfall—the only money she had ever won in all the thousands she had fed into the one-armed bandits—only happened because Bernie had been drunk in the lounge when Maryann was playing two summers before. Usually he was hanging close by, complaining about the amount of money she was wasting.

"You gotta spend it to make it, Bernie," she regularly told the big jinx as she fed the quarters and pulled the arm on her most favorite and luckiest of all slot machines.

In truth, she considered it the least lucky thing in her life that she was still stuck with Bernie. Most of her friends had gotten the big score and were widowed years ago. That was not to say Maryann hadn't been lucky in other ways. The greatest stroke of luck had come with the death of her sister's husband.

Maryann's brother-in-law had handled all the bills, and so her elderly sister Rachel was frightened half to death whenever the house tax or water bills fell through the mail slot in the front door. Maryann had played the role of kind sister and had volunteered to take care of the bills for Rachel, writing the monthly checks out of Rachel's own checkbook. If her sister had not been so trusting she might have glanced through the checkbook and noticed there were as many checks made out to "Maryann Hammelfarb" as there were to the local gas company.

As long as her sister's bank account continued to pay off, Maryann would continue to have the cash to visit the Coyote Cove Casino twice yearly, and once in the winter to take a local senior center-sponsored trip to Atlantic City.

Actually, she was often peeved that she and Bernie had to drive out of Massachusetts to get to a casino, just because their home state didn't have casinos of its own. Sometimes she thought that if it weren't for the pride she felt in Massachusetts

having given to America such great statesmen as Michael
Dukakis and Teddy Kennedy and John Kerry, she might very
well have moved someplace closer to a casino.

As she fed quarters into the machine, Maryann tried to ignore the din of the surrounding casino.

"Do you know what time the Cheyenne Smooths are coming in?" asked a man at the next slot machine.

He was a younger man, perhaps in his forties. He had a
red rash around his mouth and on his hands. Maryann had
seen a lot of people with similar rashes around the casino
floor. She assumed it must have come from the buffet, so she
had been making a point of steering clear of the shrimp.

"The Cheyenne what?" Maryann asked, annoyed that she
had successfully ditched Bernie, only to be bothered by this
itching, twitchy young stranger.

"Cheyenne Smooths," the man said, pitching his voice
low. "Word is they've got a shipment coming in today. They
were selling them at some reservations before the Chowok
massacre. Word is the Mattawantam are getting some direct
from Canada. So have you heard anything?"

Maryann's many wrinkles puckered into an angry scowl.
"I have no idea what you're talking about."

"Oh," said the young man. He glanced around.

A thrill was coursing through the crowd. Most people
were not even gambling. Faces were turning toward the main
lobby as the excited chatter grew.

"I think something's going on," the young man said, getting down from his stool.

"Excuse me," Maryann complained, "but some of us are
trying to concentrate here." She rattled her nearly empty
cup.

She was down to her last shiny quarter. She noticed as she
fed it into the machine that it was the Florida quarter, part of
the state quarter series. Many of her old friends collected the
quarters for fun. Maryann's sister Rachel used to collect
them as well, until Maryann cleaned out the cardboard display board on the dresser in her sister's bedroom and blamed
it on "that colored paperboy."

Feeding her final quarter into the machine, Maryann pulled the lever and crossed her fingers.

Tiny pictures on cylinders rolled past in a hypnotic blur. So fixated was she on the machine that she did not notice the shouting that had gone up all around her.

The three drums stopped rolling, one by one.

Jackpot, jackpot . . .

The final wheel clicked to a stop.

Jackpot!

Quarters cascaded from the slot machine.

"Woo-hoo!" Maryann whooped.

She grabbed for her empty cup. It wouldn't be big enough. Some quarters were flowing out over the tray. She climbed to her knees to scoop them up.

Screaming. Feet pounding. Finally snapping out of her euphoria, Maryann glanced up.

A casino worker had just rolled a hand truck onto the gilded red carpet in the hall above the main floor. Five boxes were stacked on the wheeled dolly. Deep blue writing on the sides of the boxes read "Cheyenne Smooths."

Pandemonium had erupted all around the casino. The man who had been speaking to Maryann bolted, knocking over his stool as he ran. The overturned stool struck the kneeling old woman hard in the shoulder.

"Ahn-ahn!" Maryann yelped.

Stomping feet kicked her quarters. She crawled desperately out on the carpet to get them, gathering them up in withered hands. A knee struck her in the temple. Quarters scattered from her hands and she fell to her side. Maryann tried to get up, but a foot stomped her wrist. Another kicked her in the side. A rib snapped. The man who kicked her tripped over Maryann and staggered to one side. Rough hands shoved him out of the way and he toppled over, smashing his head on a slot machine. He fell hard, his forehead smeared with blood.

Maryann's own fragile skin had been torn. Blood ran into her eyes. Feet all around now, like that running with the bulls nonsense they had in Spain which she saw every year on the local news. Maryann was caught in a stampede.

Feet stomped her hands, breaking more bones. She cried out in pain, but the sound was lost in the bedlam that had engulfed Coyote Cove Casino.

Men and women fell on the boxes of cigarettes. Through the blood and pain, Maryann saw bits of cardboard flying up like sawdust from a buzz saw. She spied the young man who had spoken to her, now in the middle of the melee. He was tearing at boxes and shoving packs of cigarettes into his pockets.

And in her panicked, bloodied daze on the floor of the casino, another foot suddenly kicked her in the side of the head and snapped her frail neck around a little too hard, and the world got very dark indeed and the curtain came down in the most rudely unlucky manner imaginable on what had been, until her unexpected death, the luckiest day of Maryann Hammelfarb's life.

Similar scenes played out at hundreds of locations around the United States.

On dozens of Indian reservations around the country, newborn addicts rioted for their latest fix.

On national radio an otherwise sensible talk show host who already spent a great deal of his time dismissing the dangers associated with smoking got into a live, on-air coughing fit that became a live, on-air inability to catch his breath and ended with a live, on-air heart attack. Three cases of Cheyenne Smooths were discovered in his office.

The biggest auction site on the Internet was working overtime to take down the hundreds of pages that were popping up every hour offering packs of illegal Cheyenne Smooths.

And on the streets of every major American city, a new underground industry was born overnight. A single Cheyenne Smooth was selling for seven dollars in New York, with unopened packs selling for over two hundred dollars. Street vendors were not selling them by the case. No one could afford them.

And in a glass-walled office in West Virginia, a very old man smiled a very evil, yellow-toothed smile.

"Screw FDA approval, Merkel," Edgar Rawly shouted gleefully at his assistant as he watched on television the stories of the chaos his new product was causing. "Screw even trying to sell these damned things legally in the States. I just hit the goddamn illegal tobacco lottery." The old man shouted a triumphant war cry and shoved a cigarette between withered lips. "Light me up."

"Yes, sir, Mr. Rawly, sir," said David Merkel.

$$18$$

Carl Randolph, official manager of the little munici-
pal airport in Macatchawa in the Canadian province of
Saskatchewan, had not seen such activity in his tiny terminal
since the Cheyenne Tobacco people had come to town almost a year before.

They had arrived in a flurry of activity. Trees were cut,
acres cleared, parking lots and runways expanded. Once the
facility could handle it, all sorts of people and equipment
were flown in. For a little while it was suddenly very interesting at the little airport. But the crazed activity eventually
died down, and for many months things had been back to
normal.

However, in the past twenty-four hours the buzz of activity had begun anew. There were trucks driving in from all
around the province. Little planes were coming in from the
States to meet the trucks. Boxes were loaded, the planes
would take off, and the trucks would drive away.

Carl suspected something illegal was taking place but
Cheyenne Tobacco hàd laid out a bundle for the airport up-

grades, and Carl had gotten a good bump in pay and, after many years as a glorified gofer, Carl had an official title. The city of Macatchawa was happy, Carl was happy and the men loading up the boxes seemed happy. Itchy, but happy.

For the moment things were quiet again, and it was during this break in the excitement that Carl Randolph first spied the Learjet.

It was a little blip on the radar. Macatchawa's air traffic controller, the only other employee at the small airport, had picked it up on the monitor several minutes ago, and the plane had already made radio arrangements to land.

Carl watched the plane scream down from the sky and watched the three people climb down to the tarmac.

These were not the sort of people who had been coming in and out of the airport since Cheyenne Tobacco bought the old Anderson farm on the outskirts of town. Carl Randolph had never seen a group like these three. Wondering just what sort of Yankee Doodles were invading quiet little Macatchawa now, Carl went down to meet this trio personally.

Carl could hear them talking as soon as he stepped out the screen door to the tower.

"I still say you're harboring some resentment for this whole damn country because they cheaped out about hiring you a bunch of years ago," the young white was saying as the small group walked toward the airport manager.

"We are here to right a wrong," the old Asian replied. "This weed that claimed the life of a Master of Sinanju was never supposed to see sun again. It was bad enough that the Chowok broke their word. But now even worse that they have climbed into bed with a cheapskate nation that spends its interminable winters chasing black discuses around ice with crooked sticks."

"Excuse me," Carl Randolph said. "Can I help you?"

The young white, clearly peeved, glanced at Carl.

"Sure, Dudley Do-Right," Remo said. "Why don't you toddle off and write a ten-thousand-word apology for sticking us with Jim Carrey? Or Mike Myers?"

"Remo, we need a car," Aphrodite Janise said. She was

standing behind Remo and Chiun, arms crossed, anxious to get this wasted side trip out of the way.

"Yeah, good plan," Remo said. He looked around the tiny airport. "You got rental cars?" he asked Randolph.

"Here?" Randolph said, as surprised as if the American had asked to rent an elephant.

Remo pointed at a line of five identical blue Mercurys. They were parked in what appeared to be reserved spaces in the newly enlarged parking lot. "What about those?"

"Those belong to Cheyenne Tobacco."

"Works for me," Remo said, holding out his hand. "Keys."

"Oh, you work for Cheyenne?"

"No, I don't," Remo said. He jerked a thumb over his shoulder at Aphrodite. "But her habit probably paid for all five, with Humvee money left over. Key me."

"What?" Randolph said. "Absolutely not."

Remo leaned down beside the nearest Cheyenne Tobacco company car, hooking his fingers on the frame under the door. When he stood back up, the car came with him.

Carl Randolph blinked in shock. There was no strain on the American's face, yet two tires were a foot off the ground. Then they were two feet. Then the car was creaking over onto its side, and still there was not so much as a drop of perspiration on the young American's very calm face. And then the car was on its side, but it did not stay balanced there long before it was tipping over onto its roof. The windshield shattered and it crushed the side of the car in the next space as it settled, upside down to the asphalt.

When Remo held out his hand and said "Keys" again, Carl Randolph was already running inside the building to get them.

"And I don't want the ones to either of these!" Remo shouted after him, waving toward the car on its roof and the one with the crushed side beside it. "You're not the only one who knows how Canuckistan works," Remo said to Chiun.

Randolph gave them the keys to one of the undamaged cars, as well as directions to the Anderson farm.

"It is not that I cannot accept poor countries," Chiun said

from the backseat after a few moments of silence during which he menaced the passing trees for the crime of growing out of Canadian soil. "After all, we were recently in Mexico. It is poor, and I harbor no ill will toward that filthy, backwards barbarian nation because of it. Virtually every country in Africa or South America could not afford us. The former Russian states, since the dissolution of their silly twentieth-century empire, can hardly afford cabbage for dinner, let alone the talents of the Master of Sinanju. And do not get me started on Thailand. Poor is understandable, but cheapness toward the House is unforgivable."

"But you're sure you're still not ticked over that."

In the rearview mirror, Chiun looked at Remo as if he had two heads and both of them were speaking gibberish. "How many times do I have to tell you no?"

A new sign had been erected in front of the old Anderson Farm. It read simply, "Property of Cheyenne Tobacco. Keep out."

Remo saw rows of the same big-leafed plants that had been destroyed at the Chowok reservation, although these were smaller. The first Canadian crop of the fast growing tobacco had already been harvested and processed. With the accelerated growth of the genetically modified plant, this next crop would be ready for harvest in less than two months.

They parked their car in the new driveway in front of the old farmhouse, which had been turned into a full-time home for the one permanent watchman hired by Cheyenne. At the sound of the car engine, the man on duty came out the front door and hurried down the porch stairs.

The guard wore denim jeans that had been cut into shorts at the knees, no socks, sandals and a paisley bandana. Che Guevara decorated his T-shirt, but the man's belly was so bloated the face of Castro's bloodthirsty comrade was stretched to an unrecognizable bearded smear in a beret.

"Morning, dudes and dudette," the man said in a distinct Bronx accent. "Name's Robert C. Twitchell, but my friends call me Bobby C. What can I do you gents for?"

Chiun ignored the man and padded over to the edge of the driveway. Lifting his arms high above his head, the old Korean allowed the sleeves of his kimono to slide down, exposing the flesh of his bony arms to the air. Remo knew that his teacher was gauging the wind.

"Got a match?" Remo asked the guard with a smile.

Bobby C. helpfully offered Remo a book of matches.

"Here ya go, man. But you're jumping the gun. This crop won't be ready for a whole bunch of weeks. Don't smoke myself. Least not tobacco," he added, winking broadly at Aphrodite. "Used to be a pot farm until Cheyenne came along. I can't complain. They let me grow my own private farm out behind the house, if you know what I mean." He winked again.

"You should cut the dose," Remo suggested. "It's giving you eye twitches." Crossing his arms, he turned to his teacher. Chiun was facing the other direction now, arms directed skyward as if signalling a touchdown.

There was a light breeze, which was good. Wind gusts were more dangerous, since they could double back quickly. But a light, steady breeze would carry any smoke safely away.

"What's the old dude doing?" Bobby C. asked. He did not wait for a response. "He doesn't look like he's from around these parts. I'm not from here originally either. Bronx, New York, but only until I was eighteen. Came up during Vietnam, if you know what I mean. Uncle Nazi Sam tried to send me off to kill the yellow man."

"I was in Vietnam," Remo said.

"Yeah, right. Very funny, man," Bobby C. scoffed. "You're way too young to be a Nam baby killer. Iraq baby killer in Gulf War One, maybe, but not a Nam baby killer. Hell, you're young enough to be my kid."

And then something funny happened. Bobby C. felt a chill in the air that seemed to emanate from the very cold core of the thin man with the deadest, deepest-set eyes he had ever encountered in his sixty years on the planet.

"Here's a little lesson on the real world you don't deserve

and probably won't remember," Remo said. "I've seen plenty of innocents killed in my time. The difference between our side and theirs is that we do all we can to minimize the loss to innocent life and agonize over it when it happens. They hide behind innocents or target them, and they don't give a rat's ass how many they slaughter. That's why we're the white hats. That, and the fact that we let assholes like you run around and spout off and we don't toss you in a gulag. Although you are living in Canada, so same difference."

The chill did not leave the air as Remo turned his back to Bobby C.

The guard gulped. "I got nothing against baby killers, man. I mean, somebody's got to kill them, right?"

Remo shook his head in disgust. Chiun was padding up to his pupil. "We burn," he announced.

"What?" Bobby C. said. "Whoa. No way, man."

Chiun ignored the fat man. To Remo, he said, "You and the woman take the vehicle and park down the road. I will join you when it is finished."

"Chiun, I'm not eight years old. There's no way I'm waiting in the car."

"You can't burn this stuff, dude," Bobby C. said. "After Anderson sold out, these Cheyenne people let me live here rent free. All I got to do is keep an eye on the place for them and report if anything goes wrong."

"Report hot, orange and smoke," Remo said.

Bobby C. saw that Remo's was not a face with which to argue but from which a wise man would run. But before he could race into the house and put in a call to West Virginia, the Master of Sinanju grabbed the fat man by the ear. Chiun twisted. Bobby C. howled.

"Where else is this crop being grown?" Chiun demanded.

The man spat out four other Canadian locations as well as directions to each.

"You," Chiun said to Aphrodite. "Wench with the maps. Locate these places."

Aphrodite sighed and pulled from her backpack some

maps she had found in the glove compartment of their Cheyenne Tobacco company car. "We're wasting time," she grumbled.

Chiun ignored her. He gave Bobby C's fleshy earlobe an extra twist. "Anywhere else, obeseness?"

The American expatriate dropped to his knees. "I don't know," he cried.

Chiun recognized truth and released the guard. Stumbling and rubbing his smarting earlobe, Bobby C. ran up the porch and into the house.

Remo found some gas cans near a generator in the barn. Puncturing a few holes in the cans, he hauled back and heaved them into the fields. The cans hung impossibly long in the air as they spun far out over the tobacco fields. They had rained out the last drop of gas before falling with hollow thunks deep in the leafy center of the large fields.

Strips of cloth from a chair on the porch were set ablaze and stuffed halfway into empty Coke bottles for weight. The flaming bottles sailed deep into the fields.

The fire was slow to start, burning here and there as rags ignited gasoline. There was not a lot of gas to get it started. Several times Remo thought it was about to go out, but the soft breeze worked to spread the flames. Once it blazed to life, the fire began to spread rapidly throughout the main field. Smaller fires ignited in adjacent fields. In half an hour all the fields of the small farm were burning, black smoke drifting safely off to the north.

"Mission accomplished," Remo said. "Canada's burning. Too bad it's not Quebec. Let's go." They were heading for the car when Remo suddenly noticed that something was missing. "Where's Aphrodite?"

Footsteps on the porch, and he turned to see Aphrodite hustling down the front steps of the old farmhouse.

"I had to use the ladies' room," she explained, shifting her backpack on her shoulder. She piled into the car.

"Where's Cheech?" Remo asked as he turned the key.

Aphrodite seemed surprised by the question. She glanced

toward the house. Beyond the wooden structure, the tobacco fields glowed a dangerous orange. Flames licked blue sky.

It would not take much for the fire to skip the fields to the barn and then hop over to Bobby C.'s home.

"Him?" Aphrodite said. "Oh, he said he'd be leaving right away. Said something about trying to salvage some of his personal plants out back."

"I hope he's got asbestos underwear, because in about five minutes he's gonna be a tie-dyed tiki torch."

Not caring too much if Bobby C. Twitchell went out on a pyre of pot plants, Remo turned the car around and sped down the long drive back to the main road.

Former Chinese Army General Zhii Zaw flew in style into the belly of the capitalist beast. For Zaw, that belly was Dulles International Airport, west of downtown Washington, D.C.

His private plane was a Gulfstream jet which was a luxurious step up from the simple military or cheap commercial aircraft he had flown on while a servant to the Chinese government. The plane was a frivolous waste of money, which made Zaw happy.

Zaw was an old man now, and had spent many poorer days in service to a country that would turn a dedicated soldier out into the wilderness for one small mistake. And Zaw's great sin had not even been a mistake. He had been loyal, a desperate Cassandra, warning the Trojans not to take the Wooden Horse into the city walls. And like his tragic ancient counterpart, his warnings had gone unheeded.

After freshening up in his private bathroom, Zaw found a limousine waiting on the tarmac at the bottom of the air stairs. Behind it was the black van which contained a small security team, as well as computers, faxes, cameras. Everything a world-class criminal would need on the road.

How open this nation still was. How easy it was to bribe one's way past minor inconveniences. But also how easy it was to miss the paradox. To see only the surface, not the danger that lurked just beneath America's benign facade. This did Zaw think as he stepped unmolested into his limo.

Jian was already sitting in the seat across from Zaw, angry slits of eyes visible over his dark purple mask.

The former general never asked how his bodyguard performed his little miracles. He had flown from China confident that Jian was somewhere onboard but not knowing where the young man was hidden.

The car fled the airport, followed by the nondescript van, and before long both vehicles were speeding through areas which most Americans would consider benighted but which, with their many houses and occasional strip malls, banks and movie theaters, were modern wonders compared to the primitive Chinese countryside Zaw had left the day before.

A small bed-and-breakfast would be home for the night. Zhii Zaw was no longer a young man. Traveling took much out of him these days. He wanted to be fresh for his meeting with Edgar Rawly, soon to be the late Edgar Rawly, of Cheyenne Tobacco.

Jowls bunched into a paternal smile and he nodded to the masked man seated before him. "You are wondering, Jian, why I am keeping tomorrow's meeting with Rawly."

"No, I am not," the moshuh nanren master said. "You want to look your enemy in the eye before you defeat him."

The smiling jowls sank.

Zaw had never seen the face of his bodyguard. He had always assumed the moshuh nanren was young. Jian's voice and abilities betrayed him as a younger man. But perhaps he was older than Zaw imagined. He was certainly wiser than most of the young men Zhii Zaw had encountered in his long life.

"Correct," Zaw said, disappointed. Heavy face drawn into a scowl, he sank deeper into his seat.

Zhii Zaw had spent a lifetime as a soldier constrained by lesser men who would not permit him to fight. His great enjoyment as a crime lord came not just in defeating his rivals, but in humiliating them.

Edgar Rawly thought he would dominate the Asian markets

with his new tobacco. The arrogance of the man. Zhii Zaw had met him only once, and Edgar Rawly had treated him as if the former people's general was a busboy in a Chinese restaurant. It was at the annual conference of the Pacific Tobacco Exporters and Importers Association in Japan.

Zhii Zaw had business interests both legal and illegal, and tobacco was a booming, billion-dollar business in Asia. It was a natural fit, and so Zaw had gone to the conference as a businessman interested in expanding his interests.

Zaw had hardly paid attention when the old man was wheeled into the room. He noticed that there were several Cheyenne Tobacco executives who always seemed to keep a fearful distance, as well as a woman as old as Rawly himself and a young man who seemed to be on the receiving end of most of Edgar Rawly's abuse.

The gavel had scarcely dropped on the first official PTEIA meeting of the conference before Rawly leaned to whisper loudly to his assistant. Sitting two seats down, Zhii Zaw was witness to it all.

"Merkel, shoe," Rawly had ordered.

Zaw was not certain what the command meant, until he saw the Cheyenne Tobacco CEO's young assistant get down on his hands and knees to remove his employer's mall-walker sneaker.

Rawly pounded the shoe on the edge of the table until everyone in the room was looking his way.

"Just thought I'd let you bastards know that you'll all be out of work and on a wonton soup line come this time next year." Rawly had smiled a row of stained teeth, like kernels of brownish corn. "No offense, friends. Carry on with your little conference. It'll be your last."

With that, the entire Cheyenne Tobacco delegation abandoned the conference. All except Rawly's elderly secretary, who got tangled in some coats in the cloakroom for several hours and had to be sent back to the United States on a separate flight.

After Rawly's exit, the chatter at the conference turned exclusively to Cheyenne Tobacco and its boastful CEO. Most dismissed him as a foolish old man, but their bold confident proclamations were not matched by their worried faces.

It was at this conference that Zaw was approached by a member of Edgar Rawly's entourage. Zaw alone learned of the new tobacco plant; for a fee, this disgruntled employee would deliver all Zaw would need to corner the Asian market.

Once Zaw learned from his experts the potential of the once-extinct-now-newly-revived tobacco plant, the deal had been struck. There was only one individual who would grow rich from this magnificent plant in Asia, and it would not be that egotistic old man in the wheelchair.

With Jian, as well as another level of moshuh nanren already on American soil, it would be an easy thing just to kill Rawly but that would be nowhere near as satisfying as first crushing him and breaking what was left of his arrogant spirit.

And that would be soon now. The gods were with Zhii Zaw in this venture.

On the flight, the former general had learned of the attack on Cheyenne's crops on the Indian reservation, and of the chaos the new Cheyenne cigarettes were causing. The fact that people were rioting over the cigarettes was as good as money in the bank for Zhii Zaw. And the fact that the crops had been destroyed meant that Rawly was weaker, his business collapsing, unable to legally sell his product in the United States, cut off from the Asian markets. But the end for Rawly would be betrayal from within. And few things crushed the spirit more than being the victim of treason.

The smile returned to Zhii Zaw's flabby face. He closed his eyes on the speeding countryside and intertwined his fingers over his ample belly. Nap now, billions soon.

Aphrodite was behind the map, Remo was behind the wheel and Chiun was behind them both, glaring at the bucolic countryside when, an hour after setting fire to the first Canadian Cheyenne Tobacco fields, they raced up the freshly paved road to the second farm.

The plants at the second site were far more advanced than those at the first and ready for harvest. Men in full body suits, with masks on their faces and gloves on their hands, picked leaves in the fields. The special outfits of the farmhands reminded Remo of hazardous materials suits.

"There's a picture for your next TV ad," Remo said to Aphrodite. "Fruit Loops might not be the healthiest thing in the world, but I doubt the wheat is picked by spacemen."

Aphrodite held the crumpled map in her lap. She looked tired. "If we hurry up and get rid of Rawly maybe the CSFW won't have to run any more ads."

"You mean no more eighteen-year-old grunge band rejects self-righteously hectoring me from my TV?" Remo asked. "That would almost make life worth living."

Bobby C. had apparently gotten through to corporate headquarters in West Virginia, judging by the ten very big men who surrounded Remo and Chiun the moment they exited the car.

Some held rakes, hoes and lengths of pipe. The biggest man carried a double-barreled shotgun, which he leveled on Remo's chest.

"We know what you're doing here," the man menaced. "Get back in your car and get the hell out of here."

The man was just under six foot seven and weighed over two hundred and sixty pounds. The gun looked like a child's toy in hands as big as catcher's mitts. His jaw was as square as a packing crate and little pig-like eyes glared down from above a nose that had once been broken by a two-by-four. The board had broken as well, as had the man who had been foolish enough to try to take down the behemoth with the barrel chest, sausage fingers and sloping forehead.

The gunman cast a shadow so large over Remo, Chiun and their car, it might have been used for growing mushrooms.

"I said get outta here," he repeated.

"Let me counteroffer, Sasquatch," Remo said. "You guys are just making a living here. I don't hold that against any of you. How about we just split the difference and all of you just walk away and no one gets hurt? Sound good?"

The crowd tightened around the two unarmed men.

"I take it that's a no?" Remo asked.

"No way, eh," grunted the man with the shotgun.

The gun jabbed Remo in the chest. In the car, Aphrodite sank down behind the dashboard.

Remo sighed. "Little Father, don't hurt them."

At his pupil's side, the Master of Sinanju's face was impassive. "I will not kill them," the old Korean replied. "More than that I will not promise."

"I think you're forgetting who's holding the gun here, Jackie Chan," the big man said. In punctuation, he jabbed the gun harder into Remo's chest.

"Hey, look," Remo announced suddenly, pointing behind the big man. "Isn't that Celine Dion?"

Remo was a little disappointed in Canada that all ten men turned to look. Unfortunately the gunman was already on a hair trigger and when the crowd of men spun around, a forearm struck the gunman's elbow.

The ensuing shotgun blast brought field hands up out of the plants they were harvesting and turning to the driveway like curious prairie dogs. When they beheld the tableau on the road, mouths dropped open behind sealed masks.

A thin man in a black T-shirt stood before Woody Fogle, the strongest laborer hired by Cheyenne Tobacco as part of the roving crew that toured Cheyenne's Canadian farms. The field hands had once seen Woody drag a stuck tractor out of the mud with only a length of chain and his strong back.

The behemoth that was Woody was on his knees on the driveway. His face, as big around as a trash-can lid, was bright red as he gasped for breath. The reason for his discomfort was his own shotgun. Apparently the skinny stranger in the T-shirt had split the gun between both barrels all the way up to the stock. As Woody swatted at him impotently with huge hands, the young man skipped around the big bear swipes and finished knotting the two loose ends of the smoking barrels like a bow tie around Woody Fogle's massive neck. Gagging, Woody flopped to the pavement.

Remo shrugged apologetically to the other men. "Sorry,

my bad. I swear I thought it was Celine. You guys sure do make fugly scarecrows up here."

And as one, the other men charged.

One man swung a rake at Remo's head. Remo brought two fingers against the man's temple. Not hard enough to kill, just enough to bring unconsciousness. The man collapsed to the ground next to gasping Woody.

Two men swung pipes at the Master of Sinanju. The instant before metal struck flesh, the old man who had been standing calmly before them suddenly disappeared. With their victim gone, unstoppable momentum carried both men spinning wildly. With hollow cracks each man struck the other in the side of the head. The pipes slipped from their fingers and they collapsed to the driveway. Chiun danced between their falling bodies.

Remo had found two skulls and guided them together. The two men sucked in a single gasp of pain before joining the ever growing pile of unconscious men on the ground.

A bony hand shattered a hoe, sending splinters soaring in every direction. "Ow, eh!" its owner cried. He looked at the fragments of the gardening implement in his hands. He looked angrily at the two interlopers. When he glanced up he was just in time to see the last of his comrades slip from Remo's hand and fall to the pile on the ground. The man looked at the pile that a moment before had been nine strong farmworkers. Eight were unconscious, the ninth was still red-faced and trying to pry the shotgun from around his neck. Blinking, the man looked questioningly to Remo.

"Take off, hoser," Remo suggested.

Flinging the broken halves of his hoe to the ground, the man turned and ran off down the driveway.

This time Remo was happy that he and Chiun did not have to do all the work. After seeing what short work the strangers had made of their comrades, the terrified farmworkers were only too eager to follow Remo's instructions. Tractors were brought out from the barn. As Remo and Chiun supervised, acres of tobacco plants were ground up and plowed under.

On the way in, Remo had noticed a city depot a quarter mile down the road. Piles of salted sand were mounded in anticipation of the coming Canadian winter. At Remo's direction, truckloads of the material were hauled up and spread liberally throughout the fields, polluting soil and making unsalvageable any leaves that might have survived.

Once the farm was destroyed beyond hope of repair, Remo scattered the workers after first instructing them to drag choking Woody to a hospital.

"Better take him across the border," Remo called as the caravan of cars and trucks sped away. "Your crappy rationed healthcare system won't be able to see an emergency for eighteen months." Turning to the Master of Sinanju, he said, "So who do you want me to insult next?" But his teacher was already waiting in the back of the car. Aphrodite was napping in the front seat. If his body language was any indication, in another minute Chiun would be honking the horn.

"When I reach the Void, you and I are going to have a little talk, Master To-Un," Remo grumbled. Fishing the keys from his pocket, he trudged wearily to the car.

Edgar Rawly listened to his assistant calmly lay out the details of the attacks against Cheyenne Tobacco's interests in Canada, and when the young man was through, the Cheyenne CEO picked up a stapler and heaved it into David Merkel's startled face. It bounced off the young man's forehead.

"Who the hell is doing it?" Rawly raged from his wheelchair. Globs of black spittle sprayed his knees.

"It appears to be the same three individuals who were directing the Chowok to destroy our crops on their reservation," Merkel said, rubbing his forehead.

Rawly's head bounced up and down. Although it always bounced up and down a little, this time there was no doubt the old man was nodding. "Good," he snarled. "We know who. Easier to kill them. Get someone to do it."

Merkel hesitated. "Mr. Rawly, Arvin Wollrich is dead."

"Good Christ, man, I know Wollrich is dead. I'm not senile, you know. He's not the only murdering maniac out there. I had somebody else. Before your time. Fella by the name of Anthony Marconi. Hired him out from under those Mafia bastards when they tried to get the union in here back in the Sixties. Coldest bastard I've ever seen. See if you can dig him up somewhere."

"He was on the regular payroll?"

"Yes. Get him now, dammit."

Merkel phoned the personnel department. "Sorry, Mr. Rawly, but according to personnel, Mr. Marconi died of stomach cancer in 1983."

"Bastard son of a bitch. Get me the phone numbers of his nearest male relatives. I'll show you how things get done in the real world, like they never taught you in that fancy-ass New England business school of yours."

Merkel located the number of Marconi's older brother, a retired loading dock foreman who lived in Florida. Merkel did the dialing and Rawly did the talking.

It took several hints, threats and bribes, and Rawly had to talk his way through several layers of Marconi cousins. Listening to his employer's end of the conversations, David Merkel was not sure if he should be impressed at Rawly's wheeling and dealing skills, skills that had made the Cheyenne CEO the billionaire he was today, or appalled at the ease with which Edgar Rawly was able to arrange murder.

"No, twenty. More if you can get them," Rawly barked into the phone. "They got a pattern. Looks like they're just driving from one to the next, so we know damn well where they'll hit next. This time we'll be ready for the bastards. Assemble whatever goombahs you can. We'll get you up there on a Cheyenne corporate jet. Details'll be on the plane. Here's my assistant." Rawly tossed the bulky, old-fashioned black phone to Merkel. "Get 'em to the plane, and get 'em up there fast," he growled. "Or by sundown there won't only be three corpses to mop up."

In the sitting room of a quaint little inn in rural West Virginia, former people's general Zhii Zaw was sipping weak American tea when Jian appeared before him.

"I have heard from your people who are monitoring Rawly's telephone calls," the masked man said. "I know where next my prey will be. I beg your leave to face them."

Zaw did not answer immediately. A delicate china cup touched blubbery Chinese lips. Steam rose from the tea, raising sweat on the old general's sagging face.

"Trust the wisdom of those who went before you, Jian," Zhii Zaw said at last. "The skills of the second wave outstrip those of the first. Is that not the case?"

Jian squeezed powerful fists. Veins like rope bulged on massive forearms. He nodded.

"Then accept the wisdom of your own order," Zaw said, setting cup to saucer. "I wonder why you are so anxious to waste your efforts on targets that are beneath your skills. Would you care for some tea? It is weak as water, but no worse than anything else you will get in this country."

But when the old general looked up, the masked man was gone.

19

There were dozens of workers at the next tobacco farm, along with some local police who had been warned by a phone call from Woody's friends of two crazed men and a woman marauding through Canadian farmland.

The only thing missing, Remo thought, was somebody from the Canadian Mounties sitting on a horse singing "Indian Love Call."

But Remo was happy that the cops were there. After a few brief moments of persuasion, which involved Remo's ripping the head of a steel shovel in half, the local police decided that they, probably alone of all Canadians, simply loved Americans and would do whatever Remo wanted. As long as he didn't hurt them.

They followed orders well, were good pickers and knew where the town's road salt supplies were stored. It was well after midnight by the time they were finished but when Remo and Chiun finally left the crop was destroyed and the ground was as infertile as Carthage.

They hit the next to last farm in the wee hours of the

morning. As at Bobby C. Twitchell's spread, the plants were in an early stage of growth, having only been transplanted from greenhouses three weeks before. The two workers on duty had obviously been forewarned, for at Remo's arrival they ran into the ranch house to hide. Remo could see their Mack truck baseball caps peeking out from behind curtains.

"So much for Terrance and Phillip," Remo said.

Remo was surprised not to encounter greater resistance. He had expected that things would get worse as they went along, and assumed that he and the Master of Sinanju would be battling Mounties on horseback armed with Canada's one gun by the time they reached the last farm. As it was, two workmen were not enough to destroy the crops at speed, and would only get in the way of Remo and Chiun as they worked. Remo left them cowering in the house as he and the Master of Sinanju turned their attention to Edgar Rawly's penultimate tobacco crop.

The wind was too risky for burning, so Chiun attacked the fields with a scythe in each hand. The old Korean was a one-man thresher, plants flying in his wake as he raced along destroying two rows at a time.

Remo followed suit, attacking the crops from the opposite direction. Both men were careful to keep the leaf oil from touching their flesh. When they met in the middle of the big farm three hours later, the sun of a new day was warming their backs and not a single living plant remained.

As they returned to the car, they found Aphrodite coming out of the ranch house near the big red barn and silo.

"What's that stink?" she asked.

"Some kind of chemical fertilizer we found in the barn," Remo said. "The amount we dumped should be enough to burn all the leaves, roots, and pretty much every wee sleekit cowering timorous beastie within sniffing range."

From the driveway, Aphrodite could see that some fragments of tobacco leaf had suffered chemical burns and were already shriveling brown in the hot sun.

"Where are the two brave defenders of Canadian soil?"

Remo asked, nodding to the ranch where frightened eyes no longer peered out of windows.

"Oh, them?" Aphrodite said, glancing vaguely in the direction of the house. "They're gone."

There was something odd about her tone, which Remo chalked up to a hectic two days. Despite her outward appearance, Aphrodite was ill. On top of that, she had barely gotten any sleep since they'd left Connecticut.

"Probably ran out of beer and jelly doughnuts," he said, uninterested. He glanced around for the Master of Sinanju. "Little Father, you about ready to go?"

Chiun was a little way off and staring over the remains of the latest destroyed crop.

The old Korean had grown increasingly quiet as their hours north of the border wore on. Turning from the ruined acres, he padded up to his pupil. A thoughtful expression had settled among the wrinkles of his parchment face.

"Everything okay, Chiun?"

The old man glanced back at the fields. "This would be a difficult task even for a Master of Sinanju four hundred years ago," the tiny Asian said, nodding somberly.

Without another word, he slipped into the backseat and allowed Remo to shut the door.

Aphrodite tossed her backpack to the floor in the front, and noticed Remo's mildly amused expression.

"What are you smiling about?"

"I sense a softening toward a certain recently maligned figure in our histories," Remo said, spinning his jangling key ring happily around his index finger.

And why not? Sinanju Masters were worse revisionists than the Soviets had ever been. Be the guy who figures out not to accept copper in place of gold from some ancient civilization lost to the sands of time and you get forty scrolls on your great wisdom. But be the poor schmoe who stumbles once and it's "Pook the Disgraced" or "Pook the Foolish" or "Pook the Ass-hat" or whatever insult Chiun had planned to attach to To-Un's successor in the scrolls. Remo had never liked the way Masters of Sinanju seemed so eager to turn on their own for a single misstep, so he was pleased with the fact that Pook's bio might receive at least a footnote saying that maybe—just maybe—his work destroying the Chowok tobacco was as good as could be expected for his age. It wasn't much, but at least he would not be vilified as the Master of Sinanju who failed to eradicate both the Chowok tobacco and the moshuh nanren.

According to the information supplied by Bobby C. Twitchell, the last of Cheyenne's Canadian properties was in southern Manitoba, not far over the border from North Dakota. Another six-hour drive brought them to the location Aphrodite had circled on the map.

The farm seemed to have been completely abandoned.

The tobacco plants were ready for harvest, big leaves waving gently in the soft breeze. The automatic sprinkler system was identical to the one at the Chowok reservation. Metal scaffolding rolled slowly over the fields, taking half a day to completely soak the fields before starting backwards over the same terrain. But although the power was on, someone had neglected to switch on the water. No mist sprayed from the nozzle heads affixed to the metal pipes.

The old farmhouse had fallen into disrepair. Shutters hung off windows, with some missing altogether. The warped clapboards had not seen a paintbrush in many years. But a new barn had recently been built near the ruined pile of the old one, and in the distance sunlight glinted off of greenhouses which were still under construction.

It was just too quiet. Too abandoned. "I don't like the looks of this place," Remo said.

"Maybe you scared them away," Aphrodite said.

"Maybe. And maybe not," Remo said as the three of them climbed out of the car.

Aphrodite blew a lock of hair from over her eye. "Let's just get this over with," she said, digging around in her backpack for a cigarette and lighter. "And then get on with what we should be doing which is getting rid of that evil old buzzard, Edgar Rawly."

"All things in good time," Remo said as he broke the lock on the barn and collected four scythes from the many tools arranged in neat rows along the walls.

Aphrodite was leaning against the car and smoking a cigarette as Remo and Chiun made their way to the fields, each carrying scythes in both hands. Chiun marched along as if to war, scythes crossed like swords before him.

The rows were wide between plants, but the tobacco plants themselves were as large as those at the Chowok reservation, with leaves nearly touching those in adjacent rows. As Remo and Chiun waded into the field, they were careful to sidestep the big leaves.

Hundreds of what appeared to be new hoses ran in a lattice pattern in and out the tobacco rows. Remo noted punctures that allowed water to spray up at two foot intervals along the entire interlocking network of hoses.

Up ahead, the automated overhead sprinkler system creaked closer, nozzles still dry.

"Looks like they've got two different watering systems here," Remo said. "Kind of overkill, don't you think?"

"There is no such thing as overkill," Chiun said, raising scythes high in either hand. "There is kill, and there is not kill."

A scythe blade flashed down, catching the row of plants to the elderly Korean's left. A split second after the first was unleashed, the second blade flew right. Plants did not have time to shudder from an impact they did not feel. One moment they were standing, the next they were falling away as the old man raced off, arms pumping furiously.

"You know, we could have rented a machine to do this work," Remo called.

Chiun responded, "Pfahhh. In Canadia? In a land where no people work, how would one expect to find a machine that works?"

"Good point."

As Chiun raced off, Remo followed his teacher's lead, tearing off in the opposite direction. The trick was not in the blades but in being careful where the plants landed. Attacking at speed, Remo was certain to make sure that his body was never where a single leaf fell.

In less than a minute, Remo and Chiun were a quarter of a mile away from one another and tearing through fresh rows of carefully tended plants. Green leaves flew up in their wake. Doubling back again, they passed one another in a blur, their flashing blades coming a hair away from one another as they tore off in the opposite direction.

The next circuit brought them on a close pass to the automated sprinkler. Up close it was a more complex device than it appeared at a distance. Networks of plastic tubes fed the rows of hollow pipes twenty feet above the ground. Nozzles similar to emergency fire sprinklers in office buildings were spaced along the pipes, which ran parallel to the field. The scaffolding on which the system was arranged was connected by wheels to a track that ran the entire length of the farm. Crawling remorselessly ahead, the system efficiently and methodically spread water to every inch of the big tobacco farm. Except it was not turned on.

"That's weird," Remo called as he ran. "Why would they leave this thing running if they shut off the water?"

"I already cannot fathom the minds of Americans," Chiun called out from the distance. "Do not further burden the Master of Sinanju by asking him to analyze the minds of these Canatards as well."

But, Remo knew, it was strange. Apparently the system was not working properly. Why else would Cheyenne's people have arranged all the hoses around the farm? Yet whoever had taken the trouble to roll out and connect all the hoses had not bothered to flip the off switch on the automated system.

And as if his curious thoughts were a cue, he felt a soft rumble beneath the soles of his racing loafers.

It came in at speed from a distance. Remo could sense it rolling in from the direction of the greenhouses. Somewhere unseen a spigot had been turned. The pressure tightened the hoses, and the metal scaffolding of the big watering scaffolding creaked in anticipation of the liquid that was racing toward Remo through hose and pipe.

Remo and Chiun were dead center in the field. The Master of Sinanju was passing into the shadow of the slowly rolling automated sprinklers.

It was coming in through hose and pipe. There would be no way to avoid it.

"Looks like we're going to get wet," Remo called out.

And then three distinct things happened nearly simultaneously. First, Aphrodite was suddenly screaming from the road. Remo had sensed the second thing, the thing which had caused Aphrodite to shout his name and jump up and down waving her arms, the instant before she had started to yell.

Movement of men at the periphery of the fields. They came in from woods, from road, and from around greenhouses, barns and outbuildings. More than twenty in all. They were armed, or at least acted as if they were. Remo did not sense guns, but the way they carried themselves told him that they walked with death. Each carried something strapped to his back. Remo saw the tanks, clearly saw the hoses that led to nozzles in their hands.

And in the moment he realized what the men were carrying, in the split second before the hoses and pipes around the field hissed to life, Remo suddenly caught the scent of just precisely what was being pumped through the watering system.

The hoses tightened, flooded, and launched liquid high into the air. The stinging aroma of gasoline flooded Remo's senses. It gushed out as heavy spray and thin mist. In seconds Remo's clothes were soaked through.

Far off he could see the Master of Sinanju was caught in the center of the field.

Twenty-four distinct bursts of tiny flame ignited in eruptions of orange around the field. Before Remo could shout to Chiun, the flamethrowers carried by the men around the field burst outward in brilliant orange.

Arcs of flame launched out over the field. The instant it touched the hissing mist of gasoline, the air flashed to fire.

The flames shot down to plant and hose, igniting tiny gushers of gasoline and racing crisscross around the field.

Flames licked up all around.

The instant before his clothes could burst to flame, Remo was already moving, tearing back toward the road. Speed was key, for to stop was to die. Faster he ran, and faster still. Too fast for the fire to take hold, so fast that speed itself snuffed flames before they could ignite, burning clothes, searing flesh.

As at the Chowok reservation, Remo shut down his pores against the toxic smoke that rose from the burning tobacco plants. He closed his eyes as well, racing for where he knew the road to be. When he came to the edge of the field, Remo dove through the closing wall of flame, hitting the road with his shoulder and rolling to his feet. Clothes still soaked in gasoline, but not burning. Alive.

Aphrodite jumped at his sudden appearance through the fire. "Remo, thank God!" she cried.

A man stood with a flamethrower nearby, stunned at the appearance of the hell-sent demon. He wheeled with his weapon, aiming the next arc of flame directly at Remo.

But Remo was gone.

The would-be killer felt a light tug at his back, as if some kind passing soul were helping him remove the burden of the heavy tanks he carried. But the tanks were still strapped to his shoulders and around his waist, and the burden that was being removed was the burden of life itself. The helpful little tug suddenly became a wrenching pull, and before he knew it the man was off his feet and sailing backwards out over the burning field.

On the road, Aphrodite had jumped behind the car when the man fired at Remo. She poked her head out just in time to see the shocked killer plunge into the wall of flame that had burst up all along the roadside. The tanks ignited and the man exploded like a fat, red propane-filled balloon.

Remo paid heed to neither explosion nor Aphrodite. He was glancing up and down the road.

They were alone.

"Chiun," Remo snapped. "Where's Chiun?"

Aphrodite looked out into the burning field and winced at the brilliance of the yellow flames. "He was over there last I saw. But, Remo, there's no way he could have—"

Remo was already running back toward the burning field. He had taken only three strides when the wall of flame belched out unexpectedly. He had to jump back to keep from getting burned. The fire receded, but Remo stopped at its edge, rotating his wrists in frustration. The heat was too intense, the smoke too dangerous. The longer his body fought to keep it out, the more he could feel his strength ebb.

Remo had been lucky. Nearness to the road had saved him. But Chiun had been farther out than Remo; too far out to make it back to the road before the flames became a force too great for even a Sinanju-trained body to ignore.

Helpless to act, intense heat drying tears the instant they formed, Remo backed away from the flames.

"Remo."

He heard Aphrodite call out once more, but it came at him like a voice from the bottom of a deep well.

All his life he had dealt in death.

And now it had come to him.

Chiun, his teacher, father, the only family he had ever had on this earth, was dead.

And in his grief and weakened condition he almost did not feel the pressure waves of the object flying at his back until the instant before metal touched flesh.

Slower than a bullet. Sharper than an ordinary knife blade. Unseeing, he yet understood what it was, recognized it as an opportunity to channel his pain and anger.

Without missing a step, Remo pivoted on his hip. It was a move impossible to follow with the normal human eye. One moment he was facing one direction, the next, as if his hips could swivel one hundred and eighty degrees, he was flying back in the direction he had come, his torso whirling around moments after his legs.

As he ran, Remo snatched from the air the silver throwing star that had been flung at his wide open back.

The band of masked moshuh nanren killers had concealed themselves behind tree and stone wall. Somehow they must have slowed their body rhythms to near death, for neither Remo nor Chiun had sensed their presence. Yet here they were.

With a snap, the star left Remo's fingertips. But even as he threw it, he knew his body rhythms were off.

The star should have struck its owner midforehead, splitting the skull in two. Instead, it buried itself in the killer's left eye. In place of the neat death Remo had come to expect was a sloppy mess of blood and screaming.

Another killer ended the life of his writhing comrade with the end of a merciful blade.

On a different day Remo might have been alarmed for missing so easy a target, but now the rage of loss propelled him forward.

A hail of throwing stars attacked the air around him. Harvesting them as he ran, Remo sent them zinging across the field. With fatal, distant screams, the men with flamethrowers dropped one by one. Most of the blows were fatal, but some were not. Stars struck legs and backs. Men screamed. Some scrambled to safety and disappeared into woods. Remo did not care. He merely needed to scatter the flamethrower men, remove them from the equation. That accomplished, he returned his attention to the moshuh nanren.

Two more throwing stars were hurled at him as he charged the group of men. Dodging, weaving, Remo avoided them both. Behind him, he heard the windshield of his car shatter, followed by Aphrodite's scream.

Then he was among them.

A blade slid at his gut. Remo grabbed the wrist, guiding the knife into the belly of another moshuh nanren.

Two down.

Remo felt a great weariness in his limbs. Behind him, the wind shifted. The first leading edge of the wispy black smoke cloud passed over and around him.

Another masked man drew two swords from scabbards at his back. Grunting, whizzing blades slicing air, he attacked.

A dozen, two dozen rapid-fire slashes, meant to disorient a target before the fatal blow.

Remo used the man's downward thrusts to shatter the moshuh nanren's own wrists, then snatched one of the falling swords, flipped it up onto his elbow, and with a slap of his palm, plunged it straight through the hearts of two more of the Chinese assassins. Joined on a skewer in death, the men collapsed.

Four down, four to go.

Another blade plunged at his back. Remo spun to face his attacker . . .

. . . and tripped over the two skewered men.

Remo fell hard to the ground. A polished waxwood lashing staff struck down at his chest. He rolled out of the way and sprang back to his feet. His head reeled.

Another misstep and a sword tore at his arm. Remo twisted just in time to keep flesh from being nicked, but the blade sliced the sleeve of his gasoline-soaked T-shirt.

The cloud consumed them. Remo's breath was gone, yet the moshuh nanren continued to move with confidence. And Remo realized he was facing the great Achilles heel of his discipline. Sinanju was breathing at its core, permitting its practitioners to ascend to a level unmatched by other mortals. Yet robbed of breath, unable to draw fresh oxygen into his lungs, Remo could feel the power within him ebbing.

A blow with a lashing staff landed on the meaty part of his upper back. Remo let out a reflexive grunt, which depleted the already dwindling supply of oxygen in his lungs.

One came at him with hands, launching a power fist blow at the center of Remo's chest.

In slow-motion he saw the hand come in, fingers curled, palm flat. A killing blow. And in the moment before the fatal blow struck, a single word rose from deep within the throat of the last living Master of Sinanju, and that word was, "No."

Remo would not shame his father by permitting his life to be ended by these thieving offspring of the Sun Source.

Remo's hand shot out. The straight edge of his hand

caught the flat of the moshuh nanren's palm, and with a violent crack, the bones of the Chinese killer's forearm separated up to the elbow. The force shattered bones up the arm and into the man's chest, exploding into heart and lungs.

An elbow caught a charging man in the face.

Two left.

One launched a foot for Remo's throat. Remo caught the moshuh nanren's ankle and, slipping one of the man's swords from a scabbard as he passed by, directed him into an oak tree. The man crunched. The oak did not.

The last man standing did not have time to launch a final, fatal assault in honor of his fallen brethren. With a hissing smack, Remo brought the sword through the final moshuh nanren's neck. The body stayed wobbling on its feet for a moment as the masked head rolled into a ditch.

Remo did not see the final body fall, did not hear the car drive up, nor feel Aphrodite Janise drag his unconscious body into the backseat. As he fell into darkness, all he felt was flame, and exhaustion and a growing pit of grief so deep and black and cold that it could not be obliterated by the fire of heaven's hottest star.

In a cramped black van parked in the shade at the
side of a little West Virginia bed-and-breakfast, the man Zhii
Zaw knew only as Jian studied the footage that had been re-
layed to the retired general's security detail.

Zaw was becoming more difficult to deal with. The old
general had suggested that Jian's interests were personal
and, despite claims to the contrary, not those of his employer. Of course, Jian did not admit this was the case, but he
was quietly pleased that he did not work for a fool.

From eight distinct camera angles Jian watched Edgar
Rawly's men start the fire in the field, saw the two Masters
of Sinanju vanish behind a wall of brilliant orange flame. He
was surprised to see the young white emerge from the fire
apparently unharmed.

The younger Master of Sinanju caught the first throwing
star and casually flicked it back.

One of the cameras dropped abruptly to road level and
bounced for a few seconds before it stopped.

The first moshuh nanren of the second wave was dead.

Jian watched each of the men fall in turn, their hidden cameras offering glimpses of the carnage collecting on the road. For a moment Jian began to worry that the tales of the Masters of Sinanju might be true after all.

And then the young one tripped.

He recovered quickly, and made short work of the rest. But his movements that were at first too fast to follow became slower, as if an internal battery were running low.

Some of the cameras were angled uselessly at the sky or aimed into the woods. One of the cameras had bounced into a culvert where it offered a close-up view of a mud puddle. But the remainder of the ground-level cameras attached to the corpses of the second wave of moshuh nanren offered Jian a clear view of vulnerability.

The fire was dying out and the old Master of Sinanju had not emerged from the field. There was no way he could have survived the inferno. One of them was dead.

He watched the second, younger Sinanju Master collapse, and kept a close eye on the screens as their female companion drove their car with the shattered windshield to his side. For a moment he could see only her feet and a close-up of one tire. Then he saw her dragging him into the backseat. A moment later, the car was taking off down the road. One moshuh nanren had fallen facing in the direction in which they fled. Through the blood-spattered lens, Jian watched the car disappear over a hump in the road.

Alone in the van, Jian removed his hood and unwrapped the purple mask that covered his lower face.

His skin was smooth, his hair black. Jian's would have been a kind face if not for the angry slits of eyes that hinted at the coiled fury that lay just beneath the surface.

"So, these ghosts of legend are human after all," he said, with a softness that chilled.

Wadding up his mask, he stuffed it in some refuse netting that was attached to the back of the driver's seat. He would not need it any longer. From this day forward the moshun nanren would no longer cover their faces. They had done so as a tradition based in fear. But the vaunted Masters of Sinanju were human. The white one had barely survived the second wave. And Jian now knew how to kill him.

Mark Howard pulled his car into the gravel driveway of the Melonville After Dark Motel, an hour outside Winnipeg.

Dr. Smith had given explicit instructions that he obey all Canadian rules of the road so as to not call attention to himself. As usual Dr. Smith was right. Mark's impulse was to bury the speedometer, an impulse he had forced himself to set to one side. When he finally rolled the car to a careful, controlled stop, he hopped from the car as if the seat were on fire and ran to room 16.

There was a woman loitering outside the door. Her eyes were rimmed in black, her skin a little too pale. "You got here a lot faster than I thought," she said. From her finger dangled a key attached to a plastic tag that read "16."

"Miss Janise?" Mark said.

Aphrodite Janise's omnipresent backpack was nowhere to be seen. Lips pursed, she blew a great cloud of white smoke toward the motel's office.

"You work for whatever agency he works for?" Aphrodite said. "Here's the deal on that. I've seen your boys do things that would get you all sent to prison for the next hundred years. Hell, Canada might even grow a spine and execute them for the crap they've pulled up here. I also saved Remo for you, so that means you people owe me two. One for helping your boy, the other for keeping my mouth shut."

Mark did not have time to respond. The motel-room door opened and Remo stepped out, his face expressionless.

Remo was showered and wearing fresh clothes. His gasoline-soaked rags were stuffed in a trash can in the corner of the motel bedroom.

"Remo," Mark said, surprised. When Aphrodite placed the call on behalf of CURE's enforcement arm three hours before, Remo had barely been able to speak.

"It sloughed off fast," Remo said, at the young man's amazed expression. "Let's go get Chiun."

Mark blinked confusion, glancing at Aphrodite for help. "Um, didn't you say . . . I mean, about Master Chiun . . ."

"His body," Remo said. He shut the motel-room door, flicked the cigarette from between Aphrodite's lips, and headed to Howard's rental car.

"Remo, we've wasted enough time up here already," Aphrodite argued, dogging him to the car. "We should have gone after Rawly right away. He's the reason Chiun got killed. We need to get him."

Remo turned and the face that looked at Aphrodite was so twisted in pain and sorrow that it seemed hardly human.

"Just one," Remo said. "Before there were pharaohs, there was Sinanju. Before there was Alexander, before the Caesars, there was Sinanju. There has always been one man, one Master, and now the greatest Master of all is lying dead out there. And it will not be that he will be permitted to rot like a piece of field carrion. Sinanju brings home its dead."

Remo climbed in the passenger's side of Howard's car. Aphrodite started to answer but was silenced as Mark Howard clamped his hand over her mouth. He shook his head slowly, then got in behind the wheel of his car.

Throwing up her hands in frustration, Aphrodite marched over to the Cheyenne Tobacco company car they had liberated back in Saskatchewan. Unmindful of the missing front windshield, she threw the car into reverse and, in a cloud of dust, roared out of the motel parking lot.

Mark did not follow her. "Dr. Smith only wanted me to collect you," he said quietly.

"Are you going to argue with me or help me?"

When he looked at the assistant CURE director, Remo saw that the young man's face was filled with a sadness not only for Remo but for the loss of a comrade in arms.

Putting the car in gear, Mark headed down the road in the direction opposite Aphrodite Janise.

* * *

The scene of burning chaos Remo had left at the final Cheyenne tobacco farm had been replaced with chaos of a different order. Vehicles clogged the road. Men in suits and a dozen different uniforms marched about the area. Up above, two helicopters swept back and forth.

The fire had burned itself out. The plants were destroyed, but the black ground still smoldered.

At a roadblock, Mark flashed Canadian National Defense identification which got them safely inside the cordon. Once inside, they were lost in a crowd of local, provincial and national authorities, which included representatives of eight ministers of state including Agriculture, Forestry and Mines, Federal-Provincial Relations, Multiculturalism and the Canadian Wheat Board.

Some of the moshuh nanren bodies had already been carted into ambulances, but several remained on the road.

Although he had seen much since joining CURE, Mark did not think he would ever get used to seeing the results of Remo's handiwork. Assiduously ignoring a headless body, Mark focused his attention on the other two remaining assassins.

The masks had been removed, exposing waxy faces. Wrapped around their heads were slender wires that were capped by tiny buds no larger than pencil erasers.

"They were wearing cameras," Mark commented.

Remo did not acknowledge the assistant CURE director's comment, nor the bodies of the Chinese assassins. His thoughts were focused on the center of the field, and the last spot he had seen the Master of Sinanju alive.

Few men picked around the field. Most attention was focused on the dead moshuh nanren and the bodies of the flamethrower men near the surrounding woods.

Remo had already decided what he would do. To hell with Edgar Rawly and his tobacco plant. To hell with Smith if he objected. Remo would collect the remains of his teacher and return them to Sinanju.

Chiun would be buried with the honors befitting one who had dedicated his life in service to his people. He would be given special distinction in the scrolls for the many feats he had performed in life, and for surrendering his final breath in an attempt to complete that which Masters To-Un and Pook could not. If any dared question the greatness of the man who had given Remo everything in his life that mattered, they would have to deal with Remo Williams who would see to it that their last moments on this earth were not happy ones.

All of this passed through Remo's grieving mind, but all of it would not begin without one very important thing: the body of the late Master of Sinanju.

Chiun was nowhere to be found.

Remo scanned the field. There was nothing left. The fire had completely eradicated the Cheyenne crops. Bare of plants, the field appeared much larger than it had before the fire. Raised rows where tobacco plants had been transplanted were scars across the blackened land. Hoses that had squirted gasoline had melted completely away. Much of the plastic of the big overhead watering system had burned away like mist, and what remained formed melting teardrops. The metal was burned black and no longer moved along its track.

It was difficult for Remo to get his bearings. The land looked entirely different after the fire. If not for the twisted scaffolding of the automated system he might not have been able to find the last spot where he had seen Chiun alive. And his eye might never have fallen below the unmoving apparatus and noticed the tiny bump in the earth, distinct from the plowed furrows around it.

"I don't see anything, Remo," Mark Howard said, scanning the field for any sign of the Master of Sinanju's body. "Maybe they already have him in one of the ambulances. If you don't want to, I can go ask around."

When Remo did not reply, the assistant CURE director turned to him. Remo was gone from his side. CURE's enforcement arm was racing across the charred field.

Remo dropped to his knees near the earthen bump in the twisted shadow of the automated watering system.

Digging desperately with his hands, Remo dragged blackened earth away. The aroma of fresh earth untouched by gasoline or fire flooded his senses.

At three feet down he found the sole of a simple wooden sandal. Digging deeper, his heart raced as he unearthed a pair of tiny feet. Despite the heat of the inferno that had consumed the field above, the flesh was cold.

By now Mark had run over and was scooping away loam as well. It took five minutes of careful digging to exhume the body of the Master of Sinanju.

The old Korean had known that he could not run to safety in time. He took the only option available to him, burrowing through the rich farm soil like a gopher. And that was how Remo found him. Cold as death in a makeshift hollow seven feet below the charred surface of the field.

Remo laid the body out on a bed of freshly turned earth. He did not notice the shouted voices from the road or the men who gathered around.

Careful fingers probed the old Korean's chest.

A flicker of a heartbeat. Weak, interminably long between flutters, but still beating. Yet his teacher had been in the thick of the Chowok smoke. Chiun had been exposed to far more poison than Master To-Un, who had died in a coma on the way home to Sinanju.

Remo gathered up the frail body in his arms.

Mark Howard took the lead, waving identification at all who got in their way and threatening any who tried to stop them. Behind him walked Remo, a son who knew he might lose his father for the second time that day.

21

Harold Smith stood alone on the west lawn of Fol-
croft Sanitarium and watched the stars. There was a chill
this summer night. The stars that had settled over Smith
were cold shards in an unforgiving universe.

A steady breeze blew up over Long Island Sound, feeding
the damp and filling the air with a thin salt scent. Crickets
chirped a summer chorus all around the well-tended grounds.
In the near woods, a lone tree frog sang out from the darkness.

Smith checked the glowing face of his trusty Timex and
tried to recall how many other nights there had been like this
one. There had not been a lot, but there had been enough.
Too many for Harold W. Smith.

It seemed unbelievable that anything could injure the
Master of Sinanju. The old Korean was a force of nature.
Smith had seen him face countless perils and survive.

Yet there were always risks. Chiun's and Remo's skills
were greater than any other, but in the end they were mortals
like everyone else. Smith lived with that fact each and every
time he sent the two men out on assignment.

How many times?

In the past, Chiun had been brought back to Folcroft injured on a few occasions. Remo as well. Even Mark Howard, the youngest of them all but no longer new to CURE, had been brought back in critical condition more than once.

And then there was Smith himself.

If he sat down and calculated, Smith could no doubt recall every time he had come to Folcroft as a patient. But it was a topic he chose not to dwell on. He only knew that each time he had returned injured there had been no one waiting anxiously to greet him. Most times he had not been able to tell his wife of injuries suffered in the field. During long recuperations, Maude Smith merely thought her boring old Harold was away on sanitarium business.

Yet for Smith, injury to self was preferable to standing in the cold and waiting for one of his own to be returned.

The growing thrum of rotor blades rose up over other summer night sounds. A moment later and the helicopter swooped in over the northwest trees. Branches danced wildly in cascades of light as the chopper settled to the wet grass.

Orderlies in white rushed a gurney from the sanitarium's north side doors. Remo hopped down from the helicopter's open rear door and helped slide the patient onto the gurney.

Smith was shocked at the Master of Sinanju's appearance. Although he was much older than Smith, Chiun had always seemed ageless. Indeed, as Smith aged during the decades of their association, the old Korean had remained almost unchanged for over thirty years.

The tiny figure on the gurney might have been a recently exhumed mummy. Chiun's thin tufts of hair were mottled, his face a death mask. The plastic oxygen mask that covered his nose and mouth seemed far too large for a man so small.

"How is he?" Smith asked.

Remo shot him a mute glance. Wordlessly, he followed the orderlies inside the big brick building, making certain they did not jostle their precious cargo.

Mark Howard was climbing down from the helicopter and

waving the pilot to leave. As the chopper lifted off, the assistant CURE director hustled over to Smith.

Howard's suit was covered with grime. He had taken off his necktie and stuffed it in his pocket.

"How bad is the situation with Canada?" Smith asked as the two men hurried to the building.

"We lucked out," Mark said. "I was afraid Remo was going to kill anyone who got between us and here, but the place was such a zoo up there that we eventually got lost in the insanity." At the sanitarium doors, he took Smith's arm. "But we have another problem," he said, pitching his voice low. "That CSFW woman threatened to expose us. I don't know how much she knows. Maybe not much. I tried to ask Remo on the way back, but he wouldn't talk."

Smith nodded. "Very well," he said.

"Maybe Remo can use that amnesia trick of theirs?" Mark asked hopefully. "The one that gets former presidents to forget about us?"

Barely perceptible beneath his gray Brooks Brothers suit jacket, Smith's shoulders straightened. "That is used only in rare cases, Mark," the CURE director said. "And it cannot apply to those who threaten this agency. Hopefully she does not know much. When Remo is willing to talk to us, I will make a determination on how to proceed with Ms. Janise."

Spine a rigid bulwark against the storm that was ugly necessity, Smith opened the door and hurried inside the building after Remo. Mark followed without a word.

Behind them, the sound of the helicopter faded and the cricket chorus resumed.

22

When dawn broke over Long Island Sound, the weak light of the new day burned away the dew that had gathered on the ivy of Folcroft Sanitarium's brick walls. And in a small basement hospital room, Harold W. Smith found Remo Williams in the same place he had left him four hours before, sitting at the bedside of the Master of Sinanju.

At the door, Smith noted that Remo had removed the old Korean's oxygen mask. Chiun was now breathing on his own. Smith watched the white sheet rise and fall with the slow, rhythmic breath of the frail little man.

Smith cleared his throat. "I have spoken to the doctor. He believes Master Chiun has stabilized. Although with the changes his physiology has undergone due to Sinanju training, it is difficult to know what ultimately to expect."

Remo did not tear his eyes away from the withered figure in the bed. "It's in other hands now than ours," he said.

Taking a deep breath, Smith stepped into the room. "Remo, we need to talk about the Cheyenne situation."

"No, Smitty, we really don't."

Smith had already girded himself for this conversation before coming down from his office, where he had spent a restless few hours on the couch.

"The problem is larger than we initially thought. More and more people are succumbing to this new tobacco. That other Master of Sinanju you mentioned was right to want to obliterate it four hundred years ago. This substance is dangerous."

"So's booze," Remo snapped. "Are we prohibitionists now? Women are nothing but trouble. We going to wrap them in burkas and stone them to death if they flash a little forehead? You want me to go house to house snapping off TVs 'cause people watch too much *Wheel of Fortune*?"

"Remo, right now this product is illegal. But if a path is cleared for it to be sold throughout the country, if it is brought into the light, what is happening right now in the underground economy will sweep the nation. If this were simply a product being used by individuals it would not be a concern to me. People have a right to make foolish choices. But exposure to the smoke of someone else has been proven to turn nonsmokers into addicts as well."

Remo sighed and shook his head. "Haven't you heard? There's no smoking left in this country. You already have to climb a redwood to sneak a puff, and hope to hell someone west of the Rockies doesn't catch a whiff."

"That will all change very quickly. This is not about individuals choosing a destructive path. This is about innocents who are dragged into someone else's choice. And it will not stop at our borders. We have also learned that an Asian crime lord is in the United States to meet with Rawly, presumably about distributing his Cheyenne Smooths—" Smith spoke the product's name with contempt "—in that area of the world. One Zhii Zaw, the former Chinese general."

"See Saw?" Remo asked, drawn in despite himself. "I told him and his friends to stay the hell out of America."

"Yet he is here."

"And so are the moshuh nanren."

"It had occurred to me as well that they might be

connected," Smith said. "It appears they were dogging your steps more than you realized, and it's evident they were responsible for the death of Dr. John Feathers after all."

"Feathers?" Remo said.

"It's bothered me from the start. Dr. Feathers was a Chowok Indian. Apparently he was the individual who brought the extinct plant to the attention of his employers at Cheyenne Tobacco. He is the only individual found after the CSFW ad shoot in Manhattan to be murdered in a way inconsistent with the other moshuh nanren victims, as well as the only Cheyenne Tobacco employee found dead there. But given that there were several other victims found murdered with nails in their hearts and skulls—"

"What do you mean, nails?"

"Ordinary carpentry nails. In addition to Dr. Feathers there was the chief of the Chowok tribe. He was found dead after Arvin Wollrich's attack in Montana. Then there was someone by the name of Twitchell, an expatriate American found dead at the first Canadian tobacco farm you destroyed."

"Wait, that hippie Twitchell was killed with a nail, too?" Remo asked, puzzled.

"Several nails actually. Three to the back of the skull, one to the heart. There were two other men killed in a similar fashion at another of Cheyenne's Canadian farms. I assume the moshuh nanren were a few steps behind you all the way, finally catching up to you at the last farm. They are likely connected with General Zhii Zaw."

"Maybe," Remo said, with a sad sigh. "But as far as everything else goes, you're way off."

Clearly Remo had come to a conclusion that Smith had missed. But when CURE's enforcement arm was not forthcoming, Smith forged ahead.

"Remo, it is evident that this product nearly eradicated the original Chowoks. If not for that other Sinanju Master you spoke of destroying their crops, banishing them to the West, and introducing the Lost Colony into the tribe, there is no doubt that the Chowok would have died out hundreds of years ago. Imagine that on a planetary scale. Rawly is insane for reintroducing this plant to a world grown as small as ours has. Thanks to him, we are likely witnessing the last step of mankind toward our extinction."

Taking a deep breath, Remo looked at the old man lying in bed. Chiun had never seemed so helpless. The flesh of his eyelids looked as if it might tear with every sleeping flicker of the eyes beneath. The wisps of hair above Chiun's ears appeared brittle and yellow. Remo could follow the outline of every delicate bone.

"Chiun would want you to go," Smith suggested, sensing an opening.

"Don't tell me what Chiun would have wanted," Remo said, not turning. "He only ever wanted to do whatever pig-headed thing he wanted to do. He wanted to get rid of that damned plant, and look where it got him."

"Remo, go to Rawly. Find whatever research Cheyenne has on this subject and destroy it. You have already eradicated their fields, so those crops will not be a source from which the plants can be brought back again. Eliminate the source and you will get rid of this poison. I don't know if Chiun will recover, but all the more reason for us to honor his final wish."

Remo turned a baleful eye to his employer. He said only one word, but its meaning was clear. "Don't."

Smith did not flinch at the threat.

It took many long, silent minutes for Remo to come to a decision. Finally, he leaned in close to Chiun and whispered something into the Master of Sinanju's shell-like ear.

"You once told me to bring back victory in my teeth. This time, the victory is for you," Remo said.

Laying the palm of his hand on his teacher's forehead one last time, Remo stood from his chair and, without another word to Smith, left the room.

23

It was still dark in West Virginia when Aphrodite Janise parked her car on the little dirt access road near the world headquarters of Cheyenne Tobacco, Incorporated.

It was Sunday morning and there was only one car in the big main lot, parked near the booth of the lone guard. As she chain-smoked over the next half hour, she watched several other vehicles arrive.

First was a battered old boat of a Cadillac Fleetwood that never pushed the speedometer higher than ten miles per hour. The old car scraped painfully along the side of the guard booth and bounced once, very slowly, on a landscaped traffic island on its way to a reserved parking space near the building. Through binoculars, Aphrodite watched an elderly woman in white sneakers climb out from behind the wheel and shuffle inside the glass and steel building.

Next was a sleek black limousine. Through the binoculars she watched an old Asian man get out of the back and enter the main offices. His driver stayed with the car.

Last was a yellow Rolls-Royce. She sat up straight in her seat when she saw the young man who was driving.

Aphrodite recognized David Merkel from the Campaign for a Smoke-Free World research. Merkel took a collapsible wheelchair from the trunk and disappeared beside the car. A moment later he was wheeling Edgar Rawly inside the building and Aphrodite was climbing out of her own car.

Backpack slung over her shoulder, she approached the guard booth. The guard was in his late forties and wore a gray uniform and a dark blue cap.

"Excuse me," Aphrodite said, flashing a smile as bright as the sun that was just breaking over the West Virginia treetops. "But my car broke down, and my cell phone isn't working. Could you do me a huge favor and call a tow truck?" She fumbled inside her backpack as she spoke and produced a Cheyenne Slim, which she slipped between her lips. "And if you have a light, too, you'll be my hero."

"Sure thing, ma'am," the guard said, rummaging in a drawer under his counter. "You can use my phone. You just have to dial nine first to get an—"

He straightened back up, a disposable lighter in one hand and a telephone book in the other.

It was apparent that the young woman did not need the lighter any longer, since smoke was curling from the orange tip of her lit cigarette. And while his attention was diverted she had pulled something else out of her backpack.

Aphrodite pressed the nail gun hard into the guard's chest and pulled the trigger. A loud pop and the shocked guard fell back in his seat, dropping phone book and lighter. Blood stained his shirt as he grabbed desperately for the nail protruding from the front of his crisp, gray uniform.

When Aphrodite came at him again, the guard tried grabbing for the gun at his hip, but there was no strength left in his arms.

"That's what you get for working for the evil that is Big Tobacco," Aphrodite said, puffing smoke from the side of her mouth. "Now don't wiggle. I have a meeting with Mr. Rawly, and I'd hate to be late."

Pressing the nail gun to the squirming guard's eye, she pulled the trigger once more. The man jumped once violently, then collapsed into his chair.

Aphrodite propped the body up, one elbow leaning on the counter, head in one palm and facing away from the driveway. If anyone else arrived, they would most likely think the man was asleep and merely drive onto the lot.

Stuffing her nail gun back into her backpack, she hurried to the gleaming glass building.

Zhii Zaw smiled patiently as the elderly woman shuffled into Edgar Rawly's office, a silver tea service on a pewter tray rattling in her age-speckled hands.

"Don't pay attention to Mrs. Z," Rawly instructed. "She's been a fly on our walls for the past two hundred years. You eventually learn to ignore her."

A smoldering cigarette dangled from the woman's lower lip, which was smeared with red clown makeup. Over an inch of crooked white ash hung from the cigarette's end, and when she set the service down the ash broke off and fell into Zaw's tea where it bobbed like a little tobacco corpse. Zaw left his tea untouched.

"So they tell me you're the new muckety-muck in Asian distribution," Rawly said, sticking a cigarette between his withered lips. "Didn't exactly get that by playing canasta with the ladies' sodality, did you? Well, just so you know, Chan old buddy, this might be your lucky day. Light me up."

Zhii Zaw glanced around. There was no one in the room but the former general and Edgar Rawly. Even his elderly assistant was shuffling out of the room.

"Damn, I sent him down for coffee," Rawly grumbled. "Can't drink this yak piss, pardon my French." He rummaged in the drawer of his desk for a lighter. "Anyway, like I was saying, you may have lucked out. I'd originally planned to grow the tobacco at home and export my Cheyenne Smooths from the U. S. of A., pending FDA approval. Now I say screw 'em. The past couple of days prove that the underground market's where the money is. So if you're here to talk turkey about growing and distribution in the Asian markets, lay your cards on the table. But just so you know, I'm getting most of the pie."

"Actually, Mr. Rawly, I have only stopped by to tell you that I plan to destroy you." Zaw said it neatly and confidently, as if talking about swatting a fly.

Rawly did not pause lighting his cigarette. He glanced up with rheumy eyes. "That right?" he said, puffing.

Zaw nodded. "I do not often meet with adversaries like this, but since I am going to cost you billions of dollars I thought it would be right to let you know."

"We're adversaries, are we?" Rawly said, a hint of a grin on his desiccated lips. "Strange, 'cause I only met you once in my life, and Merkel had to fill me in on that."

"Yes, you were rude, dismissive. So typically American. I wish, Mr. Rawly, that I could say that is the only reason I am going to ruin you." A faraway glint sparked fondly in Zaw's tired eyes. "There was a time in my life not too long ago when I would have found great nobility in such an act. So clean, so virtuous. Yet nobility for me is dead. What I do now, I do for money and power. Our markets will be closed to you, Mr. Rawly. There is only one distributor that matters in my hemisphere, and it is not you."

Business concluded, Zaw stood.

"I don't know what kind of cards you think you're holding, but I've gotta admire your moxie, kid," Rawly said. "But in case you haven't seen the news over in Commie Yellow-land, I've got the product everyone wants."

Despite Rawly's winning hand, a knowing smile stretched slowly across Zhii Zaw's flabby jowls.

Edgar Rawly recognized that smile. He had flashed it many times in his very long career. It was not cockiness, but secret knowledge that lifted the sagging bags of fat on either side of the retired Chinese general's face. It was a smile of a man confident in victory.

An old emotion stirred, one that Rawly felt deep in his aged, barely beating heart. It was something that had not surfaced in decades of government interference, anti-tobacco payoffs, do-gooder protests and shrinking profits. It was something Edgar Rawly had not felt since he dragged himself up, dirt poor, from the West Virginia fields of his long ago youth. The emotion was fear.

Rawly spat out his cigarette. It bounced across the floor in a spray of orange ash. Gripping the edge of his desk, he raised himself on wobbly, bowed legs. Once his legs were steady, he carefully released the desk, raising his balled fists in a pugilist's stance.

"You picked the wrong rooster's barnyard to scratch around in, sonny boy," Edgar Rawly snarled.

Yawning, David Merkel trudged out of the darkened executive cafeteria, a steaming cardboard cup of coffee in his hand. He would transfer the coffee to a mug upstairs. Merkel had brewed the coffee himself, as he did most mornings. The cafeteria staff did not come in until seven.

The capped cup was too hot, and as he walked he transferred it back and forth from one red palm to the other. Mr. Rawly liked his coffee delivered as hot as possible, even though he waited until it was lukewarm to drink it. Once Merkel had delivered his employer's morning coffee slightly cooler than Mr. Rawly liked it and wound up with the entire mugful flung across the front of his suit.

Merkel would not have to take it much longer. He had endured the abuse for more years than he ever thought he could. No more. Mr. Rawly did not know it, but his trusted assistant would soon be leaving Cheyenne Tobacco. Thoughts of liberation quickened his stride, and he was on the way to his employer's private elevator when he realized he had forgotten Mr. Rawly's cream.

"Damn," Merkel said, turning around.

He heard the pop and felt the sharp punch to his chest before he ever saw the shadow that had crept up behind him.

The elevator doors dinged open and Merkel fell back into the open car, hot coffee splattering walls and floor.

"Stop . . . what are you . . . God!"

Merkel grabbed at the nail that protruded from his sternum.

Aphrodite jumped forward, stepping on one wrist and pinning it to the floor. Pop-pop-pop! and three more nails joined the first, these directly into the heart.

David Merkel's dead hand slipped from his bloodied chest, slapping lifelessly to the pool of coffee at his side.

"Going up." Aphrodite said. The silver doors slid shut over her pretty but lined face.

Mrs. Z was chewing on a cigarette at her cluttered desk in the outermost room of Edgar Rawly's office suite. It was a perch she had occupied for as far back as she or anyone else could remember.

The old woman was collecting items in her big cloth handbag. It was common for her to gather up odds and ends from around the executive offices and cart them home, only to haul some of them back the next day. What she left at home filled rooms stacked with office supplies she had absentmindedly liberated over the course of six long decades.

When the elevator doors opened, Mrs. Z was busy stuffing a telephone book, three boxes of staples, a box of rubber bands, several fat manila envelopes, and her desk name plate into the oversized cloth bag.

She looked up and saw someone lying on the floor of the elevator. Some goldbrick stealing time from Cheyenne Tobacco. The sleeping man was not her concern.

She squinted through thick glasses at the young woman who stepped out of the car.

Mrs. Z spat a bit of soggy filter to the floor. "Do you have an appointment?" she demanded.

The young woman did not answer. Instead, she marched up to Mrs. Z's desk. She was carrying something in her hands, and might have banged the old secretary in the head with it or something had not someone else jumped unexpectedly from the shadows and grabbed the impertinent young thing. The man who had apparently been hiding in the office all along wrenched the object from the young woman's hands and hustled her into Rawly's office.

"Are you going to ravish me?" Mrs. Z asked his retreating back.

But the door slammed behind the strange pair.

Sighing a cloud of smoke, Mrs. Z stuffed a few more paper-filled manila envelopes into her bag.

Edgar Rawly and Zhii Zaw were facing one another down across Rawly's broad desk when the door sprang open. Aphrodite stumbled into the room, propelled by Jian.

Zaw was surprised once again by his personal assassin's uncovered face. He had seen the young man's bland features for the first time only the day before. Zaw was still unsure why Jian had chosen now to remove his mask. Jian had said something about "fearing wrath no more," but would not clarify further.

"What the hell is going on?" Rawly demanded of the two new arrivals. He squinted at the object Jian was dropping to the floor. "Is that a nail gun?" Recognizing Aphrodite from the Chowok surveillance cameras, he spun on Zaw anew. "You're with those bastards who were burning my tobacco and shooting nails into everybody up in Canada."

"I have no idea who these people even are," Aphrodite snapped. "I'm here because of what you did to me. You killed me, you old son of a bitch. I'm here to repay the favor." She smiled. "The nails had a poetry to them, don't you think, Mr. Coffin?"

At the use of his true name, Rawly squinted at Aphrodite. "You're one of those anti-smoking nutcases, aren't you?"

Aphrodite pulled the cigarette from between her lips and flicked it at the old man. "You got me hooked on these things when I was just a kid. 'Coffin nails.' You should have kept your real name. At least it would have been truth in advertising. Not that Big Tobacco cares about the truth."

Rawly sneered. "Where are those two bastards you were with?"

Zhii Zaw was annoyed when Jian answered the old man. But his annoyance quickly turned to panic.

"One is dead," Jian said coolly. "The younger Master of Sinanju will be coming here for you."

Zaw's head whipped around. The blood had drained from his face, turning his jowls into a sagging death mask.

"Sinanju," the old general snapped. His mind reeled as he began to put the pieces together. Manhattan, Canada. The dead. So many dead. "This? This is your obsession? This is who you have sent your men against?"

Jian nodded.

"You sent them to slaughter, you fool," Zaw growled. Rawly was forgotten, fortune and power were irrelevant. Survival became all. "We must leave here at once. Come. Now."

He waddled furiously to the door. But Jian did not fall in at his side. The young man stood fast.

"The old one was killed like the senile fool he was. The young one was weakened. I will finish him off with ease."

Zaw looked around the room, from Jian and Aphrodite to Rawly still striking a fighter's pose at his desk. The general shook his head, jowls swatting cheeks and neck like slapping hands.

"Fools," he intoned. "You are all dead." And with that Zhii Zaw stormed out the door and was gone.

Rawly dropped his balled fists, and with a self-satisfied smirk, collapsed back into his wheelchair.

"Knew that old Chinee cock-of-the-walk was all steam, no flywheel," he barked. Lighting up a fresh cigarette, he grinned at Jian. "Looks like you're out of work, sonny boy. And as luck would have it, I'm fresh out of maniacs. Welcome to the Cheyenne Tobacco family."

Jian did not speak. He pushed Aphrodite toward the large floor-to-ceiling windows. She used the opportunity to lunge at Rawly, so Jian tapped her hard on the side of the head and she collapsed to the floor. Leaving her body, the last moshuh nanren looked out the windows at the warming West Virginia day.

"So did you kill the old one or did my men?" Rawly asked. "Not one bastard's reported back to me from Canada. I figured they must be dead or running scared."

"You are correct," Jian said, still peering outside and taking special interest in the grounds below. "They are dead. But that is not to say their method did not have some merit."

"So I take it you got a plan to get that last bastard?"

Jian smiled. Reflected in the gleaming pane before him was a field of gently waving leaves. Adjacent to the parking lot at the rear of the building, the rows of tobacco stretched for a half-mile to the edge of the woods.

"He will not live to see another dawn," the young man intoned with quiet confidence.

Mark Howard brought the report down to the secu-
rity wing tucked away at the rear of Folcroft's basement.

This was CURE's special corridor, kept separate from the
rest of the sanitarium. Most of the hospital-room doors he
passed were open. Only a handful of the rooms were occupied by permanent residents of Folcroft. Passing the room
marked "Merrit M.," in which a comatose man remained in
perpetual slumber, Howard entered the room of the Master
of Sinanju.

Harold Smith sat at Chiun's bedside, his laptop computer
balanced on his bony knees.

"Thought you might find this interesting," Mark said, offering the CURE director the papers in his hand. "It looks
like Canada isn't too thrilled with Cheyenne Tobacco.
They had no idea those crops were being grown on Canadian soil. The anti-smokers up there are worse than they
are here. They're not going nuts that half of Canada was
burned, they're going nuts over Cheyenne sneaking up
there."

"That's a small comfort, I suppose," Smith said as he ran a tired eye over the report.

"It gets better. The government's swept greenhouses, barns, everything. They found the factory that was producing the cigarettes and shut it down. By the sounds of it, every last plant has been obliterated and they're ready to pin a medal on whoever destroyed them. Provided they aren't American, of course. Although some Canadian group is already taking credit, so we're even off the hook for that."

"We are not in the business of medals, Mark," Smith said, glancing up from the report to the Master of Sinanju. He was startled to see that the old man's eyes were open.

Smith hastily dumped the report and his laptop into his open briefcase. Setting all aside on the nightstand, he hurried to the elderly Korean's bedside.

"Master Chiun?"

The hazel eyes were finding focus. Smith assumed he had just opened them. As he worked on his laptop, he had been checking virtually nonstop since Remo left an hour before.

The spark of life returned to the bright, youthful eyes. A sharp intake of breath, followed by a steady exhale.

Awake and alert, Chiun looked up into Smith's overjoyed face. "Where is my son?" the Master of Sinanju demanded.

The noonday West Virginia sun hung hot over the Cheyenne Tobacco, Inc. complex as Remo drove into the parking area.

On his way in he noted the blood on the floor of the empty guard shed. There was no body but neither was there a guard. Even on a Sunday the shack should have been staffed.

There was only one car parked in the main lot, a big Cadillac Fleetwood. Remo parked a few spaces away from the dented old car and entered the building.

The executive building was wide open and empty. A mangy stuffed horse in a glass display case watched with blank marble eyes as Remo crossed the big lobby.

Remo did not encounter so much as a janitor on his way up to Edgar Rawly's office. In an outer room of the

Cheyenne CEO's suite, Remo found the only living person in the entire building. If one could call her living.

"Where the hell have you been?" Mrs. Z demanded, like a teacher scolding a wayward pupil. She had been sitting in a chair underneath a drooping fern. The elderly secretary batted fronds away as she climbed to unsteady feet. "I got things to do, you know. Been waiting here all day."

"I'd say that and then some," Remo said.

If the old woman heard him, she had not the patience to acknowledge it. "They told me you were coming. Inside. In there." She waved a veined hand toward the door marked EDGAR RAWLY. "Well, go on," she insisted. "Now I can finally get out of here. I have a life, you know."

She hefted her overstuffed cloth bag and, on shuffling sneakers, toddled toward the waiting elevator.

Remo pushed open the door to Rawly's inner sanctum. He didn't know what to expect. Probably some sort of booby trap. Instead he found a huge empty office and a big desk with a clean white sheet of paper set in its center. The paper was held in place by Nicky the Smoking Penguin, a popular Cheyenne mascot that had appealed to children for decades and that had, consequently, been dropped by Cheyenne in the wake of parental protests.

The cute little penguin in top hat and monocle puffed a lit cigarette, sending tiny plumes of smoke into the air.

Remo set the puffing Nicky doll to one side and read the note. "Look out the window, Sinanju."

The window overlooked a vast field of tobacco. A dozen yards in was a scarecrow.

Remo recognized Aphrodite immediately. Her body was tied with thick rope to a metal post and her arms were stretched wide and lashed to a wooden crossbeam. Aphrodite's head hung slack over her chest.

Remo considered leaving her where she was. The entire setup screamed trap, and even though Smith had not yet figured it out, Aphrodite was, after all, a multiple murderer, responsible for all the deaths committed with the nail gun.

She deserved whatever she got, Remo thought.

But in the end conscience won out.

Remo headed back downstairs.

When he exited the building, the Cadillac was driving off in a cloud of exhaust smoke. The old lady driver cracked a chunk of cinderblock off the corner of the empty guard shack on her way off Cheyenne Tobacco grounds.

Remo ducked around the back of the office building to the tobacco field.

Thick black interlocking hoses ran in a grid pattern around the field. The distant breeze carried the faint scent of gasoline to his delicate senses. Mindful of the lessons of Canada and certain now that he was being watched, Remo headed through the field toward Aphrodite.

Upon entering the field, Remo detected another scent, something different from recent experience. As he walked, he casually brushed the tips of his fingers against a big tobacco leaf and realized instantly that he was correct.

He continued along the path between rows of tobacco plants until he reached Aphrodite.

Remo had known even before entering the field that she was dead. Judging by the ghastly bruise on her temple, a single blow had finished her off.

The fatal injury was a knockoff of a Sinanju blow, similar to the forehead blows he had witnessed at the New York morgue. Seeing the Sinanju method robbed of all artistry by lesser hands, Remo felt anew his anger toward the moshuh nanren, whose theft of Sinanju skills had surely cost the House of Sinanju business and thus had robbed food from the mouths of the people of Chiun's small Korean village.

It was at that moment, when his quiet anger was roiling, that he saw the smooth, young Chinese face.

Jian had appeared like a ghost around the far side of the executive office building, near a large garage that, judging by the equipment Remo spied through the open door, was used for groundskeeping services. Two huge spigots fed the irrigation system.

Remo had no doubt that somewhere along the vast network of hoses the line had been tapped. It would not be water that squirted from hoses and nozzles.

"Your thieving face should be covered, moshuh nanren scum," Remo called.

Jian smiled. "For a long time it was," he replied. "That time has ended. We fear Sinanju no more."

And giving a mighty wrench with both hands, the Chinese assassin spun the pair of spigots. As the irrigation system rumbled to life, Jian lit a Cheyenne Tobacco promotional lighter and tossed the flame into the field. The lighter landed the instant the gasoline erupted from the hoses.

A wall of flame exploded near Jian. He watched it race back across the field, engulfing the area where the young white Master of Sinanju stood helplessly.

A similar fire had killed the old one and weakened the young one. Even if the white survived, he would stagger from the flames, charred, vulnerable and ready for death.

But something strange happened in the infinitesimally short instant before the gas shot up at Remo's feet and the fire engulfed the field. For a split second, Jian could have sworn that the young white disappeared, as if the earth had opened up and swallowed him whole.

Of course that was preposterous. The brilliant yellow fire was simply playing tricks on his eyes.

Jian stepped to the edge of the field and waited. He expected nothing to emerge, but if the white fell through the flames he would deal him a merciful death. And the moshuh nanren would take their rightful place as the greatest martial warriors on the face of the planet.

Jian's confidence in the supremacy of his order was short-lived.

A voice suddenly thundered, seemingly from the flames. But it was not born of fire but of something more elemental, and the words that boomed from beyond time and space echoed within Jian's frightened ears.

"I am created Shiva, the Destroyer; death, the shatterer of

worlds. The dead night tiger made whole by the Master of Sinanju. What is this dog meat that stands before me?"

And rising up from the tilled earth that surrounded the tobacco field, unsinged, unharmed, and with death in his eyes, was the young white Sinanju Master.

Jian's startled eyes barely had time to register the hole in the ground that fed into the tunnel through which Remo had burrowed beneath the fire.

The moshuh nanren grabbed for a sword and brought the deadly sharp blade swinging down at Remo's head.

The blade shattered along with most of the bones beneath Jian's elbows. The moshuh nanren dropped to his knees.

"Crawling on your knees," Remo said, grabbing the young man by the throat. "It's a start. Now beg for your life."

Remo squeezed.

Jian's eyes bugged from their sockets as the exquisite pain of the hundred little breaks in his neck electrified his spine and sent spasms of shock throughout his body.

"Please," Jian gasped.

Remo's face was stone. "Tell it to my ancestors. They'll show you as much mercy as me. Before you go to them, one question. Any more of you left out there?"

"I am the last moshuh nanren," Jian choked.

Remo knew that he was telling the truth. "Got that right, kid," he said, and planted his fist so deep in Jian's face, daylight shone through.

He was wiping the blood on the Chinese assassin's tunic when he heard the growing sound of a helicopter. He met the Army aircraft as it was settling to the center of the empty parking lot out front. When he saw the worried face peering desperately out of the window, Remo's heart soared.

The door burst open and the Master of Sinanju exploded out, flouncing through the lot.

"My son!" the old Korean cried. He had seen the fire from the sky and even now withdrew from the smoke that was heading on the wind into the parking area.

"Not to worry, Little Father," Remo said. "Dopey moshuh

nanren didn't even know this was regular tobacco. It's crap on your lungs, but nothing like that Chowok stuff."

Remo could not mask his joy for seeing his teacher whole again, nor could Chiun hide his own great relief.

"So how did you beat the curse of To-Un, Little Father?"

"The smoke did not enter my lungs, but it attacked my breathing skin in the brief moments before I was able to find safety. It took time for my body to purge the toxins. Not that I had any other choice but to return from near death. 'I will bring back victory in my teeth,' Remo, are hardly appropriate last words to your father. I will clearly have to stick around a few more decades to give you time to come up with something more appropriate. Why are you smiling like an imbecile?"

"I was thinking. In a way, you died in Canada and were reborn here."

"Yes. First that nation does not want to pay me, then it tries to murder me. I have shaken the dust of Canadia from my sandals, and hope never to return." Chiun stuffed his hands inside opposing kimono sleeves. "But if you ever again say I was born in America, I will disown you."

From where they stood Chiun could see most of the field. The fire was burning out, and the lowering flames had revealed the cross on which hung Aphrodite's remains. Remo followed his teacher's gaze. The fire had not blazed long enough or hot enough to incinerate the corpse.

"Well, she sort of lied to us, which isn't easy. When I asked her if she was responsible for the bodies in Manhattan, she was telling the truth. She was only responsible for *one* body up there. That Feathers guy." Remo sighed. "I guess it's fitting. She died the way she lived. Blackened and reeking of tobacco."

"Why did she kill so many?" Chiun asked.

Remo shrugged. "Just anger, I suppose."

Chiun clucked. "One should not kill out of anger. As a general rule. It destroys the artistry."

"I'll keep that in mind," Remo said.

"What of the moshuh nanren?"

Remo grinned. "You finished To-Un's work with the tobacco, I handled Pook's with those Chinese thieves. Figures it's up to the two of us to straighten out everyone else's mess. Speaking of which, c'mon, we have more work to do. You up to it?"

"Don't be rude, white thing. Lead on."

25

Zhii Zaw, former general in the People's Army of the People's Republic of China, felt the icy grip of fear relax its clenching hold on his bowels.

The drive back to Washington had been torturous. He had expected the young Master of Sinanju to leap out from behind every stop sign and mailbox. But as the miles between Zaw and West Virginia grew, his earlier panic ebbed.

Jian had stayed at Cheyenne Tobacco to confront the young Master of Sinanju and was doubtless dead by now. The last of the vaunted moshuh nanren was no more.

But in this was a stroke of luck for the former general. Zaw's own experience had taught him that these Korean master assassins did not take much time eliminating their enemies. There would be no questioning. When he found Jian on Edgar Rawly's property, he would assume that the moshuh nanren had been working for Rawly all along.

Yes, it was not only possible, it was probable. That young master would dispatch Jian so quickly he would never learn of Zhii Zaw's connection to all of this.

Zhii Zaw had met the younger Master of Sinanju once five years before. Zaw was supposed to be meeting with an American traitor who was passing secrets off to the People's Republic. Instead the young Master of Sinanju had shown up at the hotel rendezvous in Cancun. When he left, the hotel room was awash in blood and Zaw had a message to return to the leadership in Beijing. No more stealing American secrets or the Yangtze would flow free with their blood.

Zaw had delivered the message exactly as he had been told, and as a result had been drummed out of the military and forced into his current life of crime. China's Communist leadership did not take threats well.

Zaw considered himself lucky that he had not been taken out to a field and shot in the back of the head. But it was a risk worth taking, for he considered himself even luckier that he had done as the white instructed and therefore would never have to meet the young Master of Sinanju again.

All that had been put at risk by Jian, the foolish moshuh nanren who had not told his employer that the men he was determined to kill were from Sinanju. But Jian was dead now and, quite probably, in death had served his master much better than he ever had in life.

Gates opened and the limousine raced onto the tarmac at Dulles International Airport. The car was pulling to a stop beside Zaw's jet when his cell phone buzzed.

The voice on the other end of the line was angry. "Well I'm here at the godawful airport. Everyone's so noisy. I've got everything you wanted."

Zaw could not believe his luck. He had been ready to flee the United States without his prize, the secret to the Chowok tobacco plant. Quickly, he made arrangements for his Cheyenne contact to meet him at his plane.

Clicking the phone shut, he hurried up the air stairs. The engines were already fired up.

Jian had paid in blood for the general's freedom. There was now no connection between Zhii Zaw and Edgar Rawly.

Smiling amid the flabby folds of his face, Zaw hustled into his private quarters.

There were two men waiting inside.

"Hey Tubba Goo," Remo said. "I could've sworn I told you a long time ago to stay out of this rice paddy."

The aged Master of Sinanju stood at Remo's side. "See, Chinese mongrel, what happens to those who hire lesser assassins when Sinanju's rates are perfectly reasonable."

And Chiun was at Zhii Zaw's side, hands pressed against either side of the former general's head. He squeezed. Zaw howled.

"Wait, stop the presses, Little Father," Remo said. "He was hooked in with Rawly. We've got to make sure he doesn't have any of those plants, too."

"I do not," Zaw cried to Remo. He tried to turn his head, but could not move in Chiun's vise-like grip. "I swear, Master of Sinanju, I do not." His voice suddenly struck a hopeful chord. "But I can tell you who does."

Remo thought he was beyond surprise, but he could not refrain from an "I'll be damned" at Zaw's confession. When they had wrung all the information they were going to out of the former general, Chiun dragged the whimpering man to the door of the plane.

"For the sin of hiring cheap help, pray that we do not meet in the next life."

With a wrench, Zaw was off his feet and sailing back toward the fuselage-mounted engine above and behind the wing. He did not feel the impact that ended his life, nor the explosive pop of fire and smoke.

Zaw had been thrown through the engine like a bird sucked through at an altitude of twenty thousand feet. What little there was of him that spat out the far side spattered the hot tarmac. By the time the alarms went off around the airport and sounds of emergency vehicles rose in the distance, Remo and Chiun were already gone.

Agnes Zeigert shuffled through the busy terminal at Dulles International Airport.

There were alarms going off and people running all over. That was all people did these days, run. Run, run, run.

Agnes shuffled on.

In her tired hand was her big cloth handbag, in which was all the data that Agnes Zeigert's Chinese partner needed. Agnes had access to everything at Cheyenne Tobacco, including Rawly's private helicopter, which had flown her to Dulles.

Her moment to shine had been a long time coming. At one time she had been an advocate of equal rights for women. She had even been mentioned in a college textbook a few years back. Unfortunately, Agnes had been late to the suffragette movement and early to the feminist age, and had been forced to take a job with Cheyenne Tobacco to pay the bills. She did not remember her early life any longer. She vaguely remembered years of sexual harassment by Edgar Rawly. Worst of all, she remembered when she got too old and the harassment stopped.

"I'll show him, non-harassing old buzzard."

As she shuffled along, the crowds around her thinned. People were streaming for the exits. There was some sort of crazy announcement over the public address system about a possible terrorist act out on a runway. Through a large window, Agnes saw emergency vehicles surrounding a plane. Smoke was rising from a spot just behind its wing.

Nothing to do with her. Agnes hobbled down an empty corridor and into a ladies' room. After taking care of business, she had her lipstick out and was smearing it around her mouth when in the big wall mirror she saw the door behind her open. Two men entered the room.

"What the dickens are you doing?" Agnes demanded.

The men did not speak. The old one looked like General Zhii Zaw, whom Agnes had met after getting lost in a closet at the Pacific Tobacco Exporters and Importers Association conference the previous year. The young one stuck a trash barrel up under the door handle.

"You work for that Chinese fella?" Agnes snarled. "Tell him to keep his shirt on. I'll be there directly."

"Don't hurry, Miss Z," Remo said. "They'll be scooping him out of swimming pools from here to Virginia Beach for the next two months."

The dawn was slow in coming, but Agnes eventually realized that these two meant to do her harm. Clutching her bag close, she backed against the sink.

"Hold it right there, you jokers," she snarled. "I'm not some shrinking violet you're dealing with."

To prove it, Agnes tried to blow her rape whistle. Remo reached over and crushed it flat between two fingers. Agnes blew. No sound came. Much spit did. Remo and Chiun stepped back to avoid the spray.

"Hold on, hold on," Agnes muttered. She dropped her useless whistle and fished in her handbag. After much rattling of all the odds and ends she had liberated from work, she produced a can of Mace. "Aha!" she cried.

She launched a stream of Mace directly in Remo's face. At least she thought she did. The young man moved and somehow the can exploded back into Agnes's face and hair. The only thing that kept it from her eyes and nose were the enormous glasses that shielded her eyes and pinched off her nasal passages.

Agnes tried to send a sneaker into Remo's crotch. The shoe flew off, banged against a wall and splashed down in a toilet.

Agnes sighed in resignation. "All right, do your worst."

She started to unbutton her dirty blouse.

Chiun turned away, aghast. The old Korean sent a fluttering hand up over his delicate eyes.

"What the hell are you doing?" Remo asked.

"You're going to rape me, aren't you?"

"Lady, it was safe for you to stop worrying about that when they stopped selling war bonds."

There was disappointment on her heavily creased face. "Is he going to rape me?" She pointed at Chiun.

"Remo, make it stop," Chiun cried, horrified, from beneath his shielding hands.

"No one is going to—" Remo had to pull her hands away from her blouse buttons. "Geez, knock it off. We're here for all the Chowok tobacco stuff you stole."

Remo did not want to have to torture a little old lady, even if she was Edgar Rawly's secretary, but found that he would not have to.

"Oh, tish-tosh," she sighed. "Here."

She handed over her bag. It was filled with computer disks, paper folders, packs of Cheyenne Smooths and several plastic Ziploc bags containing samples of Chowok tobacco leaves.

"I've got it all up here anyway," Agnes boasted. "I'm not senile, you know. What I don't remember, I know how to find. I can get it from Edgar again."

"Better hurry. He won't be around for long," Remo said.

This took her off her game, but only for a moment. "Even better. I'm his beneficiary. I had him sign all the paperwork over the years. I now own enough Cheyenne Tobacco stock to start production right away. I don't even have to go to foreign dealers."

She stuck out her tongue triumphantly. Remo turned to the Master of Sinanju.

"What do we do with her?"

"She cannot be allowed to spread this evil."

"But she's like a thousand years old. I can't bump off some old lady who's a thousand years old. I think it says so in the Bible."

Chiun sighed. "I must do everything around here."

Near the sink, Agnes had planted a cigarette between her lips and was rummaging through her bag for a light. She noticed the Master of Sinanju approaching. Agnes sighed. All men were after the same thing. Might as well just give in to them.

"Oh, if you must," she said, closing her eyes. "Just be gentle with me."

He was.

When the furor over the poor Chinese businessman who had gotten himself accidentally sucked through a jet engine finally subsided and a work crew noticed the jammed door on the tucked-away ladies' room, a second tragedy was discovered. A sweet little old lady had apparently slipped while tossing a cigarette into one of the toilets, hit her head on the tank and drowned in the bowl.

The airport's carefully crafted statement to the press read in part, "This tragic accident is just one of the many health and safety reasons why smoking is not allowed in our terminals, and why we hope that in the future, in addition to the usual health cautions, packs of cigarettes will offer the new label WARNING: MAY CAUSE TOILET DROWNING DEATHS AMONG THE ELDERLY."

26

In a little park in Washington, D.C., away from the main pathways, Remo set a fire in a cement trash receptacle and watched it burn.

Into the flames he fed the computer CDs, paperwork and other material Agnes Zeigert had taken from Cheyenne Tobacco headquarters. He threw in the tobacco leaves without taking them out of their plastic bags and stuffed the promo knapsack down on top of them. He and the Master of Sinanju were careful to stand upwind as they watched the fire flare and then slowly die to glowing embers.

"Smitty will have to take care of whatever's on the computers and in the labs at their headquarters," Remo said. "I guess we can give it a pass, too, if you want."

Chiun nodded. "We will finish this, as it was not finished four hundred years ago."

Remo noted the contemplative look on his teacher's face. "I think Masters To-Un and Pook can finally rest in peace, Little Father."

The Master of Sinanju stroked his thread of beard as he

considered his pupil's words. "It was unfair to call To-Un 'disgraced' in the scrolls. That wrong will be righted."

"Good for him."

"And if he failed just a little it was probably because he was distracted by worry."

"Abso—What?"

Chiun looked up at Remo, a puzzled expression on his wizened face. "Obviously To-Un had trained an incompetent as an heir. Pook could not even eliminate a few pesky Chinese assassins. How inept is that? To-Un was a Master of Sinanju trained to the pinnacle of perfection, who had performed his duties flawlessly in a lifetime of service to his people, only to have it all undone because he was doubtless fretting over that oaf Pook. It must have been a terrible burden for him, Remo. Believe me, I know."

"Little Father, as long as you're rewriting history, can't you give Pook a break, too?"

Chiun was appalled at the very suggestion. "Our sacred scrolls are not written in sand, to be scrawled over at a whim. Time has vindicated To-Un, not Pook."

"Yeah? Just wait'll I start rewriting the scrolls."

A tiny smile played at the corners of the elderly Korean's lips. "There is hope for you yet."

27

Orange and red fire smeared the brilliant blue can-
vas of the Nevada sky. The sun was setting in Hollywood
colors over rust mountains and green-dusted yellow prairies.

A lone rider on a horse sat on a bluff and stared at God's
great world, attempting to glean the meaning of all existence
from sky and land. He held this pose for as long as he could,
ten seconds in all, before his thin frame was racked with a
violent coughing spasm.

Tearing away the manly cigarette that was between his
lips, the rider sucked down a massive glob of snot, hocked
up a huge phlegmball, and loogied all to the Nevada dirt.

"P-tooey," said Edgar Rawly. "Godammit, who gave me
that Coke on the plane? It's making me cough like shit."

"Cut."

The lone rider was not so alone. A dozen men hustled into
sight from behind the cameras that had been filming Rawly's
latest commercial. The director, who specialized in music
videos, was growing nervous. It had taken half an hour just
to balance Rawly on the horse. Now they were running the

risk of losing a perfect sunset because the old man could not hold off coughing up his lungs for just five minutes.

"I'm telling you, Coke makes me cough," Rawly growled.

"We're losing the light, Mr. Rawly," the director said.

"Relax, Hitchcock. I'm picking up the tab here. We're taking five."

The director glanced at what was left of the perfect sunset, shook his head, and turned to the crew.

"Okay, five minutes everybody!" When the crowd dispersed, only one man remained near Rawly. Eyeing the horse nervously, he nearly dropped his clipboard when the animal's tail swished in his direction.

"Can't stand these TV bastards, Merkel," Rawly said.

"Um, sir, Mr. Merkel is dead. I'm Branley."

"I know that," Rawly snapped. "I'm not senile you know." Grunting, he stared at the fire-red mountains. "John Schien directed all our commercials in the Fifties. Black and white but, God, he was a genius. This is for Japanese TV. Can't run TV ads in the US. Japanese love that artsy-fartsy crap. Give Schien a call, Merkel."

The man who was not David Merkel nodded and hustled off to make some calls, little realizing that John Schien had suffered heart failure after a bout of pneumonia, all cancer related, back in 1964.

Alone, Edgar Rawly looked off at the horizon and the setting sun. It was hard not to have big thoughts in this setting. Rawly's thoughts were of all the smokers that were being conceived and born around the world at this very moment. It gave him a warm feeling in his heart.

But then he thought of the anti-smoking campaigns, and mental images turned to all the pink-lunged children who would never lift a single cigarette in their little hands. Considering all the profit that would be lost by Cheyenne Tobacco, a manly mist came to Edgar Rawly's rheumy old eyes.

"This is it," Rawly snapped. He pointed at his own moist eyes. "This is exactly the look I want. Get that bastard direc-
back here now."

Mr. Rawly's new assistant had been on the phone. Branley hustled over to the vans and cars and horse trailer that had hauled them all out to the desert.

"Hurry up, you dumb bastard," Rawly bellowed. A warm desert breeze kissed his weathered face and he could feel his manly moist eyes beginning to dry.

Rawly's shout agitated the horse, which swished its tail angrily. Rawly hated this breathing horse. He had wanted to have Misty flown out from West Virginia, but everyone said the old stuffed horse just was not working. Bastards.

The crew was somewhere behind him. He could not wave to them, or turn in the saddle. They had balanced him very carefully and he was afraid to shift his weight lest he end up hanging sideways from this wretched beast.

Rawly stared straight ahead.

The shot was now almost certainly ruined. His eyes were dry as the dust below his horse's hoofs. Maybe they could be moistened, but Rawly was suspicious of Visine and Murine. Everything seemed to cause cancer these days.

Thinking evil thoughts about the forces that were allied against him, Edgar Rawly suddenly spied something in the distance. Near some rocks, positioned so that no one could see them but him, were two men.

It was no mirage. They were there, clear as day; an old coot in a bathrobe and a young guy in a T-shirt. Rawly was infuriated to see that neither of the men was smoking.

What kind of nancy boys was this country producing these days? In the great age of tobacco, all real men smoked. The Duke, Bogie, Old Blue Eyes. Hell, even Ricky Ricardo smoked. Now here were these two fruits standing out in the middle of the desert, neither of them smoking. Probably some sort of damned hippies out communing with nature. It certainly looked that way, especially when they both reached down and picked something up off of the ground.

The young one smiled and waved.

Suddenly Edgar Rawly recognized the two men. He had never seen their faces, but he had seen enough. These were the two who had invaded the Chowok reservation, killed

Arvin Wollrich and destroyed Rawly's crops in Canada. These were the two rat bastards who had set back production of his beloved Cheyenne Smooths by months. Rawly had left that Chinese killer back at corporate HQ in West Virginia, giving him carte blanche to kill the young one. And here was not only the young one, alive and well, but alongside him was the old one, whom Rawly had been told was dead.

Then the young one was flicking something off his open palm. The old one did the same an instant later.

They weren't as slow coming in as they appeared to be, for there was no way they could have stayed aloft if they were as sluggish as they seemed. Yet as fast as they must be moving, somehow they were slow enough so that even Edgar Rawly's ancient eyes could make out exactly what they were.

The two pebbles made a beeline from the fingertips of the men to the rear of Edgar Rawly's horse. At the last moment there seemed to be an extra burst of speed, and the tiny stones became invisible blurs. They struck the flanks of the Appaloosa, one after the other.

With a terrified whinny, the horse reared up on its hind legs. When Edgar Rawly was flung from the saddle, his right foot remained firmly in the stirrup. His manly boot was still lodged in the stirrup when the Appaloosa took off like one of the four horses late for the Apocalypse.

Remo smiled as he watched the last, great American tobacco executive's brains get bashed out on Nevada rocks.

As Rawly's horse galloped away, it was chased into the sunset by a hysterical ad crew, wranglers and Cheyenne employees.

Taking a deep breath, and exhaling happily, Remo turned to the Master of Sinanju. "Welcome to Cheyenne country, Little Father."

Remo Williams and Chiun go toe-to-toe
with Death itself in . . .

THE NEW DESTROYER:

DEAD RECKONING

Warren Murphy and James Mullaney

Coming in April from Tor Books

TOR® A TOR PAPERBACK
ISBN-13: 978-0-7653-5761-8   ISBN-10: 0-7653-5761-5

www.tor.com

His name was Remo, and the courtroom had not changed. It was the same ugly, depressing chamber he remembered from that day more than thirty years ago when the state of New Jersey decided that it was in the best interest of the people that an innocent man be executed.

The walls were still the same ghastly green he remembered, more appropriate to the exterior of a strip-mall car wash than to the interior of a court of law. At some point in the past the hard benches had been stripped and revarnished, but that was decades ago as well, so the state of disrepair Remo found them in was about the same as he recalled. On the bench where Remo sat at the back of the room, a car thief artist had invested a few pretrial moments in carving a penknife engraving of a naked woman in the solid oak. The same fluorescent fixtures hung from the water-damaged ceiling, although Remo imagined that the buzzing bulbs had been changed since he last sat and waited to hear the words black-robed judge.

e judge. Now that was different. The judge was not the

same one Remo had faced as a defendant, back when he was young and naive enough to trust that he would find justice in a system that seemed determined to railroad an innocent man. The judge in that kangaroo trial had been a tired, bloated lifetime civil servant more interested in protecting his job than meting out justice. This new judge, who had just entered the room from a door behind the bench, was a tired, bloated lifetime civil servant as well but a good two inches shorter than the last one.

"All rise!"

The courtroom obeyed the order of the burly bailiff. Feet shuffled as men and women clambered to their feet. Remo stood with the packed crowd, keeping a special eye on the individual who was seated at the defense table.

Another change, a different defendant. Where once Remo had sat was a woman of about fifty. Her hair was cut in the page-boy style of the boy on the paint can, but on her it was as cute as a silk ribbon on a mudslide. Her rough skin was decorated with eczema blotches, her thick neck was like an inflated inner tube of doughy flesh, and her body had the same blockish shape and squared corners as a mailbox.

During his trial, Remo had been nervous, but this woman seemed unconcerned with her circumstances, and as the audience took once more to benches and chairs, she leaned in to the younger of her two lawyers and laughed.

Remo found it strange that someone could laugh with their life in the balance.

In Constance Arnold's case, it was life as she had known it, the comfort of an occupation that would be forever lost to her if the proceedings this day went against her.

Arnold was a lawyer who had been found guilty the previous year of passing information from her terrorist clients to operatives in the international al-Khobar terrorist organization. Whereas aid to the British in the Revolution, to the South in the Civil War or to the Nazis in World War II would have brought a severe penalty, usually involving the perpetrator swinging from the end of a rope, Constance Arnold's sentence for treason had been nine months in a federal health-spa penitentiary and suspension of her law license. She was in court this day to have the license restored and the record of the conviction expunged.

In front of the court, the ruddy-faced judge made a show of shuffling through some papers for a few minutes. The name plate on the bench identified him as Judge Harmon Gates.

Remo recalled that there had been no paper shuffling during his trial. The court had no windows, so Remo's judge had merely stared at the wall for most of the proceedings.

Although Remo had not known it at the time, the outcome of his own trial had been determined long before a dead drug pusher was found beaten to a pulp in an alley, with the badge of Newark beat cop Remo Williams clutched in his dead hand.

Almost before the bloodstains had dried, Remo had been arrested, tried and executed. Luckily for Remo, the electric chair had been rigged to not work. He had awakened from death in an ivy-covered building on Long Island Sound, and from there had embarked on a new life and a new mission.

The building was Folcroft Sanitarium, cover to CURE, America's most secret crime-fighting agency. Trained there to the peak of human perfection, Remo was to become the agency's one-man enforcement arm. For years he had toiled away in secret, eliminating the enemies of America at home and abroad. And now his covert life had seemingly come full cycle. Remo Williams, that innocent man who had been framed in order to fight for truth, justice and the American way, now found himself back in the courtroom where it had all begun, observing the hearing of a woman who had betrayed everything for which Remo, CURE and America stood.

At the defendant's table, Constance Arnold listened to a few whispered words from the younger of her two lawyers and laughed again. Smiling, she shook her head and her bangs bobbed appreciatively. A broad grin on her face, she turned her attention to Judge Gates.

The judge had finished shuffling his papers. "Get up here, of you," Gates growled from the bench.

Lawyers from both sides approached the bench. Remo noted that unlike his trial, the jury box was empty for Constance Arnold's hearing.

Constance remained seated, a smug smile on her toad-like face, as she drummed her fingers on the desk before her.

The room was full, but there were not many reporters present. A few men and women scratched notes on lined paper. No cameras whirred, since the judge had banned all video equipment.

This phase of the Arnold affair had drawn little interest. Indeed, the press had seemed to go out of its way to look elsewhere during her trial the previous year. Remo's trial had been similarly ignored by the media. Back then there had been a few second stringers from some of the smaller New Jersey and New York papers.

Remo could focus his hearing better than others could focus their vision, and had he chosen to, he could have picked up every sound coming from the front of the room, including the whistling noise of the judge breathing through knots of wiry white nose hair. But Remo found little of interest in what lawyers had to say, and that went double for judges.

As lawyers and judge yammered softly, the crowd waited expectantly; the handful of reporters scribbled furiously; and Constance Arnold smiled knowingly, while Remo examined his fingernails and recalled the phone conversation with Upstairs the previous afternoon.

"You want me to whack a lawyer, and it's not even my birthday?" Remo had asked. "How much will I owe you?"

"This is a serious matter," Remo's employer had insisted, his voice the audio equivalent of a bag of squeezed lemons. "Constance Arnold was attorney to several high profile terrorist clients, including the so-called Deaf Mullah as well as Mustafa Mohammed, that 9/11 hijacker."

"Yeah," Remo said agreeably. "But she's a lawyer. Everybody gets a lawyer, right? The Constitution. Blah, blah, blah. Why's she on the list?"

"Because she is the worst of the lot. She would visit her clients in prison along with an interpreter and then allow the interpreter and client to carry on separate conversations to send out orders to terrorist groups. It was only by luck that Arnold was apprehended."

"Wait a minute . . . Arnold. I remember her now, 'cause she had the same name as the talking pig on TV. Same face too. Wasn't she convicted?"

The voice on the other end of the line grew so sour Remo swore he felt the phone receiver pucker in his hand.

"She could have been sentenced to twenty-four years and even that would have been too lenient. Instead she got nine months. Judicial insanity. Even so, she served her time, and I would be willing to turn a blind eye on her past crimes if not for this hearing. She sees the same judge who passed sentence on her, and I think she might just get her right to practice law restored. If that happens, she'll be right back passing messages between terrorists and getting Americans killed. We can't let that happen."

"Enough," Remo said. "You had me at 'kill the lawyer.' "

"Do not take this lightly," said Harold Smith, Remo's employer. "These are perilous times."

"They're always perilous, Smitty."

"Not like now," Smith said. "Distance and oceans no longer protect us from our enemies. We have a difficult enough time defending ourselves from forces without. Treason from within needs to be punished."

"Okay. I'll zap her in her house."

"No." Smith's voice was rock steady. "This needs to be more public than that. The press will no doubt be present for her hearing tomorrow. A sudden apparent heart attack after the ruling might send a message. Our enemies are superstitious in a great many ways. If even one of them believes that some supernatural force somehow intervened and struck this woman down, that might be one less attack we will have to deal with down the road."

"I'm the hand of God. Gotcha," Remo said.